SON OF THE FLAME

A.M. DYER

MISTY HOUSE PRESS

Paperback: 978-0-6454629-6-8

Ebook: 978-0-6454629-7-5

This is the first edition of this publication

Printed in Australia and Internationally.

Published by Misty House Press

Mistyhousepress@gmail.com

SON OF THE FLAME

A.M. DYER

MISTY HOUSE PRESS

This book is dedicated to my loving parents,

Wayne and Michelle Dyer.

Thank you for your love and support.

CHAPTER ONE

Everything else became insignificant when Gytha heard the name from the traveller girl's mouth. The mention of her son consumed her entire self. If she hadn't already tended to the king, she might have abandoned the mission that had brought her to Ravinshore in the first place. Some might have held the light of the king and the kingdom first, but for Gytha, the throne of Ravinshore wouldn't have stood a chance if she'd had to choose one to save. There would have been no choice when it came to her child, and she wouldn't have hesitated. Not a heartbeat. Not this time.

Gytha would have scorched the Red Flame to the ground if she hadn't found him. Then she would have turned the fire onto the village, and Queen's Hill would have felt the heat of the flames ten times worse than that of its Order. There would have been no telling if the entire kingdom would have been spared if she had never had the chance to speak with him. How the conflict ended hadn't mattered to her — she'd only cared about telling her son the truth.

Her wrath was far from over, even after the Orders' attempts were thwarted and Olinander came out unscathed in the end. This allowed her to breathe after she'd learned everything that had been happening in her long absence. But it wasn't enough.

Gytha stared at Thorne from where she sat in the common cabin with the other passengers on the Flea, bound for Edenborough. This was a judgment she needed to see to personally, not just because he was a vile being and only ever poisoned everything he touched, but in part to prove to herself that she wasn't completely useless as a mother. She was patient. She wanted to savour it. She wanted to relish every bit of this as she counted all of the sins committed on her son while she'd been gone. This man was going to bear all of the hell that had been locked away, all of the rage she had buried from being apart from her son for so long, all of the anguish from when she had returned to find his guardian dead and him barely clutching at life on the floor of a filthy dungeon. This would be the watcher's penance.

Vengeful as Gytha was, however, she was conscious that they were not alone on the ship. Whatever she did would have consequences within the confines of the vessel, with its children and babies and unknowing travellers. She could rip him apart from the inside out right now and draw the attention of everyone. Or she could continue to watch him enjoying the illusion of sanctuary till she could tear it out of him, someplace away from the eyes surrounding them, until those eyes found what was left of him afterwards.

In the cabin on the lower deck, as the ship drifted towards Edenborough, a surreptitious quiet fell over the inhabitance of the vessel. Gytha watched like a huntress as her prey breathed in the oblivion of the sentence passed on his life through his fickle endeavours. Then the quiet vanished as the breeze eased in from the sea south of the three kingdoms. A loud shrill came from the other side of the ship, snapping the attention of the huntress, her prey, and the clueless passengers and crew on the main deck to the undisturbed sea.

The cry came from a woman carrying a child wrapped in a grey shawl. The mother continued to scream at what had become of her baby. It took only a moment before Gytha rose from her seat and moved towards the woman to see for herself.

"Help me! Help my baby!" the ginger-haired woman cried with an eastern accent as she jerked her head up and caught the eyes of the Grand Sorceress. "Someone, please, help my baby!" the mother begged.

Nearby, another mother held her toddler closer instinctively in the fear and uncertainty of what could be wrong. A couple of other women joined Gytha in approaching the crying woman. Eyes peered at them sceptically from a safe distance. The knocks on the ship's wood from the footsteps as others approached from the cabins played third in the chorus of the bellowing of the panicked mother and the crowd's murmuring. The Grand

Sorceress took the child from the mother's hands and rushed towards a table.

"What happened?" Gytha asked.

"I – I don't know, I swear it, I don't know! I – I – I fed her one moment, and she was smiling at me after, but out of nowhere, she stopped, and then she coughed and her colour just . . . changed!" The animated mother has now been flanked by a man and woman whose task it would be to subdue her should the worst come to pass in this ship in the middle of the sea.

It was apparent indeed that the child's colour was unnatural. A greyish cast over her brown skin painted the image to everyone close by, and not just the Grand Sorceress, who could feel the life ebbing out of the infant. Gytha glanced at the mother and the people around her.

"Hold her," she instructed.

At once, the man and the woman grabbed the arms and shoulders of the mother without question.

"Wait! Wait! What is it? Let me be!" The confused mother wriggled in their hands.

"Quick, give me your knife," Gytha said to another man standing just behind the mother, and the pinch on the man's face did not stop him from obeying as he unsheathed the small dagger from his belt and handed it to Gytha.

Gytha ignored the sounds of the disturbed mother and the questions from the other passengers as she took the blade to the babe's hand and slit about half an inch into her palm. Gytha handed the knife back to the man and used her hands to part the baby's lips so the child would find air quickly when she sought it. The sorceress placed her left hand on the child's bleeding palm so she could feel her blood, and she placed her right hand over the child's chest.

"What – what is she doing!" the crazed mother cried, struggling to break her restraints, only to watch in horror as arcane threads led from the Gytha's hands into the babies, and slowly wrapped around the child's body, focused on the infant's chest.

"Firmus a enterius," Gytha whispered as she leaned over the child, blowing a soft breeze at the baby's face. "Come on, little one," she said.

The entire cabin fell quiet, except for the panicked sobs of the mother. Many hoped something would change with Gytha breeze. They watched and waited for something to manifest even as the child remained unmoving, breathless, ghostly, and unnatural.

"Come on . . ." Gytha gripped a tiny bit harder at the child's hand, feeling as the magic worked into the body to sneak life back into her blood and snatch her from the jaws of death. The sea itself seemed to hold the ship still as the Grand Sorceress leaned in one more time and blew yet again at the child's face. Gytha felt a thud beneath her hand, then another, and she felt the body twitch. Slowly, the baby's colour turned, and she twitched even harder before coughing and letting out a bellow that was instant music, sending everyone into a loud rejoice.

"There you are," Gytha said.

The child cried harder, and soon all of the death left her colour. Gytha focused on the cut palm and the wound closed with only a tiny scar. She picked up the child and nodded at the people holding the desperate mother. They freed her, and Gytha handed the breathing child back into her teary mother's hands.

"Oh, thank you! Thank you! Thank you . . ." the mother cried as she fell to her knees, holding her baby tightly to herself, pulling her away to plant a deep kiss on her small head and then holding her tighter again.

"Feed her, and she will be fine," Gytha said to the mother.

The woman nodded aggressively and was helped to a seat by the other women. The Grand Sorceress looked away from the small crowd toward her prey. She was met with the coldness of Thorne's absence. Before she could react, a loud explosion sent the ship rocking, and the passengers were thrown across the hold.

* * *

To flee was not weakness. Wisdom demanded that a great warrior know when he needed to step back should his enemies gain the advantage. Becoming a martyr and losing the war wasn't a sign of a great mind.

Thorne's injured hand could barely form a fist as he thought about the events that had brought him here. He had lost the battle, but the war would wait for him. He knew it. Those who would witness his plan's eventual success would certainly not forget. They would be there when he returned. And he would, when those who thought they had seen the last of him least expected it, the Orders would take what had belonged to them since they had been declared the guardians of the kingdoms. Walera would take what belonged to it. It was impossible to kill the idea as deeply rooted as the Orders reigning over the three kingdoms. Otto and his betraying lips had been right about one thing: plans for the Order to take power wouldn't succeed overnight – it had been years in the making, and those years undoubtedly had sown seeds that a little challenge wouldn't easily gust away.

Thorne's efforts, and those of his watchers, may have been thwarted. He had never predicted that the king would survive, let alone that there would be anyone strong or skilled enough to save him from the Egro. He ground his jaw as he thought about Wylie. He had lived in obscurity only to show up and turn out again to be a bane, a bastard whose blood-kin had proved to be nothing but the same thing. Thorne wondered at the coincidence that the mother of that same bastard had come to the king's aid. His body grew cold as he remembered her face when she had turned her horror on him, and he had felt the magic tearing out of him before she had been cut short. A flame burned in his heart, one that would consume whatever was left of that family when he returned. Quietly or loudly, he would find them all and make sure he didn't leave anything to chance again.

For all those he had foreseen as possible challenges to do away with – advisors, counsels, commanders of armies, palatines, aldermen and kings – a pathetic reunion with an insufferable troublemaker and a family of vigilantes wasn't something he had anticipated to be his greatest threat.

The quiet vanished from Thorne's thoughts as the scream of the panicked mother took hold of the cabin. He watched as she bawled, and everyone turned towards her and the dying child. Thorne didn't move from his seat, watching from a distance while the passengers moved to the tune of the horror in front of them. It wasn't his business to be concerned with, save for how insufferable the woman's cry was becoming on a trip he had hoped would be uneventful. He wasn't looking to stand out. He was resigned to ignore the woman's woe as best he could and looked away until he heard the voice of an old woman.

Thorne watched as a Seemingly random passenger took the infant away from the mother. He watched as this old woman took control and slit the child's palm. He wouldn't have been suspicious of only that. She looked dressed and sounded normal. She could have been no more than an old hag for all he knew. But as the woman slowly revealed her true self and her arcane threads flowed out of her as she uttered the words, Thorne froze in place, and his eyes went wide. Those threads sent alarms off in his head, ones he could certainly not ignore. It was all too much for him to doubt. A sorceress who was also a healer, bringing back a child from the brink of death.

Thorne knew he had only one choice. Waiting one more moment to be sure of her identity, watching the changing colours of the arcane threads that reminded him at once of the hands that had ripped his power out of him, would be the last mistake of his life. That kind of power didn't simply wander onto a ship to Edenborough and blend in with the common folk in an open cabin. He knew.

Thorne rose and hurried out of the cabin to the ship's main deck. He passed some people – crewmen who wanted to know who had screamed – but didn't stop until he reached the quarter deck and the sea's breeze blew into his frightened face. He turned briskly, only to see nothing but the water surrounding the ship. The Lord Watcher clung to the rail of the boat as he peered into the distance. Edenborough was barely a thin silhouette more than a mile north. He couldn't risk it. If there was even half a chance that she was who he thought she was, Thorne knew there was no way he would survive if she found him. He looked at his hands, the scars where his threads had been ripped away and his magic butchered. Even at his full strength, he had hardly been able to put a dent into her efforts. That encounter had shown him the ugly side of his mortality, and he knew that if she saw him, it would spell the certainty of an end for one of them, and the odds were not in his favour.

And so, he dug quickly into the small satchel he travelled with and brought out his last resort. Breath bated and heart pounding in his chest, the Lord Watcher stared at the Alzeibier.

"What the hell is happening down there?"

Thorne snapped his gaze to the boatswain who trudged from the other side of the quarter-deck towards him, seemingly late to the party with a bottle in his hand. At once, the mastermind of Walera saw his chance. Thorne slid the ring on the index finger of his left hand. The black jewellery felt harmless. It would remain so until he fed it.

Thorne moved quickly, giving the boatswain no time to react, and all the sailor saw as he turned was the swing of a hand from a hooded man standing by the rail close to the mizzen mast. The boatswain's eyes widened, and he felt the pinch in his throat before the air mixed with the blood. The pain was the last thing he felt as the shock consumed his body, and he dropped the bottle. Thorne quickly turned the blade to his skin and slit his palm. He looked up as the stunned boatswain grabbed his slit throat uselessly, and the sorcerer didn't waste a moment before he wrapped the hand with the ring around the man's bleeding throat before he could fall.

Thorne's hand quickly became covered in thick red blood. The ring would taste the magic in his own blood but instead feed on the essence of the man he had killed. It was a luxury Wylie hadn't had when he had used the ring to save his nephew. Thorne held the boatswain's bleeding neck in place, feeling the ring draw from both of them, sparing his essence even as it felt like he was pulling at his soul. He watched the veins of his own hands run towards the enchanted ring as the life drained out of the boatswain.

A loud gasp sounded behind him, and Thorne snapped around, releasing the dead sailor and waving his arm toward the man standing there. Infused with power from the now-fed Alzeibier ring, Thorne watched as the man was thrown against the main mast and impaled by the yards. Confident of his abilities, the Lord Watcher quickly wove a portal spell. The air sizzled as if he had torn through it, and the portal appeared to manifest his escape.

Thorne moved to step into the portal but turned around in a heartbeat. Now that he was almost guaranteed his survival, he balled his hands into fists and buried them into the floor of the deck, sending an explosive force through and ripping the ship apart. The sea had no mercy as it began to make its claim with the precarious vessel. Only then did the Lord Watcher jump into his portal, dooming everyone on the Flea.

* * *

Old Ron took the bucket from his youngest son and moved to the stable, where he poured the apples into the horse feeder. He stood there for a moment until his son joined him, dropping a handful of hay in the corner of the shed before grabbing the shovel and beginning to haul away the beast's shit, mixing it with dirt and the hay in the wheelbarrow. Old Ron brushed the horse's back as it ate, and his hand wandered in the direction of the small scar towards the rear of the animal. At once, he was reminded of where it had come from, where he had been, who he had been with, and everything about that night before it had all gone to shit, and a King's Guard was no longer something they could call themselves.

Old Ron thought of the ambush and how Wylie's blade had been the only thing that had stopped a spear from ripping through his chest. He thought of what had become of Wylie. Old Ron had seen the house and had heard what was being whispered by folks who thought they knew the carpenter. Ron could recognize the signs of the desolation left behind by the watchers, and even if Wylie hadn't taken the ring, Old Ron would have still known what had happened there.

There was only so much he could do as he searched for Olin, hoping that perhaps there was a chance the boy had survived, at least. It was impossible to doubt Wyle had managed to do something with the ring and not something good. Ron breathed deep as he remembered his friend's refusal to tell him why he had needed the Alzeibier, despite how much he had pressed. The knowledge would only have doomed him. Old Ron looked at his son, cleaning up after the horse, utterly oblivious to what could have been, and he wondered if he had made the right decision to stay in Hunter's Grove, to remain in Ravinshore.

His son stopped shovelling and stood. Old Ron followed the boy's gaze, turning to the house where his wife was leading a strange woman towards them.

"Ron," his wife called.

Old Ron stepped towards them, looking from his wife to the commonly dressed young woman. A child stood with her, a girl barely five years of age. "Yes," he answered.

"She's here for you," his wife said.

Ron frowned as his mind quickly searched for where he could have made an acquaintance he couldn't remember. "How can I help you?" he asked at once.

"Are you Old Ron?" the young woman asked.

"Who's asking?"

"She is," the woman said, her hands on the child's shoulders.

Old Ron's eyes dropped at the child. "What?"

"She is Ilda's. Gytha has asked me to bring her to you. She says you will take care of her."

His eyes widened as he looked back at the woman, the child, his wife and then back at the woman. Old Ron's jaw almost slid off his face before he spoke, "Gytha? Ilda, you say? Where did you come from? How did you . . . Where —"

"I'm sorry, it's a long journey to Ovien, and I must get back tonight. Gytha said to tell you that Ilda was the child's guardian, and now you are. She asked that I deliver the child, nothing more."

"Wait, is she there? Is Gytha in Ovien?" Old Ron asked.

"No, she's not in the village. And before you ask, I don't know where she is. I've only followed her instructions, and I must be on my way now." The young woman nudged the girl gently towards her new guardian. "Her name is Ella," she said. "And you should know that she neither speaks nor hears like common folk. I must go now. Be well."

They watched, utterly perplexed, as the young woman hurried away. Old Ron looked to his wife and the child in front of him.

CHAPTER TWO

King Ranald wanted them dead. He wanted all of them gone. They had appeared and died before him, but Ranald was far from at ease after what he had discovered. His eyes were wide and his breath heavy as he stood by a window in the smaller of his court rooms. The larger one had been abandoned temporarily in the aftermath of the event hours earlier.

"Your Majesty." The group curtseyed while making their way into the room. King Ranald turned and scanned their eyes one after the other as they arranged themselves a few yards away.

Once the last of them had made it in, Ranald nodded, and two guards approached the alderman.

"You will do well to allow the guards to make certain that you are not carrying a weapon in my court," the king said.

A perplexed look ran across the faces of all four aldermen as the guards searched quickly for anything that had the semblance of a weapon, particularly a blade.

"You Majesty's, this is —"

"I do not care how you think this looks, Alderman Kon. After what I have witnessed today, I am hardly in the mind to let down my defences, even in the presence of old acquaintances. Be grateful that I am allowing you to keep your garments on and you are not all stripped to nakedness to satisfy my distrust."

Alderman Kon looked from the king to his fellow aldermen as the guards finished their search and found nothing. The guards stepped several paces towards the wall, significantly away from the king. Whatever questions Kon had, whatever questions any of them had, would ultimately come secondary to addressing the news that had brought the Aldermen of Queen's Hill to the palace in such urgency.

"Your Majesty, we came as soon as we heard," Alderman Kon said before anyone else could.

"Is that so?" the king asked, a hint of suspicion in his voice.

"Yes, of course, Your Majesty," Alderman Simoen answered. "We are all still in terrible shock, and what we heard is still hardly believable to our ears."

King Ranald took turns looking at each of their faces as if trying to discover something hidden. "Shocked? My court was not only turned into a slaughterhouse, Alderman. But I came inches from death". —he gestured, pinching two of his fingers together — "at the hands of the guardsmen I thought were there to protect me, palace guards, who turned out to be assassins, watchers in disguise. The Red Flame had its blade at my throat, in my court. In my palace! In my own bloody kingdom!" he shouted. The aldermen gasped and exchanged glances again. "I watched them slit the throat of my palatine right before my eyes! So, believe everything you heard, and do not tell me how shocked you are."

"To all the gods —"

"Leave the gods out of this. They have done nothing. This was the hands of the Red Flame, and I want it to end. Heads will roll, and the Order will answer for its crimes."

The words took a moment to register for the seemingly oblivious aldermen. They were trying to process the repercussions for the kingdom. If the Order had not only turned against the throne but had tried to kill the king. Sovereign as the king was, there was a reason why the Order existed and why only the king's power was revered more than that of the Red Flame.

"Your Majesty, there is no excuse for what has happened. None. But I do not think I am the only one who thinks declaring war on the Red Flame is the wisest thing to do," Alderman Kon answered.

"I disagree," Alderman Simoen said. "If a bold attempt on the king's life is not enough to demand answers from the Order, then what the hell is?"

"Demand answers, not declare war," Kon noted. "Surely we cannot forget what the Order is."

"No one has, and just as well, no one has forgotten that they answer ultimately to His Majesty, the king," Simoen answered.

"If this doesn't demand war, I don't care what does," King Ranald said. "I will make the Order pay. If it takes a civil war to ensure that every single one who had a hand in this answers with their head, then Queen's Hill will burn. The purpose of the Order means nothing if not to protect me and this kingdom, and they have declared that they have the complete opposite intentions. My court was violated, and those vile entities invaded my sanctuary. Whatever it takes, they will answer for it. They all will!"

* * *

The east was just as shocked by what had almost befallen it. It was only a matter of time before the news spread across Ravinshore and the rest of the three kingdoms, and Queen's Hill learned that they weren't the only ones who had almost fallen under the siege of their Order. The passages of Ravinshore's castle were almost ghostly, locked down to everyone but a handful of personnel. The King's First Guards, handpicked by King Edmond himself, guarded the walls around the castle, and service to the royal family only came from the hands of servants picked by Ole and Ariana personally. Every other servant, maid, guard, groundsmen and palace help that had perfunctory duties were barred from entering.

The walls seemed to echo sounds from every corner of the castle. Even the silence felt as though it still carried the remainder of the noises that had filled the castle's halls, passages, and crevices hours before. The air was thick with the stench of horror and blood. They could all feel it, even in the safety of the throne room, as the doors parted and Ole walked into the presence of the king and the queen.

"Your Highness, Her Grace." He bowed.

"Anything?" King Edmond asked at once.

Ole rose from the bow and shook his head. "No, Your Highness. Nothing at all."

"He cannot have merely disappeared. If he's not dead, he's somewhere in this kingdom," the king said.

"If he is alive, he probably knows that he's been defeated, and the best thing for him to do would be to make himself as scarce from Ravinshore as he can, Your Highness," Ole said.

"And what about his minions? What about Walera? It still stands. He could be hiding there, for all anyone knows," Ariana said from her seat next to the king's throne.

"The King's Guards have been to Walera, Your Grace. It's still under the control of the Order, but they have chosen to disclose that the Lord Watcher is not there. That was their response to the impending invasion of the King's Garrison camped at the gates of the Watcher's Den," Ole answered.

"He's not dead. He's somewhere hiding and licking his wounds, and that does not comfort me," King Edmond said. "How is it possible that I missed this? How did I not sense this coming?"

"As much as it turns my stomach to say this, if we had figured it out any sooner, then the Order wouldn't be what it is. The secrecy and the shadows are what the Order thrives on. This is why I'm not confident that Walera is still standing, and what's left of the Order's power remains in their hands. It doesn't feel right," Queen Ariana said, her fist balling on the chair's arm.

They fell quiet. Both Ole and the king could hear the anger in the queen's voice. It was similar to the rage in Edmond's voice when the Grand Sorceress had kept them in the bed-chamber during the heat of the attack on the palace. He had felt powerless. They were not powerless now; regardless of how hard it was to see it, Walera had failed. It wasn't likely that it would make any more moves for the throne with the king still alive. A retreat had been their only option after the attack on the palace had failed. Even if the mastermind hadn't disappeared and Thorne was still somewhere in Walera, The Lord Watcher would know that he was all but done for. His one shot had failed. Edmond's survival had been unexpected. The Order's power would always be secondary as long as the king lived.

Their other targets were pieces that could be replaced anytime. All those the Order had cut down still answered to the crown.

"Leave us," the king said to Ole.

"Your Highness." Ole bowed, turned, and made his way out of the room.

The door closed, and Edmond turned towards his queen.

"The watchers that were captured are in the dungeons. They could know where he is," Ariana said.

"It's unlikely he would risk knowledge of his escape falling to the watchers who would let themselves be captured. You said it yourself. The Order exists in secrecy. To them, it is death or service. Thorne isn't the kind of bastard to confide in anyone else about his plans to flee should it fail. And whether or not he imagined his plans would falter, I feel that he has buried himself as far as he can," Edmond answered.

"Still! We have to try. I will ask if I have to make the demand myself. If it is death or service, then that is all I need – I am prepared to carve an answer out of them. Since they do not fear death, they can go ahead and wait for their Lord Watcher in hell," Queen Ariana answered, her eyes wide with anger. "We cannot sit by and do nothing!"

She rose but froze when she felt a grip on her wrist. Ariana looked down at her hand as Edmond rose from his seat and walked to her. Her chest rose and fell quickly with her breath, and her whole body was stiff with the ire that his hands came to diffuse. Edmond stopped in front of her and took her other hand in his. He could feel her trembling. She continued to breathe heavily, and he knew that his hands were the only thing keeping the heads of the prisoners in the dungeon in place. He knew what she was capable of. Edmond knew.

He released her left hand and raised his hand to her face instead so he could look deeper into her eyes. Behind the rage and hunger for revenge, Edmond searched for the love of his life.

"They almost had you," she said, almost stuttering. "They almost had our . . . our children, Edmond."

"I know, and I am so, so sorry," Edmond said, holding her in place, feeling as her trembling grew. He gripped harder at her hand and held her face still. Edmond watched as her lips quivered, and he watched as tears crept over her eyes as though he had been expecting it. Edmond wrapped his hands around his wife just as her knees seemed to give way, and she fell against his chest. He held her tight as he listened to the sobs that no one else in the kingdom could boast of hearing. For as ferocious as she could be when she needed to, Ariana rarely knew when she was on the verge of tears. The King of Ravinshore held his queen, who had kept it all at bay while he was slumbering towards death and was now falling apart in his arms.

CHAPTER THREE

T he sun had set on Queen's Hill. Dusk gave no better than the day, which had seen the fate of the three kingdoms nearly go up in flames and pool with blood. The cascade of events and revelations made it seem like a wild dream they could wake from. But with every moment that passed where the memories didn't give way to a cruel awakening, they had to accept that fate had swept across their lives.

Levyna stared at Olin as he tried to force a habit of normalcy by sitting still, peering out at nothing in the distance beyond the window of the house. He had been that way almost all night, and she was sure he hadn't shut his eyes at all. He hadn't been looking out the window in the dead of night, but she had sensed his restlessness, had felt it. It was as though his heart was uneasy. It was odd that she couldn't merely read his thoughts as she had earlier. Olin turned around. It was already too late. He had seen her. She couldn't pretend that she hadn't been staring at him.

"Are you alright?" he asked as he pulled away from the window.

Levyna nodded. He had been asking that almost every hour she had been awake since the events at the Queen's Hill palace. "I'm fine, but I could ask you the same question," she said.

"You could." He stared at her. "And I will tell you that I'm fine."

"And I would still think that you're lying."

"What makes you think that?"

"Because I'm unable to see whatever is bothering you right now."

"I would think there are things you aren't so eager to share with me either," Olin answered as he moved towards the table, holding the scrolls he had scribbled to pass the time while everyone slept. He picked one up and set it down just as quickly. The former sciff turned back at her. Her gaze drifted away this time.

"I don't mean to pry," she said.

"I know," he answered. "There's no doubt that this . . . feels strange even as it feels natural at the same time."

Levyna knew precisely what he meant. It was unexpected and unimaginable how they had connected, how they were connected, and it felt effortless when they were around each other, even if it had been only a day and a half. It felt like they had been conscious of each other even before Posdel had given them a name for what they were.

"Did you see something new?" Olin asked to divert the conversation away from himself.

Levyna shook her head. "No. Nothing since what I saw earlier," she answered.

The phoenix. Olin had suggested it represented rebirth, and Posdel had agreed, saying the bird was a creature of magic whose power was connected to the sun and, as it meant redemption, it could just as easily mean death. This dream felt different, unlike the ones she had seen before, where many of the signs related to a person. There was no one she knew in the kingdom who went by the symbol of the phoenix. The fact that no one knew of Levyna's powers meant that the burden of finding the dream's true meaning would continue to haunt her, and unless she stumbled across the answer close to home, she would be plagued with never knowing.

There were a handful of people who could tap into a seer's dream, but they would need to know about her gift, a decision that had been left hanging following the events of the past few days.

And that was hardly the only thing Levyna needed help with. Her gift of travelling unprovoked through her spectre was something she needed to understand better. She wasn't the only one struggling with a new power either. Olin's powers had manifested, but he was far from in control of them. The things he had done at Queen's Hill may have been positive, but there were always secrets beneath every magic. That was what Posdel had said. They were eventually going to learn how their magic worked to test their levels of power. Still, that knowledge wouldn't be gained overnight, even if they seemed to have overcome the shock at the reality of the fact that their bodies were literal vessels of magic.

When Posdel said there was more to magic than just the gift, Levyna had found herself hardly thinking about what it would mean to be a seer and a traveller simultaneously. Her prominent thought had been of Olin, and the image of him as he had set Vernon on fire, scorching the man before he realized what was happening to him. What kind of power made someone do that? Even though she realized the urgency of what he had done and why it had been necessary. And it was a fate she had wished on the one who killed her father, but seeing Olin in that light for the first time brought questions to her mind. Questions she hoped Olin had been too distracted to hear.

They had sought Posdel's counsel, of course. After all, he was the one who had revealed what they were. So it was natural for Olin to retreat to Posdel's home after the madness at the palace, and Levyna had found herself unmovable despite her mother's reservations. Levyna had told her mother before her mother had left that she had hardly felt there was a place where she could be at peace other than here. What Levyna had not said, and what her mother had added in her head, was that it was a person with whom she had suddenly found peace. So while one mother left with promises to be back soon, and only because Levyna had promised she would be okay with a smile on her face that hadn't been there since her father's death, another mother's absence weighed heavily in the room.

Posdel was a powerful and skilled mage, but even he would be the first to admit that the presence of a Grand Sorceress would do a world of good for the children who were searching the depths of their magic, even if one of them wasn't her child. There were things she could do that she knew would save them both the trouble of having to discover it for themselves, but most of all, her presence would have soothed Olin. For the mage, it went without saying that the company would go a long way in sparing him from thinking about his fallen apprentice.

Levyna had asked about Gytha after her mother had left, and Olin's response had been uncertain. His mother had told him she needed to attend to something and that she would be back, but that promise had felt as real as the ones he couldn't remember hearing when he had been nothing more than a toddler, and she'd disappeared the first time. Olin had no idea where she was going or what she was up to. she was gone again. For all he knew, the mission that brought her to Ravinshore and out of the shadows was finished, and she had gone back to wherever she came from. For all he knew, it would take another nineteen years before he set his eyes on her again if he was lucky.

Olin tried not to let his feeling slip free, but Levyna knew. She could feel it off Olin as he turned back to the scrolls on his desk and picked up the charcoal.

"We need to find out more about the phoenix," Olin said, bringing her mind back to the dream they had been discussing. "It could be just as urgent as the ones before it." Olin ran his hands across the scroll as he continued to sketch.

"I agree, but other than Posdel, if we want to find answers about a seer's dream, we would have to go where my mother went days ago, and even that is not a certainty," Levyna said as she pulled herself from the seat and moved towards the table. Olin glanced at her as she walked, and a thought crept into his head that he had forgotten to hide. "Not that I have any offence to it, but I'm not that desperate for help," she answered.

Olin sighed. "I'm sorry, I didn't mean that you are, but I cannot stop thinking that your mother was right and you should have gone with her. This place reeks of sweat and liquor and the uncertainties of masculine minds. It is not fit for someone like you. That's the truth, and you know it. It's not to say that you cannot handle your grit," he said.

"Then don't say it. I might be young, but I'm far from naïve. I understand where I am and how much of a contrast it is to my home at the palace. I'm not desperate to return, not just because of the memories I fear it now holds, but because here feels different, and it feels good."

"There are things you need, things —"

"Yes, Olin. And I will make do. I don't fall completely apart in the absence of a maid, contrary to what's in your head."

Olin let out a heavy breath. "That's not what's in my head, and you know it."

"It's what it sounds like. Don't worry about me. I'll make do, and mother will be back soon anyway with things I might need. Unless you're the one who's desperate to have me leave," she said as he picked up the scroll in front of the pile.

How could he be? Her appearance was what had saved him when he had been out of his depth and near death. Besides the fact that magic connected them, it felt like he was rooted with her company, which was not something Olin thought himself famous for. But between trying to save King Edmond and losing the people closest to him, he was beginning to feel that standing still at times could have less consequences than wandering. "I don't want you to leave, and if you don't know that, then there's probably something wrong with the link, and it needs to be looked at. I'm glad you're here. I can be glad and worried at the same time," he said.

"Don't be, please. I'm not here by chance this time. I chose to be here."

His face pulled into a mock frown. "I thought you said you've never been here before?"

She struck the scroll playfully against his arm. "You know what I mean."

He did. Their second time meeting had been under the strangest of circumstances. Neither of them could fully explain it, even now. Levyna's spectre hadn't visited him by choice, though it hadn't been purely chance either, as her mind had been seeking him even if she hadn't consciously wanted to go to him.

"I do," he said out loud, nodding. He stared into her eyes, looking up at her from his seat. It was crazy how it seemed they were living in an illusion of normalcy, even after they had both witnessed two kingdoms almost fall to ruins the day before. But though the urgency was still there and the air was still thick with the threat of the Order's treason, Olin found himself a moment to breathe for the first time in what seemed like a while.

"Alright, so if you're done staring, perhaps we should find Posdel and tell him that we need to find out who this is referring to?" Levyna said, picking up the scroll on which he had drawn the image of a phoenix just as she had seen it in her dream.

* * *

The Watcher's Den of the Red Flame was afire with the heat of the chaos the attack had left behind. The failed attack on the king bore stiffness in the minds of the watchers as the doors opened and six people entered the large room. At the centre of the room was a large table etched with the symbol of a flame. Seven tall seats surrounded the table, with six of them shorter than the one at the head. A lit brazier burnt in a corner, and torches hung on the walls, positioned between carved symbols of flames surrounding the crown.

The six watchers took the seats, save for the tallest. When they were settled, they reached for their faces, pulled their masks off, and sat them on the table. The First Watchers of the Red Flame joined the Lord Watcher to form the circle of the Order's hierarchy, one that the death of the Lord Watcher had broken.

"This chaos has gone on long enough. The Order needs to get in front of it," Eden, the highest ranked and First Watcher, said.

"This happened due to poor judgment. I think many of us would agree," the Second Watcher said.

"Don't be too quick to give voice to what's in your head," the Third Watcher spoke, his words directed at the second. "There might be a kink in the plan, and it doesn't mean the plan is wrong."

"The Order has become villainous overnight, even after everything it has stood for in the past. I don't think anyone here truly believes completely that this is the path to take," the Second Watcher said.

"Are you saying you don't think the Order's intentions are valid?" Eden asked.

"No. I don't mean that," Second answered.

"Then what do you mean?" Eden said.

The Second Watcher looked at the faces across the table. "The Red Flame's motive has always been to serve the interest of its kingdom, Queen's Hill, even against its throne. I don't count that. But since when was this Order subjugated to Walera? Have we all accepted that?"

"Walera brought the plan that has been waiting decades to life," Third said.

"But whose plan was it?" Second demanded.

"What are you fishing for, watcher?" Eden's deep voice demanded.

"The flame of this Order burns in my veins, and it will continue till the moment I take my last breath, but have we not failed the Order by conceding to a mission that was doomed from the start? Do we still serve Queen's Hill?" Second asked. His pause doused the room in silence before he spoke again. "Do we serve

Queen's Hill by what we have done and are doing, or are we being made puppets for another's goal?"

"Everything we do is in service of this kingdom, everything!" the Fourth Watcher said.

Eden stood and sauntered, hands behind his back, towards one of the lit torches.

"And how are we sure about that?" Second pointed at the empty seat in the circle. "Our Lord Watcher has disappeared before the heat of the battle, and we have gone ahead regardless, even as the uncertainty lingers. The Red Flame edges closer to losing its identity and becoming mercenaries for an outsider because we have been convinced that was what we needed to do. For the first time, the Red Flame has tried to end its king, and we see nothing wrong with it because —"

The rest of the sentence was lost in his throat as his eyes bugged. The end of a stiletto dagger stuck out of his neck.

Eden pulled the knife out quickly, allowing the blood to run down the watcher's throat while he clutched at his neck, staring confused at the faces of other watchers, who merely sat there and watched until his breath failed and he dropped his head to the table before sliding off the chair and falling to the floor.

"Well, is there anyone else who wishes to speak fickle of this Order?" Eden asked.

"It was always his problem; he never knew when to stop talking," Third said.

"Yes, he never did." Eden looked down at the body as he walked towards the tallest of the seats at the table. "He was flawed, but he was right about one thing: the Order cannot continue to look precarious. Liston's role needs to be filled as we continue on this path. We might have failed one strike, but we are not merely crawling back into the shadows to die. We will get what we are after."

"Then we decide now. Who will it be?" the Fourth Watcher asked.

"I know Liston's wishes as he did himself, as I do Thorne's. Hence I do not see the need for any confusion as to who the new Lord Watcher should be." Eden looked at each of their faces.

The Fourth Watcher reached for his left hand and pulled off his gauntlet, placing it on the table. He looked up at Eden and nodded. The Third Watcher followed suit, and then the Fifth. The Sixth Watcher looked at the gauntlets on the table, at the faces of the unmasked watchers – faces that bore the secrets of Queen's Hill across the last decade – and he looked at Eden, who tilted his head to the side as he waited.

"What will it be, watcher?" the Fourth Watcher asked.

The Sixth exhaled as he got on his feet. He reached for his gauntlet and pulled it off, dropping it on the table like the rest. "Eden," he said as he nodded.

Eden smiled wryly.

"And in the conscience of this circle, the Lord Watcher shall be the Eden, son of Arrius," the Fourth Watcher rose as the other two followed.

And so the Red Flame's circle grew smaller but firmer, with a new lord and one less watcher and a shared goal to finish what they had failed the day before.

Paid to the Rodamann relations by the relatives hand down with picture of lord and his . . . that has unto a maiden . . . up to be only that coming and called to . . . up to prove it

CHAPTER FOUR

T he horses trotted through the gatehouse. Damiran didn't fail to notice the quiet and how ghostly the grounds seemed as his convoy rolled towards the front of the castle. It was a complete contrast to the last time he had been there a year before when he had come to celebrate a feast with family. The grounds had been crawling with servants and faces of people he had known since childhood, cousins and nephews and a wild bunch of the extended family. He saw a few servants and guards standing at the gates and the door. He might not have lived in

Queen's Hill for the last five years, but he knew for sure when something was wrong.

Damiran walked through the doors to find the king raising his head from his hand. A fractured smile pulled on Ranald's face as he saw him.

"Cousin!" the king said.

"Your Majesty." Damiran bowed before he stepped closer to the throne, but he halted at once when the guards inched towards him. Perplexed, he looked from one to the other and then to the king.

"Oh, you will have to tender your sword. You'll have it back once we're done," King Ranald said.

Surprise showed on Damiran's face as he looked at the king, wondering whether he meant it. "Your Majesty, we have known each other since we were children. What fear could you possibly have of my sword in your court?"

"I know, Damiran. It's not that I'm worried about you. I worry about what others could take advantage of," Ranald said. "Please, hand the guard the blade so we can talk."

Damiran blinked at the King's Guard standing by for his weapon and gave him a once-over before he undid his sword belt and handed it over. He watched as the guard walked away with it. Damiran turned his gaze back to his cousin, who nodded and pointed at the row of seats to his left.

"I received word and set out as soon as the messenger left. I must first ask you, Your Majesty, are you well?"

Ranald exhaled and nodded. Typical of Damiran. His cousin hadn't changed, which warmed his heart, despite everything that had happened. It was good to know that the first thing that came to Damiran's mind was his well-being. Damiran was a couple of years older than he was, and despite their mothers being sisters and Ranald having siblings of his own, his cousin had always been the one he was closest to. It was with Damiran that he had shared most of the best of his teenage and adolescent memories. Before anyone else, his cousin had been the one he had confided in about most things, and many had thought that Damiran would go on to become pivotal to Ranald's reign over Queen's Hill. But it hadn't turned out as expected after rumours grew of Damiran's involvement in a compromising relationship. He had never been able to shake them.

Damiran had moved as far away as he could afterwards, leaving Queen's Hill for Maedro merely a year after Ranald's father passed and Ranald had been crowned the king ahead of his half-brother. Damiran's appearance a year ago had been the first in almost a decade. They had thought the reunion would last them for another five years or so before he returned. Ranald had never been able to get his cousin to stay, even after becoming king, and he had always respected Damiran's decision to exclude himself from all court affairs. The attack, however, had pushed King Ranald to overlook his cousin's reservations that made him stay away. His brush with death had forced him to search for the one he had always seen as an ally.

"I'm alive, Damiran, even though I sometimes wonder how it is possible. I'm alive despite what the Order has attempted," King Ranald said. "I shouldn't let the shock bother me, but I cannot help the feeling that they have invaded everywhere. I stood in a room with my guards and palatine and watched as they emerged. Watchers. It was a horrible experience that opened my eyes to the truth. I have had an enemy at my back all along, one who has just been waiting for the right time."

Damiran's face pulled into a frown. It looked as though words failed him. "What about the queen? The prince and the princess?" he asked.

"My family is fine. I plan to send them away soon. Thankfully, none of them were in the room when it happened, but that's a risk I'm not willing to take again."

"Do we know why the Red Flame has suddenly turned, besides the obvious?"

"It is the obvious, cousin. And the madness you must have heard is that the Red Flame was not in this alone. Walera played a part in it," Ranald answered.

"What? That is . . ."

"I had the same look as the one on your face when the news was brought to my attention, Damiran. The disbelief was so great that I felt insulted, but it immediately cleared after I watched the assassin's attempt to snatch my life away. Watchers in disguise. I had thought it ridiculous, and so had Palatine Cyrus, who was wrongly suspected of being an accomplice to the Order's plan."

"Cyrus? What happened to Fredrick?"

Ranald chuckled. "They had gotten to him days before with no one the wiser. He died in his bathing bowl, of all places. They had him out of the way, and, when I think about it now, I imagine it was because he would have quickly sensed something was wrong. Fredrick would have discovered the truth."

"Or they could have just taken him out early to make it easier to get to you," Damian said.

"Maybe. Well, they did. It was shocking, and I was still on the verge of recovering from his death, with Cyrus taking his place. It appeared that my new palatine had met with one of the hands that would plot his own end too, and he never knew. Fredrick's wife and daughter appeared in the court to claim that he could be the assassin, only to watch his throat be slit from behind."

"It was not him?"

"Unless the role he had to play involved his own death, Cyrus was as shocked as the rest of us until he died. My death would have been certain, Damiran, had it not been for Fiona, her daughter, a mage, and a Ravinshore boy. It would all have been over. You would have returned to Queen's Hill and been greeted with my dead body on the palace floor. My enemies would have won. I tell you now that I have never been more grateful to be interrupted by strangers before, cousin," King Ranald said.

The shock was also in Damiran's breath. "And I am grateful to them, Your Majesty. Did they tell you how they came to learn the intentions of the Red Flame?"

"That is a story I could hardly believe either, but it all came down to the boy – a sciff from Walera itself – who overheard it all and set out to reveal the plot."

Damiran's brow arched. "A sciff, you say? And he survived the Order?"

"He looks to be more than just a sciff, and he certainly had a lot of luck on his side, too."

"So he overheard Walera's plans to have you killed?"

"Not quite. He witnessed the plot of King Edmond of Ravinshore's demise. Can you believe that? He overheard the Lord Watcher of Walera talking about how Edmond wouldn't survive his illness. Apparently, he had been poisoned, and they were waiting for his slow death to signal the onset of their larger plan, and when that failed, they moved to attack like savages." King Ranald paused and looked away. The thought came to him suddenly that he could have just as easily been subjected to a similar fate as his Ravinshore counterpart – poisoned without being the wiser. And he probably wouldn't have lasted as long as Edmond had, with Egro draining the essence from his body. King Ranald's face grew pale as he looked briskly from his cousin to the guards and then to the room's doors and windows.

"Your Majesty?" Damiran said.

"Damiran. There are only so many reasons the Order could have for what they have done and what they have tried to do, and honestly, I don't care what that reason is. They believed they can do as they please and get away with it, and I seem to be surrounded by chickens pretending to be foxes themselves. I have asked you here because I realize how empty my circle is. I want to end the Red Flame. I don't just want them to pay. I want the Order to end for good."

Damiran exhaled, and his face pulled at his cousin's words. Behind the king's statement, he could hear the anger, the frustration, and, more than anything, the panic of realizing that he had an enemy like the Order of his kingdom who couldn't be easily silenced with the wave of a hand. The king had been the one to give the Order its power and freedom to do as needed to protect the kingdom. Ranald might not have been there when his ancestors had chosen to put a group of assassins in charge of the kingdom's safety six hundred years ago, but he was on the throne now, and it was his problem to bear.

* * *

"I asked around as you demanded. No one saw anything," Giodin said from behind the counter of his merchant's stall, and Posdel's face pulled into a frown at the words.

"What do you mean no one saw anything? Someone should have seen something. Someone is bound to see something. It couldn't have just disappeared."

Giodin turned his palms up and shook his head, his response no different from what it had been before. "I don't know what you expected me to say. I asked everyone I could, everyone, who would know about something like that happening on the street, and no one claims to have seen anything."

"But that can't be. It's impossible. I saw it with my own eyes – I saw her with my own eyes. I saw the knife hit her neck, and I saw her drop to the ground. And then I went after the one who did it. She definitely couldn't have just gotten up and walked away, so someone must have carried her body," Posdel explained.

"Look, other than Yondi, I haven't heard of anybody found on the street. If there had been, I would have heard about it for sure. You know people talk to me," Giodin said. "But you say she could have been taken – why would anyone do that? What business could anyone have with a dead body?"

"Many things and none I can think of that are good," Posdel said, sighing. There were those who did unspeakable things to the dead. It was uncommon but not completely unheard of. The thought was abhorrent for him to even allow in his head. But as Giodin had said: people talked in Queen's Hill, especially when it came to something like this. If anyone on the streets had seen Moreen's body, he would have heard of it. He had heard about Yondi before his blood had dried on the cobblestone.

The aftermath of the troubles with the Order had led him to think about his apprentice and inevitably remember the circumstance of his death. Posdel, after abandoning the betraying cousin to go after the watcher in a chase that had eventually led him into the den of the hunters themselves, had gone back in search of her body only to be told it had never been found.

Not that it had been taken, it had simply never been found. It was as though she had never died there, and even though he knew what happened to her in the end, Posdel couldn't quite shake the curiosity of the mystery. A body did not just disappear. The possibility had crossed his mind that the ones who had cut her down had taken her. That was a slightly more plausible scenario than the alternative, even if he could see no reason why the Order would murder Moreen in the open only to steal away her body afterwards. Posdel knew first-hand that the Red Flame had never really bothered to conceal the trail they left behind, not since they had grown reckless and desperate. The sight of Yondi's body face-down on the ground was a painful reminder that Red Flame didn't care about evidence. Only actions.

Even if it had been the watchers, it would have taken time for them to get to her unless others had been standing by in wait. Posdel had thought it through, and it made no sense. He couldn't shake the curiosity. It wasn't that he was oh so passionate about the remains of the young woman, but he couldn't help but remember how quickly he had abandoned her to her death, and a feeling of guilt crept over him. He had condemned her in his mind when he realized what she'd done. He hadn't cared when she'd said she hadn't known what would happen to her cousin after leading the watchers to him. Nothing of the ache in her voice as she'd spoken her confession had moved him. She had been one of them, had chosen them over her own family, and there was no excusing that as far as he was concerned.

Moreen deserved what came to her, and it had felt better not coming from his own hands. That was what Posdel had told himself. It suddenly hadn't mattered that she was no stranger, that he had housed her countless times when she'd come visiting her cousin. Posdel had seen the blood spurt from her throat, and he hadn't made a move to try and do anything to save her or ease her pain. She deserved it, and instead of pondering what would become of her, he had gone after her attacker instead. Not because he considered her murder a terrible injustice but in the hope that he could at least get his hands on those who'd killed Yondi.

"Look, if you want, I'll continue to ask around. In fact, you don't have to mention it all. I'll keep the word out on the street for anyone who might have seen or heard something about it."

"You don't have to, Giodin."

"No, I want to. Truly. It's the least I can do. I know who she was to Yondi. You know, He wouldn't stop talking about her whenever she came around. I can only assume that whoever killed Yondi got to her too. It's sad. But the disappearance of her body is a mystery, and I think we owe it to your boy to find out the truth," Giodin said.

His boy. The urge to correct the merchant drowned as quickly as it came. Giodin was oblivious to the truth of what had happened to Yondi at his cousin's hands, and Posdel saw no need to ruin the memory.

"I don't think I'm the only one in this market who will miss him," Giodin said.

At that, Posdel had no doubts.

* * *

"I think I need to go to Ravinshore," Olin said.

Posdel held the bowl of soup in his hand, glared at him, then glanced at Levyna too. "Is that so?" he asked.

"Yes. I know it's probably a little too soon, but it has been days. I want to know if Wylie has been buried," Olin said.

"Of course," Posdel said. "You should do that. But do you think now is the right time for you to go?"

"It's obvious that the Order has more important things to worry about now that their plan is out. I don't think anyone would be concerned about an old sciff anymore," Olin answered. "I know it doesn't mean that the Order is completely done with me. I'm not ignorant of that."

"But you still want to go?" Posdel asked.

"I feel that I should. I feel that I need to," Olin said.

Posdel looked at Levyna, who still hadn't said a word to Olin's declaration. "You know you don't need my permission to go wherever you want, Olin. I can only try and talk you into understanding why doing something else might be a better decision. I don't think going back to Ravinshore for the reason that isn't urgent is wise. You might be right that the Orders have bigger problems than you, but, like you once said to Yondi, they cannot be underestimated. Don't think that they have completely forgotten about you."

"I know that," Olin said.

Posdel sighed. "I cannot keep you here, but Levyna's mother made me give my word that she would be safe."

"And she will be," Olin said.

"Safe here," Posdel stressed.

"Yes," Olin said.

Levyna snapped her gaze to him. "What?"

"You need to stay. It's safer that way."

"How can you be sure? And what about you?" Levyna asked. "You sound as if you don't know what could be lying in wait for you there."

"I don't know." Olin shrugged. "Which is why it would be best not to risk the both of us."

Levyna stared at him in confusion, searching his brown eyes for what she was missing, for what had changed since their discussion about finding the meaning of the phoenix dream. Something they had planned to do together.

Where is this coming from? she asked him.

It's just something I feel like I need to do, he answered.

Why do I feel like there's more to it?

Why do you care, Levyna? What does it matter if there's more!

Levyna heard the shout ringing through her head as Olin's forehead creased with a frown. She gasped, frowned, and stepped away from him. Olin turned and headed out of the house, more for the need to keep himself from saying something he would regret than him setting out on the journey to Ravinshore at that moment. Levyna dropped back to her seat, trying not to appear too affected by what he had said.

Posdel dropped the bowl on the table, glanced at the door, and then back at her. "I'm guessing that conversation did not end well."

"I don't know. He has looked off all day, and we talked earlier about trying to figure out who the phoenix was referring to or what it meant. We were going to . . ." Levyna trailed off.

"I cannot claim to have known him for long. Still, I can tell that he has trouble accepting that he doesn't have to carry all of his burdens alone. I don't think he means that you should stay behind because he would rather not have your company, but he has lost people going up against the Orders, and I believe that leaves its mark, regardless of what you are to him or perhaps, especially because of it."

"I am not some maiden who would need to be saved. I did not ask for our paths and our magic to cross."

"I feel you know that more than just your magic is linked, which is why you're so worried about him leaving alone."

"It makes no sense. None of it does."

"It can be like that sometimes. Sometimes because of the magic, other times it's more. I cannot claim to know exactly how it is for you. Frankly, not many people know the experience of having their magic linked to another. Neither of you have had the most convenient experience learning about it, with your losses and the chaos the Orders have thrown the kingdoms into."

Levyna exhaled. She knew there was truth to Posdel's words. She'd been able to feel Olin from the first touch of his hand, back when she had been dealing with dreaming her father's death, and he had been struggling to escape the watchers, and it had only grown since. "I just don't understand the sudden change of heart, the need to go to Ravinshore now."

"If there's anyone who would know besides him, it's you," Posdel told her.

"But I don't . . ." Levyna quieted herself as she thought about it. There was one reason she'd sensed when he'd looked off into the distance earlier. She'd ignored it, unsure of whether he had wanted her to know. "Could it be?"

"What?"

"His mother."

Posdel sighed. "It wouldn't be crazy, after all."

"If he thinks that perhaps she's there, somewhere."

"It would quite frankly make more sense than burying the dead while watchers swarm."

Levyna looked at Posdel. "If that's true, you must let me go with him. I fear he thinks she has abandoned him again. He shouldn't have to go through it alone."

"Levyna, the only real reason your mother has allowed you to stay with us is because I gave her my word that I would keep you safe. I failed that task for one ward. I am not eager to repeat the experience," Posdel said.

"You know I could leave, and you wouldn't be able to stop me, right?"

"Your body would still be here."

"I could leave completely."

"And then I would be forced to either keep you here with a spell or go after you."

CHAPTER FIVE

Fiona tried not to think about what had happened the last time she had been in the palace as she was led to the throne room's doors.

Fiona stood at the threshold, and a part of her tried to block out the event, especially as she was conscious of the fact that she was not accompanied by the pertes – her daughter and her partner, Olin – or a mage. Fiona was aware of how the palace suddenly reminded her of her mortality. Forces that had taken her husband had attacked the king, and her daughter had been caught between them. Levyna had been one of the reasons why the king was still alive, why two kingdoms still had their rulers despite the efforts of the Orders. But she had done that by getting in the way.

When Levyna had asked to stay with Posdel, Fiona's first instincts had been against it, but then a part of her had been somewhat relieved at the idea that her daughter would be away from the focal point of any violence that may come in the future. That was why she had agreed to let her remain in the company of the mage and Olin. And though both of them were still somewhat strangers, they had proven with every minute that they would put themselves in front of Levyna if there were ever trouble. Fiona had seen that and how her daughter reacted when it came to the boy from Ravinshore. Fiona was terrified of what the grief of losing her father would turn her daughter into, what the guilt would make of her. She had seen glimpses of those fears the morning before Fredrick's death, which tormented her. Levyna had started talking about the boy. It had seemed as though she had something to take her grief away.

Or at least push it to the side.

It hadn't been the best order of events – going from losing her father to having to witness other men die in front of her. It had been a baptism by blood, but somehow Levyna had managed to look somewhat more confident and at peace even after everything they had been through. Fiona wasn't sure whether it was the magic, what Posdel had done, the connection with the boy from Ravinshore, or that Levyna had realized her potential to save someone, but her daughter looked to have earned a year's worth of confidence in two nights.

Fiona sighed deeply. Her thoughts settled on her daughter. the doors opened, and she stepped into the throne room. She almost froze in place, and her legs suddenly felt weighted as she realized what she had walked into. When she had asked to meet with the king, it had only been because she wanted to apologize for the wrong assumptions she and her daughter had made about Cyrus concerning her husband's death and also see if the king was doing well. She hadn't been expecting an audience like the one before her. Heads turned towards the door as she entered. She hadn't known that King Ranald was busy with guests.

"Ah! Lady Fiona!" The king's voice carried a distinct excitement from his seat on the throne, and he raised his hand, beckoning her even as she approached.

Fiona walked the length of the aisle a fair distance from the throne where she curtseyed. "Your Majesty. I must apologize if I have intruded in your court yet again. I was of the opinion that the guards would inform you of my request for an audience, tell you it was not urgent, and relay to me that you had something important going on. I am terribly sorry, Your Majesty," she said.

"No, please. Don't be. I wanted you here. You have nothing to apologize for," King Ranald said.

Fiona raised her face as she realized that the king had not been confused. She blinked and glanced to her left, where she found a familiar face she hadn't seen in a while.

"As a matter of fact, it's you we have been waiting for," Ranald said.

Fiona's brows raised. "Me? Is everything alright, Your Highness?" she asked.

"Considering the circumstances, all is well at this very moment. I am sure you remember my dear cousin, Damiran?"

Fiona glanced at the familiar face. She nodded. "Yes, I do."

"Good! He has returned on account of what happened. I'm also sure you remember the aldermen," the king said.

"Of course, Your Majesty, I remember all of them," Fiona answered, her gaze staying on the king's cousin.

"Well, when you said you needed an audience, I thought there would be no better time to let the news out than now," King Ranald began. "I was utterly oblivious to what was lying in wait for me until Fiona and her party manifested in the middle of my court. She had just lost her husband to the hands of the watchers, yet she led her daughter and friends here to thwart the effort of the Watchers of the Red Flame. If they had been only a moment later, there's no telling what could have happened. But they weren't.

"It's quite easy to forget just how important those that surround you are. Because of that, I want to thank Fiona for being a trustworthy friend in my time of great need," the king said.

Fiona curtsied at the king's words, trying not to feel like a charlatan as he heaped praises on her even though all she had done was accompany her daughter and the rest here – those who'd had the powers and had done something to protect the king and the kingdom.

"Her husband was my palatine for many years, and he was the very best I could have wished for. I might not have seen it before, but I think it is deserving now," King Ranald said, his words rolling off his tongue but hardly helping the curiosity in the faces of the Damiran and the aldermen as to what the king's plan was. "And so, I am naming Lady Fiona as my palatine – the Palatine of Queen's Hill."

"What?" Fiona said, shocked, her voice rising above the others that clamoured for the king to repeat himself.

Damiran's gaze snapped from his cousin to Fiona and back. It seemed the king's words were a surprise to everyone and especially to the woman herself. Damiran struggled to hide the disbelief in his expression as Ranald sat on his throne, smiled, and nodded.

"Yes," the king said. "That is what will be."

"Your Majesty, I . . . I am afraid I don't think I am the right person to be your palatine, Your Highness."

"That is untrue, Lady Fiona. Your husband had the job for many years, and you watched him do it. You watched him serve, and you served with him. I would only ask that you continue that service. You are the one I have chosen to be my palatine, Lady Fiona, and that is final."

Fiona's eyes remained wide as she looked from the king back towards the familiar face of his cousin. Damiran's gaze held steely on her, and she wasn't sure what to make of it. She wasn't sure what to make of the expression on the faces of the aldermen, either. At that moment, she felt like she wanted time to stop so she could breathe and understand what fate was bringing her way. But she didn't even have time to react to the news of her new title and role. She had walked into the room an outsider to the court and was now to take her place at the king's left side as his most trusted hand.

Fate wasn't done moving the pieces around Fiona and her daughter.

* * *

Before the old king of Queen's Hill had died, many thought there was a chance that he would let someone else have the throne rather than his son, Ranald. It hadn't been a secret that the king had a soft spot for his older son all through his life, and many assumed that the older prince would end up being the one kneeling on the day of the coronation. But it hadn't turned out the way anyone expected, and despite the way the king had favoured his first son, he had never been the crown prince. And then the day came that his younger half-brother was named the heir to the throne.

There had been questions, several, that wrapped around what had happened to cause the king to change his mind. But, ultimately, there was no way to know what had influenced the king's decision.

When the elder prince had failed to gain his birthright, he had moved from the palace castle to an estate some distance away. Their father had planned for Ranald to take charge and his brother to be the one who helped him from the sidelines, but Petr hadn't lasted more than the perfunctory period in his role after his failure to gain the crown. He hadn't declared his intentions of reclaiming it. He hadn't declared that he hated his father. He hadn't actively sought out avenues to act against his brother's throne. But he found ways all the same.

Damiran descended from his horse and watched the prince release an arrow at the bird in the sky. It fell to the ground with a thud. A small dog hurried towards the dead bird and came back, holding the kill in its jaws. The dog dropped the bird on the ground next to the prince, who was taller than King Ranald but had the same hair and look.

"Your aim is still as perfect as ever," Damiran said from a few yards away, and the prince turned. The look on his face was not one of complete delight.

"I get by," the prince said. "Damiran."

"Cousin."

"You found your way to Queen's Hill just when the time is right." The prince turned away and pulled the arrow from the dead bird. The arrowhead was still intact. He fixed the arrow's nock, guided by the feathers to the nocking points on the string, and lined it with the bow's grip before he aimed again.

"There was no way I could ignore a call from the king after the attack. I would have come sooner had I been aware of what was happening."

A redness seemed to appear on the side of the prince's face as Damiran mentioned the word 'king.' Petr tensed from his jaw to his arm as he followed the sight of another bird in the distance, breath still as he released the arrow. A soft quack was heard from afar, and then a thud somewhere in the bushes. The dog took off at once and disappeared after the target.

"Like I said: when the time is right," Petr said.

Damiran exhaled. To Petr, losing the crown had felt like a betrayal from everyone in the circle of the royal family. While he honoured calls to the palace and feasts that involved family, he never truly looked like the old self he had been when he'd thought he would be the kingdom's next ruler. He refused all his brother's attempts to pull him close to the throne. Petr wasn't interested in being an alderman, a palatine, an advisor, a commander, or an emissary. He made no claims whatsoever and made no efforts to cling to power, just as he had promised. But though he has tried to shoulder himself out of the title, he was still a Prince of Queen's Hill.

"Petr, I know you must know what happened at the palace."

"Good fetch, you." The prince knelt by his dog and eased the bird out of his jaw. He rubbed the head and patted the back of his hunting companion before he pulled the arrow out of the bird again. "The entire kingdom has probably heard by now."

"Then you must know that the throne and the kingdom of Ravinshore is under attack. There's a fair chance it won't stop with a single attempt at the king's life. Even if the Order has retreated, the king has not. He wants answers, and heads will roll."

"The last I recall, it was his head they wanted. Does it not sound fair that he wants theirs in return?" Petr asked as he tied the feet of his four kills together.

"Yes, but remember who we're talking about here, cousin. It's not just some hopeless man or group in over their heads. It's the Order. The Red Flame."

"So?"

Damiran sighed at being made to labour with the explanation. "I know you know what that means, Petr. The king can demand only so many heads before he has something else on his hands. He's hinting at a war against the Order in his own kingdom."

Petr rose. "I still don't understand what the problem is and why you have come to bother me, Damiran. The king does whatever he thinks is right."

"There's no way you can say that with a straight face, Petr. Not about the King of Queen's Hill. No way. No matter what you think you're trying to prove, you have just as much to lose if the kingdom is plunged into a civil war, and perhaps, even more, should the Red Fame conquer the throne of Queen's Hill. You cannot possibly be at peace with the idea that the throne could burn at any moment if it isn't already!" Damiran noticed the twitch in his cousin's brown eyes, the one he could never hide, no matter how much indifference he tried to pretend. Damiran knew that Petr could see it just as he could.

"You still haven't answered my question, cousin. What do you expect from me?" Petr moved his bow and arrow to the side.

"I think there is something more happening."

"What do you mean?"

"I think the king is . . . suffering a lot of stress," Damiran said.

"Did you not just a moment ago say that the Red Flame tried to kill him? How can he not be stressed?"

"I know, but listen, you must understand what I'm saying. This . . . this seems to be something else. With the way he talks and the way, he has been acting ever since my arrival. I've picked up hints that there might be a need to worry about him."

"You have to explain what you mean, Damiran, do not jumble words."

"Ranald saw something when his guards almost killed him, something I fear might have harmed him. Broken something. Much more than his common trust for people. I said he speaks too quickly, like an easterner who doesn't know when to stop. His eyes are almost dead from lack of sleep, and his thoughts are cleaving towards mortality with every other sentence. He is even beginning to make utterly questionable decisions – he has made Fiona, the wife of his dead palatine, his new palatine, Petr." Damiran wasn't mistaken. Petr reacted again, this time, both of the prince's brows twitched. "He doesn't let anyone close to him during court. This evening he wore armour underneath his robe. I don't know what will come next, but I suspect it will be worse than making the wife of the old palatine his new palatine just because she helped save his life."

Petr fell quiet. Damiran could imagine the picture in his head.

"I don't think I am the only one who is noticing the signs, cousin. And it's early. You asked why I'm here. I want you to consider coming to the palace. Your presence could help steady the course your brother is leading the kingdom towards. There are people who need to see that Queen's Hill is more than King Ranald."

"Is it?" Petr asked. "Is he not the king? Is the kingdom not his to make or break?"

Damiran scoffed and shook his head. "No, Petr. And again, I know that deep down, you don't believe that. All of this . . . is yours too. It is ours. Ranald might be the one with the crown on his head and his ass on the throne, but nothing anyone can say will wither away the fact that you always...always have a part to play in the affairs of Queen's Hill. I have tried to stay away for years, and so have you. Ranald has tried to do it on his own, but clearly, something has given the Order the confidence that they can come for the throne of Queen's Hill and just take it as though it were bread from a simple child. You had your reasons for staying away, as did I. Unless you're going to tell me that you don't care whether your father's throne is taken over by a bunch of watchers when the Red Flame finds its way back. You must see reason in what I am saying. Ranald doesn't know what he is asking for. He is too . . . confused."

Petr exhaled as he looked at his dog chasing a moth. The prince pulled his gaze back to his cousin before he reached down, grabbing the rope around his kill's feet and walking towards his horse tied nearby. "All you have said of Ranald's behaviour – none of it is too damning for him to shake."

"Oh, Petr . . ."

"This is my kingdom, and that is my father's throne. But it is not my throne – he never meant it to be." Petr hung the rope of birds from the side of the saddle before mounting his horse. "Let the King of Queen's Hill fight the battle for his kingdom as he seems fit, cousin. Leave me out of it." He clicked his teeth and nudged the horse to a trot before he whistled for his mutt, who abandoned the moths to chase after the horse.

Damiran watched as the prince slowly grew into a tiny figure in the distance. Whispers and chatters had stirred his own abandonment of Queen's Hill, but there was nothing his self-exile had cost him that could possibly be compared to what Petr continued to turn his back on as he rode away from anything and everything that involved the throne of Queen's Hill. If the prince had any sort of a plan, Damiran couldn't see it, couldn't imagine it. Was his apathy because he knew Ranald would never last and he would get his chance then? If that was it, why not try now when he could have two for the price of one. He will need to get close to the throne and make his case for leadership while keeping the Order away from the kingdom's seat.

Petr said his brother would shake whatever it was. Damiran mounted his horse and turned in the opposite direction, thinking the prince had sounded just like someone who hadn't seen for himself what the King of Queen's Hill was becoming.

CHAPTER SIX

Their faces looked too precise, too focused. Ranald could tell. Every face that entered and left his court, he searched for the signs, and they all looked similar, they all looked the same, all but a few of them anyway.

Ranald had woken from his sleep, sure that he had heard a creak. It had come from the door and moved to the windows. Blade in hand, Ranald had gotten up to confirm he had defiantly bolted them shut. Then he'd seen what looked like a shadow moving beneath the door, and that had caused him to freeze for almost an entire hour, staring and waiting. He could never be too sure when they would come again. He could never be too sure who it would be. After he had eventually returned to bed, he again heard the creaking of wood, even with the windows and the doors unmoving. Finally, he had abandoned the comfort of his bed for a chair, where he had spent the rest of the night waiting, dagger in hand.

Now that he was looking at their faces again, almost all of them were changing. He kept them at bay and couldn't allow them to get too close. Only a few of them felt real and didn't make him conscious of the sword he now carried even as he sat on his throne in court in his palace. To his left was the woman who had brought the party that had saved him, and to his right was his cousin, who he trusted more than anyone else. At least he was sure they were loyal and safe, even though the rest of the court looked increasingly suspicious. With them at his side, Ranald didn't feel completely overwhelmed.

The king exhaled and looked ahead as the messenger arrived.

"Your Majesty." The messenger bowed before the court.

"Speak," Ranald said, conscious of the man and what he was holding.

"A message to My Lord from the Order."

Ranald stiffened. He looked from his palatine to his cousin. "They send a message and no messenger. Do they really expect that me to honour whatever it is they have to say," he said, referring to the note in the messenger's hand. "I'm not interested in hearing written words. Let them know that! I want hell to rain on them for what they did and what they tried to do. Send it back at once!" the king ended with a shout.

"Yes, Your Majesty." The messenger bowed and turned to leave.

"Wait!" Fiona called out, causing a stir in the court. Her presence was unusual, to begin with, and now she dared to counter an order from the king. Whispers and quiet questions followed her interjection. "Your Majesty, I think perhaps you should reconsider sending back the message without knowing what it is," she said.

"I've said I'm not interested in hearing whatever they have to say, especially when they cower behind scribbled words," the king answered.

"Of course, Your Highness, they are hiding behind words, but it could be to our advantage to know what is on their minds. Why can't the Order send a delegate? If anything, I think we can be sure they are aware you are far from being in an accommodating mood. They know they have messed up the sheets, for lack of a better term. Whatever your judgment will be, and deserving as it is, I think knowing why they have reached out could be to your advantage," Fiona said, holding her head up.

King Ranald stared at her with a partly-formed frown on his face. He looked back at Damiran and then at the messenger who was still standing, waiting to spring into action should the king repeat his prior order; the messenger would not be slow enough to hesitate. Ranald looked back at his palatine, the face he had chosen to remind him of a sanctuary that would not be merely a figurehead. "Fine, lets' hear what it is," he said.

Fiona nodded and signalled to the messenger, who hurriedly approached and handed her the small scroll.

King Ranald watched the handover carefully, his eyes locked on every muscle the messenger moved as he bowed, turned, and hurried out of the court. The palatine snapped the seal on the scroll and opened it to read; a part of the king's mind was watching every movement of her muscles, too fearing there was perhaps something he had missed that the Order could have managed to get to her, to hold something over her, to turn her against him.

Fiona read the message herself first before she conveyed it to the court. It was brief. "The Order of the Red Flame is requesting a White Indulgence with His Highness," she said.

"A White Indulgence?" King Ranald asked.

"Yes. They seek to meet without arms. They want to have a dialogue," Damiran said, his voice carrying much farther than that of the Palatine.

The king scoffed. "Do they take me for a fool? Do they think I would really walk straight into another trap and allow them yet another chance to attack so they can finish what they started? How stupid must the Order think I am not to see their trick for the second time?" He laughed, his panicky voice echoing alone through the room.

As Ranald laughed, he tried to hide the trembling in his gut at the possibility that he could be forced into a situation like the previous attack. The memory of the blood and the idea of it happening again began to dissolve down his throat and chest. King Ranald could suddenly feel his heart pounding and chest tightening as he laughed. His laughter dwindled as he quickly realized that his breath was caught and his breathing had turned laboured. The king coughed and slowly moved his hands to his chest.

Fiona's eyes did not leave him. She saw his struggle for what it was. "Your Majesty," she said, rising to her feet as she spotted the edge of his ear turn red. She spun to Damiran. "Clear the room!"

"You cannot —" an alderman tried to argue.

"Clear the room!" the palatine ordered again, and this time the thunder in her voice was unmistakable as she moved towards the king quickly.

"You heard her. Get out, all of you!" Damiran said to those still dragging their feet in their exodus from the throne room.

"You too!" Fiona barked at the guards, who didn't seem sure the order applied to them in the king's state.

The two guards at the door stepped out, and the doors closed, leaving Fiona and Damiran alone with the king.

"They are gone, Your Majesty, it's alright. You're alright. You have to breathe," she said.

Damiran stood and watched in silence as the palatine placed her hand over the king's and nodded slowly, inhaling and exhaling deeply so the king could imitate her as he opened his eyes.

"It's alright, take it very slowly, breathe in with your nose and breathe out with your mouth," she said. "You are alright," she said.

Damiran watched as Ranald followed suit, taking the breaths very slowly, eyes locked on the woman in front of him. The king's eyes gradually widened as he began to recover control of his breathing, and his cousin watched till he looked like he had returned to himself.

There was a moment of quiet. Both Fiona and Damiran remained in the room, observing the king. The last time Damiran had seen Ranald panic like that was when he had been a teenager, over two decades ago. Damiran couldn't help but wonder if Petr could see this, would he still agree that his brother could shake off his reaction to the mere thought of having an audience with the Red Flame?

"I had no idea it was happening again," Damiran said.

"It's not," the king said brashly. "It is not. And I forbid you from speaking of it."

"Of course." Damiran bowed.

Another moment passed without anyone saying anything, as though the other two were trying to weigh the king's breaths before they could speak mentally.

"I think there is no one who will question Your Majesty if he does not seek to honour the Order's request," Damiran said.

Fiona glanced at him. "No one will question His Majesty's choice, but that does not necessarily mean that he should not at least consider the idea," she said.

"Why do you say that? Do you not see . . .?"

"See what?" Fiona asked, wondering if he would dare mention something the king had just forbidden them from talking about.

"If His Majesty does not think it is the best thing to do, then there certainly is no reason for him to honour the Indulgence, except perhaps on his own terms."

"Of course, His Majesty's terms would, by all means, overrule whatever terms the Order requests for the Indulgence. But we would both agree that it would be in the best interest of harmonious discord for the terms of both sides to be honoured," the palatine said.

"Would you two stop talking as if I'm not right here?" the king said.

"Apologies, Your Majesty," Damiran said as he and Fiona bowed.

"I have decided to accept the request for the White Indulgence, no arms. I want to hear what they have to say and how they plan to pay for what they have done," Ranald declared.

Damiran's face creased, and he darted a glance at Fiona, who seemed surprised, before turning back to his cousin. "Your Majesty, are you sure that is something you're ready for?"

Ranald always knew his cousin to be a clever one. Hence he was not surprised to hear him subtly hint at what he could not say. "There will never be a perfect time to deal with this. I want it over with as quickly as possible so that I can pass judgment. I want to end the Order, that is certainly still my plan, but perhaps it's time I listen to my palatine once again and see how I can use their thoughts to my advantage. But, whatever becomes of that Indulgence, they can be certain of the fact that I am delivering penance for what they have done, even if I cannot do it during the Indulgence itself," the king said. "The Order will never forget that they have crossed their worst enemy."

Fiona swallowed hard. The fact that the king was willing to meet with the Order was not a perfect answer but was certainly better than the alternative, which would see Queen's Hill painted with the blood of innocent lives who would have no say in the tides of war. Even if it were for her daughter's safety, Fiona would take the king's sudden change of heart over his initial stance of a blind attack on the Order, something which she couldn't imagine would lead to a bloodless resolution.

They had been forbidden from talking of it, but Fiona could still think about it. She had spotted the signs of the king's panic attack because it was familiar. It was something she had used to see in her brother when they had been much younger, which was how she'd known how to help. She also knew that the last thing the king and the kingdom needed was for word to somehow make it out of the room where the king had suffered an attack. People wouldn't care that it was the first attack in decades. They wouldn't understand that it had been caused by the thought of facing a massacre in what was meant to be his sanctuary. Nearly everyone in the kingdom would assume a panic attack made their king feeble-hearted. That wasn't something Queen's Hill needed to deal with right now.

"To my terms of the White Indulgence, you will add that I meet the Order only if their Lord Watcher is present."

"Of course," Fiona said.

"And one more thing. There will be no watchers with magic in attendance. None at all."

* * *

Fiona's heart fluttered in her chest as she stepped through the doors, out of the throne room, and into the halls where she found her daughter waiting.

"Levyna?" she said.

"Yes, Mother," Levyna answered.

Fiona moved to her quickly and held her. "Are you okay? Are you really here? Is everything alright? Is Olin alright?" she asked frantically as her eyes scanned her child from chestnut hair to feet.

"I'm fine, Mother. And no, I'm not really here," she said.

Breath seemed to return to Fiona at the realization that it was only her daughter's spectre she was talking to, and the true Levyna was still far away from the palace. "Come. Away from here," she said as she took her daughter's hand and led her out of the open hallway. They walked through the passages into a room meant for the palatine's business.

"Are you sure you're fine? Are you safe? Everything is okay?"

"Yes, Mother. I swear I'm safe," Levyna answered. She only needed one glance to identify the room. "This used to be Father's," she said.

Fiona came to the realization quickly too. "Yes, it used to be. But now I guess it's mine."

"What?"

"The room, it's mine to use now," Fiona said.

"I don't understand, Mother."

"Fiona, King Ranald has made me the palatine. I have replaced Cyrus."

Levyna pulled back as she searched her mother's eyes, wondering if perhaps it was a joke. "Mother? Are you being serious?"

"Yes. Yes, I am. It all happened so suddenly, I wasn't even asked. I came to pay my respects, and His Majesty practically ordered me to take the role in the presence of a full court. I wasn't thinking it, and I certainly wasn't expecting it, and yet there it was."

"How is it even possible? Is that something that can be done?"

"Well, I mean, the choice of the palatine is always at the king's discretion, and they are traditionally whoever the king considers to be his closest counsel."

"And King Ranald believes that you are his closest counsel?"

"Maybe. I'm not so certain about that, especially since Damiran, his cousin, is around."

"Lord Damiran is in Queen's Hill?"

"Yes, he has been for the past couple of days. I would have thought for sure that he would be a far more appropriate choice than I."

"I mean, he is the king's cousin and one-time confidant. It would have been less surprising."

"Well, I have no idea why King Ranald didn't choose him instead. I mean, beyond the fact that His Majesty feels somewhat indebted to me for being there when you saved his life. I think he considers me someone he can trust."

Levyna nodded. "That makes sense. And since you say it is the king's decision, there's no one to argue."

"I did try, but I was quieted quicker than I could finish the statement. He wouldn't hear of it. I'm sorry you have to find out this way," Fiona said. "I was hoping to tell you when I visited."

"No, please, Mother, do not apologize. You have nothing to be sorry for. I'm glad that I came and found out. I'm happy for you. Despite everything that has happened that is still happening, this is delightful. I'm proud of you."

Fiona's lips quivered as she pulled her daughter closer and kissed her forehead. "Thank you, my love. That means a lot to me. Now, tell me the truth: is something bothering you?" She pulled away, took her daughter's hands in her own and looked into her eyes.

Levyna averted her gaze but felt her mother's grip tighten.

"Tell me."

"It's Olin."

"Is he okay?"

"Yes, he's fine. At least, I think he is."

"You think? Did something happen?"

"Maybe. He's been a little off since yesterday. He seems to be keeping to himself, not that I'm being a bother, but he stares off, lost in his thoughts. I can hardly feel him. We had a plan to try and find the phoenix —"

"The phoenix?"

"Yes. I . . . it, in my dream. And I don't know who it could be referring to. Posdel told us a bunch of things, but since none of us knows who bears a phoenix sign or what it represents, we were planning on going to the same place you did when I had the dream about Father, to maybe find someone who can see more about the dream."

"You want to go to Kelegro?"

"We wanted to until Olin suddenly changed his mind and said that he wanted to go to Ravinshore instead."

"Ravinshore? Did something happen again?"

"No, I don't know. He said he wants to go and see if he can bury his uncle, but I don't believe that's really it, and Posdel doesn't either. We think it might be because of his mother. We think he's going to Ravinshore to find her."

"She has not returned?"

"No, she hasn't. And I fear he thinks that she might be gone again, that she might have abandoned him again."

Fiona exhaled. She could understand why the young man would want to return to Ravinshore before the storm was hardly over. "And you're worried something might happen to him."

"Yes, especially since he won't let me go with him." Levyna looked up at her mother's face and quickly spoke. "I want to, Mother, please."

"Levyna . . ."

"You know that I'm already wherever he is, in part. I'm only here because Posdel threatened to chain me with a spell if I try to follow Olin."

Levyna snorted. "He sounds like a good man."

"Mother . . ."

"It's dangerous, Levyna. And I think Olin knows that, which is why he asked you not to come."

"It is dangerous, and he will be alone. If I am there, it will not be so bad. Two parts of one, remember?"

"How long do you plan to remind me of this pertes thing?"

"Only until I know you have seen reason in it. I promise, Mother, we will be safe. Please."

Fiona stared at her daughter as an array of thoughts flooded her mind. The main one was how alive Levyna seemed when she spoke of the boy, and Fiona knew it had not been an exaggeration when Levyna had said that half of her was already wherever Olin was.

CHAPTER SEVEN

S outh of the Black River in the kingdom of hills, Crow
Cave grows cold as the sun disappears behind the thick
clouds, and nightfall brings a wave of chills to the village that
lasts through the night. It was believed that where the land
was situated – at the tail end and junction of two valleys –
brought the intense cold, but some argued that the Black River's
breeze was the source of the icy chill, regardless of the season. A
stranger might wonder about the name – Crow Cave. Why that
one, when many other things could have been used as the title
for the town? Either the ever-present breeze or, better yet, the

Black River itself. But there was already a River's Tail, though it was down south in Duken and not in Queen's Hill, so the predominantly rive-based villagers of Crow Cave hardly had a say in what the village was named.

Over a hundred years ago, a traveller and his family – his heavily pregnant wife and their four-year-old son – had found themselves stuck on the side of a path in the middle of the valley in the dead of winter when a wheel broke on the wagon carrying the wife and child. The traveller, who was a farmer and no craftsman, had chased after the wheel and brought it back but then realized there was nothing he could do to fix it. And if they hadn't had enough to worry about, the storm had begun to blow in from a distance. The snow began to fall heavier. The wind began to gust stronger and stronger, causing an avalanche of snow and ice that crushed their horse, the family's only means of travel.

They had been prepared to abandon all of their belongings on the broken-down wagon – a few sacks of possessions weren't worth their lives, the very lives they'd left their home to save, fleeing a creditor who'd threatened to take their soon-to-be-born child as repayment for their debts. After hearing that, the man and his wife decided that fleeing was all they had left, and the storm hadn't dissuaded them. They hoped the storm would do quite the opposite, and they had looked for the heavy winds and the thick snow to serve as their cover and obscure their escape from the eyes of the creditor. They chose to take their chance in the wild unknown rather than with a neighbour who wouldn't be stopped if he chose to carve out the child from the belly of the mother.

Watching the horse neigh in agony as its blood quickly stained the snow red, the man and his family had known they needed to find another way to survive the storm. It had been too far to return home on foot, even if it hadn't meant that they would walk back into the hands of their creditor. There had been no hope that someone would pass by unless they were crazy and desperate enough to be out in the storm. The path had no shelter to provide them with warmth they could see. The woman was too pregnant to run. The snow would swallow their legs up to their knees. The man carried the young child on his back while his wife trudged behind him. All but the child in the womb had been wrapped in layers of clothing to keep the heat inside.

Minutes passed as they had walked north of their abandoned life, and then the woman had stopped, knees quivering as she'd felt the child coming. She could not possibly make it another step. The man had looked around rapidly, breath steaming the air as his eyes searched. Nothing had been on the horizon, not that the snow had let him see. His wife had fallen to her knees, and her grunts had begun to sound in the rhythm of labour. It was unimaginable. It looked as though this would be their fate. The man dropped to the ground next to his wife. He was horrified at the thought of delivering their child in the open, in the middle of the storm, where they were liable to freeze until he had felt the tug of his son's small hand.

The snow had not stopped, yet the man had followed his son's finger and saw birds circling a few yards to the left. Then the birds had flown towards the family, circling once, then had flown back to the same spot. Seeing that there was nothing else they could do, the man lifted his wife and stumbled towards the crows, each step feeling like it would be their last. They followed the birds, with the boy walking ahead until a cave appeared.

The crows had circled until the family was inside, after which they stopped and landed inside with them. The little boy had watched as his father set his mother on the ground, and her pained grunts had grown louder. Suddenly, there had been no need for a fire or warmth as the birds, scores of them, had started glowing red, circling the family as the man had delivered his child. Each of the crows had given off enough heat to keep a human child warm, and the birds had remained glowing through the storm and through the night until, one after the other, the lights had gone out for good.

In the actual cave of crows, every ten years or so, one bird was spotted but hardly ever seen again. And as the origin of its name was one of the most chilling stories in Queen's Hill, and quite possibly the three kingdoms, it gave the village the feeling of a haven that always protects those who find their way there.

But if most of the settlers of Crow Cave thought of the village as safe, surely one of them knew that the same could not be said of him because he knew what he was.

He picked up the empty baskets and threw them in the back of his wagon with a smile. He couldn't know there would be a time when crows wouldn't come to his rescue. He had been the storm himself many times. He hadn't been wild in his display of power. Of course, he hadn't left a path of loud shrills and a chorus of bellowing after he'd left the scene. He had done his deeds in the shadows.

For a man like him, who wore the mask of a fisherman with no bride and no child, he must have known that there would be a day, an evening when the breeze eased, and he would sit on his chair, watching as the rabbit roasted on the open fire. It must have crossed his mind many times that there would be a time he would see past the fire to find a shadow moving swiftly, and he would pretend not to be alarmed, picking up the cup by his side as he furtively reached for a dagger. Surely there must have been a moment when he thought of the day he would not be quick enough, and the shadow would strike, its dagger finding his heart from behind, nailing him to the seat.

The fisherman would see his mask fall, and he would see no crow in sight when his storm came to face him. He watched as the life slowly dripped out of him, but not before he was shoved into the open fire where he could only writhe, remembering all he had done for the Order, for the Red Flame. The watcher would die without answering the mystery of how his true identity had been discovered as he roasted in the fire he had lit.

* * *

"Olin!"

He pants as he pushes the brushes aside and hurries through the field, legs pushing him with a quick burst of strength as he stamps across the ground. The thrill of the chase consumes his entire body.

"Olinander!"

He hears the call, but he is not interested in answering, not until he gets to where he's headed. This is a battle only the strong-willed can survive. The slap of the wind rattling against his skin as he breezes past is fuel for his body. There is no stopping him. He glances back and catches sight of his uncle to be sure that he's following, and Olin smiles when he sees his uncle still trailing him, though the expression on the man's face isn't pleased as he chases after the boy. But Olin is still not prepared to close the distance between them. He continues to dart ahead, certain that if he stops, his uncle will catch him and stop him from reaching adventure. Olin doesn't bother looking back now that he is past the tall brushes, and he can see the open field in front of him and past the field: the river.

"Enough, Olinander! Stop right now! Don't make me catch you. You won't like what I'll do when I get my hands on you!"

But Olin wants to know, not just because he wants to drive his uncle crazy. This is what he spends his day wishing for – a chance at an adventure, at learning secrets. Olin hears Wylie curse as he tears down the slope, sliding on his back towards the bottom till his feet land on the black soil in the mud of the bank. The ten-year-old heart pumps with excitement in the barrel of his chest, and he doesn't bother to take his clothes off before he jumps into the river.

"Bloody hell!"

Olin laughs as he lifts his head from beneath the water and looks up to see his uncle just sliding down the slope. Wylie's eyes fixate on his figure in the water. Olin's laughter continues even as the coldness drowns his skin, and the boy can feel the thrill his muscles have obtained through the run to surrender to the water. Olin waves at Wylie, beckoning for his uncle to join him in the hope that it would diffuse the anger on his face. But Wylie stands frozen, hands akimbo, looking on in disbelief with his breaths steaming.

Olin continues to giggle carefree until he feels a tug at his leg below the water. Then his smile is replaced by a frown, and he stills as he looks down, then back up at his uncle, just before he is swiftly yanked below the water.

"Olin!"

Olin hears his uncle's voice again, falling in the distance as he's pulled deeper. He cannot see what caught his leg and tries to pull away, but it only appears to make it worse. He's pulled further down, and soon his hands cannot even reach the water's surface. It doesn't take long for the fear to begin strangling him as he struggles for breath. Then Olin feels motion in the water as his uncle dives in, trying to reach him as he's pulled further down. Olin sees his uncle's figure above him, and Wylie grabs at his hand to pull him up. But the illusion of rescue is lost as he watches his uncle pulled in the opposite direction, this time with a force ten times stronger than the one tugging Olin down. Olin watches, eyes full of horror, as his uncle disappears into the bottom of the river, and he can't stop it, can't even free himself. The rush he'd hoped to gain turns on its head as he struggles to escape.

Olin's hope is momentarily rekindled as he sees yet another hand reach for him in the water. He sees the body dive in to try to reach him, and his eyes grow wider as Yondi finally gives up his attempts to pull him and reaches for what has latched onto his leg. Yondi tries to pry it off him. Olin needs to breathe, but his eyes remain open, albeit only barely, but enough for him to catch the moment they both realize it's a hand holding Olin below the water. Fear borders on insanity as both look down to see the face below as it manifests from the darkness of the river.

And it is Olin himself.

Olin's mouth opens in a silent scream just before his friend is yanked below. He watches as blood trickles into the water from Yondi's pierced throat before he, too, disappears into the darkness. And finally, everything turns blurry as his eyes close, and the only thing left is silence in the wake of his quest for adventure.

* * *

"Olin. Olin!"

Olin gasped awake, sucking air with every muscle in his throat and chest as he sprung up with eyes wide. He exhaled and blinked his eyes into focus. By his side was Levyna, who had a look of worry plastered on her face. Not far from her, coming in through the door with a bundle of firewood in his hand, Posdel stopped short as he took in the scene. Olin regained his breath but couldn't do anything to hide what Levyna had seen and what Posdel's eyes read.

"He might never tell me, but maybe he'll finally tell you," Posdel said, closing the door as he turned to drop the chopped wood in front of the fireplace. The mage raised his fingers and waved them gently at the fireplace, and the wood already inside caught fire. Turning around, he walked towards the part of the large room he loved the most, facing his shelf.

"Olin? What is it?" Levyna asked.

A crease pulled on his face as he swallowed hard and shook his head. "It's nothing. Just a strange dream," Olin answered.

"I remember you said something similar the day you almost burnt my bed down," Posdel said, not offering them a glance. He was familiar with how Olin would respond.

Olin glanced at the man, then at his own hands as if to be sure they weren't on fire. They were not, and neither was the bed. Levyna touched his arm, and he stared at her hands.

Levyna could read it off him, the fear and the panic and . . . resentment. It was Levyna's turn to frown as she sensed that resentment among the mixture of emotions in Olin. Resentment towards himself. She stared at him, and he said nothing still. Olin lifted his head and swept his hair back in some attempt to pull the thoughts away from his mind. Finally, Levyna met his eyes. He didn't look like someone who'd had a simple strange dream. Something else was troubling him, and he still wouldn't tell her what it was.

Do you not wish me to know? She asked.

No, I don't. And if you have any value for your own wellbeing, you'll cease pestering me, Levyna.

Olin saw the shock in her eyes at the words, and it was Levyna's turn to pull her hand away from his arm, get up, and walk out of the house.

Posdel watched the young woman leave and finally glanced at Olin. He had half expected the sciff to be in Ravinshore by now, but Olin had returned, despite his resolve to leave. He wouldn't be surprised if the young man disappeared in the middle of the night.

Posdel had a fair idea why Olin would be pushing away the one person that fate had put in his path to accompany him. He had witnessed many deaths, some of which had been caused by his actions. And Levyna was sliding into a similar role to those he had lost. Combined with the thoughts of losing his mother again, there was a chance that Olin, the daring sciff, was prepared to run himself unarmed into Ravinshore among the eyes of the watchers. The boy, not even fully realizing his powers, was beginning to feel the cracks beneath it all. And if there was anything Posdel knew, it was that cracks like that could shift even the most fearless of minds.

The mage walked to the shelf and plucked a few bottles of potions to examine. His hand strayed as he replaced them, and the next bottle Posdel picked up was wine.

CHAPTER EIGHT

E den exhaled as he stared at the attire hanging on the wall.
He'd seen it many times before. He'd had many conversations in this room with it hanging in that corner. The brazier threw shadows of light across it, highlighting the features of the armour even in the dullness of daylight.

It wasn't common for watchers to have relatives in the Order, but Eden could be considered an exception. It wasn't something many people knew, of course, at least none who lived since the death of Laiton, his predecessor. Eden learned of his relation to a past watcher when he'd stumbled upon armour left by the Lord Watcher before Laiton. It had struck at some memory, one he couldn't quite place. And when he'd seen the mark inked inside the wrist, a tiny symbol of a flame, it had given him a second clue. Eden had been curious until he'd seen the ring on Laiton's finger – a brass band – and he'd remembered he'd seen it before, on his grandfather.

Eden couldn't remember ever seeing his mother's father in his full costume as a watcher. It was obvious his family didn't know what he truly was, and even though he still couldn't place the memory of the hooded vest and gauntlet with the red stripes, he still remembered seeing that mark on his grandfather's hand. He also remembered that brass band. Later, when he'd joined the Order, he'd learned that his grandfather had been a ghost watcher for decades before taking the reins and becoming the Lord Watcher of the Order. Discovering he was a descendant of a Lord Watcher had rooted his heart in the Order even more. It had gone from being more than just service. Now it was about blood for him, about following the footsteps of his grandfather, which was why it had taken minimal effort for him to see what Thorne, the Lord Watcher of the Order of Walera, had planned. And to see his plan for what it truly was – a chance for the Order to take its rightful place in the kingdom, to be something more than mercenaries that worked in the shadows. His devotion to the Order hadn't been enough. This was the chance for the Red Flame to take the reins over the kingdom. It was a tune his heart beats for. Eden hadn't needed convincing to see himself as the Lord of Queen's Hill after the Red Flame took charge. The role would suit him and would make his grandfather proud.

Of course, Eden had known that Thorne had his own plans, not all of which held the Red Flame's best interest at heart, but he had been willing to take the chance to see power land in the hands of the Order. Thorne had spoken, and Laiton, who had been the Lord Watcher, had spent years debating it with his circle. In truth, they had only hesitated because Laiton had been too much of a coward to accept the cost. Laiton's cowardice made Eden's actions a service to the Order and the kingdom of Queen's Hill rather than a betrayal. It was Thorne who had suggested before their plan had begun. The First Watcher was the next Lord Watcher, and all Laiton had done was give him more reason to get him out of the way.

Killing Laiton had been simpler than Eden had expected. He'd used a stone mite that had crawled into the man's ear and paralysed him. Then Eden had simply covered the Lord Watcher's nose and mouth until the life had left him. Laiton's eyes had been filled with disdain and anger that couldn't stop his fate. Eden had made sure the Lord Watcher knew who he was – who his grandfather had been – and why it had been his duty to do what needed to be done. Laiton had felt no pain beyond perhaps the betrayal as his heart had broken while pumping futility. He'd hardly struggled against his own First Watcher's assault, but it had been inevitable, as far as Eden was concerned. There was perhaps some irony to how it had ended for Laiton. He'd been the one to teach Eden about the powers of the rare stone mite from the caves of the Dark Hills, and on his first kill as a watcher, Eden had used the stone to get rid of his mark.

Now, long after the deed had been done, the new Lord Watcher turned away from the armour to the people that were entering the room. Each wore the full gear of a watcher, including masks. The watchers raised their right hands to their chests in salute, a gesture recognized by Eden's nod.

"We have received a response from the palace," the Third Watcher said.

"And?" Eden asked.

"King Ranald has accepted the proposal of a White Indulgence."

"Is that so?" The Lord Watcher said. "I have to say. I wasn't sure he would be so easily convinced. I was half-certain he would simply return the messenger's head. But it seems he's not as crazy as I had assumed after all."

"It's possible he's realized he doesn't have many options. He must know the alternative isn't something he can afford," Fourth answered.

"Of course, but we must not be so naïve as to think he is completely hopeless. Bitter as it may sound, there's a reason the Order has served the kingdom in the past. Our failure to turn the tides isn't something he will easily forget," the Lord Watcher said.

"Though the king has agreed to the terms of the Indulgence – no weapons in the room and no attack from either side – he has also added demand of his own. There will be no watchers capable of magic in attendance," the Third Watcher added.

"He still has much to fear. I don't blame him for that. Send word that we accept the new terms. Though we have asked for White Indulgence, we will not walk in completely powerless. You will come with us," Eden said to the Third Watcher.

"Do you think that wise?" Third asked hesitantly.

"It seems you have forgotten to whom you are speaking, watcher." The Lord Watcher's voice held an edge of anger. Perhaps the sudden change in power had left some of the circle forgetting that Eden was now in charge.

The Third Watcher straightened. "I apologize, My Lord. What I meant to say is that we might be better off not giving the king any reasons to suspect hostility if that is indeed still the plan."

"It is. Nothing has changed, even if the pieces have been moved," Eden answered. "We convince Ranald that the attack was a grievous error in judgment, a passing moment where the Order allowed itself to be influenced by the idea of a mad lord. Laiton's death will serve us greatly in this."

"Permit me, Lord Watcher, but would that not be seen as a sign that the Order is weak? That it was enough for one watcher to influence the Red Flame so much?" the Fifth Watcher said.

"No. It will be the opposite, you see. We arrive looking like a bunch of loyalists from an Order with a few misled members, and we swear our utmost devotion to him and the crown of Queen's Hill. We say that we do not wish for war or any harm to come to him. We remind him that we are on his side until he feels comfortable. He needs to feel like he is in control again. Ranald has never been the smartest, and ever since Frederick was killed, he has been surrounded by a clueless bunch. He will not see this for what it is," Eden answered. "He will not suspect any hostility as we will not give him a chance to." He turned to the Third Watcher and again gave the order, "You will come, but you will do everything to bury your magic. Don't even think of a spell when you're there. Not unless it doesn't go as planned."

"And if that happens, what should I do, Lord Watcher?" Third asked.

"Whatever you have to do to ensure Ranald does not walk out of that room alive," Eden answered.

Third swallowed, understanding what he was being asked to do. Almost certainly a death sentence, should he fail. However, that was less likely if the king kept his word and brought no defence to the meeting. But, as the Red Flame was prepared to defy the terms of the Indulgence, they would be naïve to think that the king wouldn't follow suit.

"The Red Flame has attempted to take the king's life once, and it's safe to say that he's aware of our similar attacks on Palatine Fredrick and the commander. How can we be sure that the king is able to look past that and come to an agreement?" Third asked.

"Because, as I said before, he knows what it would mean if the Order turns against him completely. It's why his garrison has been guarding us without taking action. Even though his life was nearly lost, Ranald will not risk war by being impulsive, no matter how scared he is. Which means we are at an advantage," the Lord Watcher said. "He will listen to what we have to say, and we will pretend that the Order is willing to recognize the king as the sovereign power over Queen's Hill, and then Ranald will let down his defences, which will buy us time."

"Time for what?" the Sixth Watcher asked.

"To bring to life the plan that was always meant to be. This time without rogue elements. Our patience won't last fortnights – it will be soon, very soon, and since Ranald has no doubt grown wary of the company that surrounds him, he will certainly not suspect what is coming. So, let him know we are prepared for the Indulgence."

"Of course, Lord Watcher." Third nodded.

"Lord Watcher, what do we intend to do with the new counsel the king has surrounded himself with?"

Eden stepped away and walked towards the chair set up like a throne in the hall. The Lord Watcher made himself comfortable before he answered. "Ranald is scared and brought his scandalous old cousin from exile and made Fredrick's wife the palatine. It's hardly anything to worry about. If it turns out that either of them will be a problem, then we will get rid of them. I'm not concerned, and you shouldn't be either. Neither of them has even half as much hold as Fredrick did in the kingdom. Without Fredrick, Ranald is even less competent than he was before."

"You said the Order won't give up, but surely we cannot ignore the fact that Ranald is conscious of the threat that surrounds him, as you have said. The watchers closest to him have all been silenced. How, then, do we intend to get what we want?"

A small smile grew on Eden's face as he shook his head. "You speak as though your faith in the Order is nothing. The ghosts around him have been unmasked, but that doesn't mean that is where the Order ends. It doesn't matter how much he cowers. The heat of the Red Flame never dies."

CHAPTER NINE

O lin finally decided to leave for Ravinshore. Previously, either the palace or Black Castle would have been safe for him, but now he was less inclined to seek either of them. He had called Hunter's Grove home for years. It was where he'd grown and had spent the better part of his teenage years. He knew who lived in each house, whose farms had the best birds and whose children were menaces.

Now Olin was standing in front of the house he had called home. His uncle's house. He was rooted, staring at the door for what seemed like an eternity, unable to move forward.

Olin scanned the front of the house. It stood out from many of those around it, making it evident that the carpenter who'd lived there had known what he'd been doing. The windows were newer than the doors, and the wood looked much less aged. Wylie had changed them about a year before. The wooden slab of the door was just as he remembered, with the addition of a broken handle, something that had marked the beginning of that horrible night. In the owner's absence, a few wayward plants had grown through the crevices. The stones that marked the fire pit outside were still there, and when Olin looked at them, it felt as though he could see the fire the last time Wylie had set it. There was a small stool outside, not far from the door, and he pictured his uncle sitting and working while Olin did his chores. He pictured Wylie teaching him how to skin his first rabbit when he'd been eleven. Then Olin suddenly felt his body stiffen as he remembered something else.

The dream.

Olin still couldn't move as the thought of the night it all changed came to his mind. Every time he thought he could bring himself to step closer, he remembered the dream. He hadn't needed any interpreter to know its meaning. Olin thought of the attack. He had slept through the beginning of the attack, and each time he tried to step towards the door, he remembered Wylie's wrecked body after being stabbed by the watcher's blade, remembered how his uncle had shoved him through the portal. Olin was stiff. Fear, anger, regret, and resentment. He had it all.

And she could feel it.

Olin sighed. "I thought I told you to stay away?" he asked, not turning around. He'd been conscious of her from the moment he'd arrived. It was almost impossible for him not to feel her presence.

Levyna stepped out from behind him and came to his side, stepping as tenderly as possible, as though careful not to add to his upset emotions. He saw her chestnut brown hair out of the corner of his eye as she slowly turned to face him, even as he remained staring at the house.

"Yes, I know what you said, and I may very well be wrong, but I think I know why you said that. And I don't care. Before you say anything, you should know that my mother is aware, and so is Posdel," she answered. He said nothing and still didn't turn. She could feel the weight of his silence with every exhale. "There was no way I was letting you do this alone, regardless of what you said."

Olin tried to think of a new argument to persuade her to rethink her decision. He didn't like being needlessly unkind, but Olin hoped if he showed a little more teeth, it would show her the idea was terrible. But the ache of unpleasant emotions running through him was eerily familiar. It felt the same as that day on the streets of Queen's Hill when a mage's apprentice had accompanied him, his accomplice and friend, and though Olin had protested, he'd been relieved at his presence in a battered, wayward corner of his mind. That same wayward corner was delighted at the fact that she was here, even if he'd partly hoped that she would have listened and stayed away.

"This isn't Queen's Hill. This is Ravinshore. This is Walera territory, Levyna."

"I know, and it doesn't scare me. Whatever you do or do not have about being here, it's split halfway with me," she answered. Right then, she was almost positive that the Order of Walera wasn't the most imminent concern at the moment. "You should stop worrying about me and understand that I can make my own decisions too, despite what you say, and I choose to be here, with my friend," she said. "I will not force you to talk to me or let me feel whatever is bothering you, but I will be here."

Olin exhaled and finally glanced at her, their eyes meeting as she turned to him. He said nothing as he stepped forward and eventually opened the door, letting it go as it swung aside on its own, making that familiar squeaking noise. The house was exactly how it had always been, except for one thing. The entire room was trashed, evidence of what had happened that night.

They stopped over the threshold onto dry blood, and Olin's memory flashed back to the fight, the watcher bleeding out. To the left of the room were marks and cracks on the wall from the shields and the pulses the mages had battled with. A piece of mouldy bread was on the floor next to the puddle of dried-out soup. Olin moved his gaze quickly to the right, where he remembered the second watcher had landed, and he could almost see the impression where Wylie had thrown him into the wall. Of course, Olin knew what had happened to that watcher, and he hadn't taken his last breath.

Finally, Olin looked at the dark brown pattern on the floor where Wylie had been standing. There was no point in guessing. He knew who the blood belonged to, he saw it drip out himself.

Olin swallowed hard as he felt Levyna's hand on his arm. He had said he would get Wylie's body and bury it, but Olin wasn't sure he had ever really believed it would be here. He led the way as he searched the bed chamber, where they found a scorched sheet on the floor. Olin picked it up and looked at it, and he held his breath for a moment as he saw the handprint. He glanced furtively over at Levyna, who saw it too before he dropped the sheet and moved on. The kitchen, like everywhere else, was empty of what he wanted.

Wylie was gone.

Just like she was gone.

Levyna wasn't sure how much of it he could have expected to change, but she didn't think Olin believed that the other person he was hoping to find would be in the house. She watched as he looked at the remains of his life before, seeing the horrors of the aftermath of Walera's attack. He'd told her what had happened, and she'd felt his emotions, but it still hadn't done justice to how much terror had consumed him during the attack.

Olin reached for the wall to his right as they walked back into the living room and removed the sword belt hanging there. Levyna watched as he undid the one he was wearing, pulled the sword out and replaced it in the scabbard of the new belt he strapped around his waist.

It's Wylie's, he said, and Levyna nodded.

* * *

There was only one place to go after he'd had no luck with the house. As far as he knew, if Wylie's body had been at the house after the watchers had left, it would certainly not have disappeared. There was a greater chance that someone had come and taken it. Olin appreciated the quiet that came with Levyna's presence, but his eyes were peeled as they walked through the streets all the way to the house of one of the few people Wylie had ever trusted when he'd been alive. Olin ignored the eyes that peered in their direction – in his direction – as he led the way to the hunter's house.

Old Ron looked like he had seen a ghost as he snapped his head up from what he was doing and stared at the young man as he approached. "By the gods. Olin!"

Typically, this would be where Olin's face would pull into a toothy smile, and he would hurry to embrace his uncle's friend – someone who was like an uncle to him too. But there was hardly a fracture of excitement on the boy's face. Olin noticed as Old Ron's little boy darted out from behind the house, no doubt after hearing who his father had shouted.

"Old Ron," Olin said.

"By the gods. Oh, boy!" Old Ron exclaimed as he wrapped his arms around Olin in a tight embrace, pulled away, and then took the young man's face in his hands. "You're alive," he said, face pinched in relief.

Olin wanted to say that it was despite what he'd done that he was still alive. "So it appears," was what he said instead before Old Ron's youngest son ran towards him and threw his arms around the visitor. Olin knew that he would have to suffer at least one more as Sara, Old Ron's seemingly ageless wife, appeared from the house and mirrored her husband's previous actions, only she was a tad more tearful than Ron had been.

"I couldn't possibly be more grateful," Old Ron said.

Olin didn't miss Old Ron and his family staring in the direction of the young woman beside him, and he wasted no time. "This is Levyna. She's a friend from Queen's Hill," he said. Levyna performed a brief curtsy even though she wasn't in the presence of nobles.

"Queen's Hill?" Old Ron's brows pulled up. "There's a lot you have to tell us."

"Welcome, Levyna." Sara moved towards the young woman as the guests were nudged towards the house.

Old Ron's youngest held Olin's hands. The boy seemed to have grown inches taller than the last time he'd been here weeks before. As they stepped into the house, Olin saw a new face, a young girl with skin paler than both Old Ron and his wife and with eyes that pierced right to his soul.

* * *

"I worried like a man going insane. I think I might have for a minute. I had no idea where you were," Old Ron began to say.

"I'm sorry. It has been a very challenging few days, and I left very . . . It hadn't really been something planned when I left Ravinshore," Olin answered.

"We thought as much. Wylie . . ." Old Ron paused as though to acknowledge the name. Olin's reaction all but confirmed what

Old Ron had gone from fearing to being sure of, even if he had had no actual proof. "Is he . . .?"

Olin's face pinched. "I thought you would have known."

"I do, or at least I figured. When I went to the house and I saw . . . and neither of you were there . . . I knew one of two things had happened – either you had been killed or they had taken you. The blood suggested the watchers hadn't taken you without a fight. Not seeing Wylie after his visit was a confirmation."

"His visit?" Olin asked.

" Yes. That night, he came here to get something. You probably won't know what it was, but when he told me he needed it, I realized at once how much trouble he was expecting, even though he wouldn't explain. He thought that if he told me, he would be risking our lives. He wouldn't let me come with him either, the stubborn bastard. He just took the ring and left."

The ring. Olin remembered now. The images played back in his head – he'd seen it on Wylie's hand during the attack, and he remembered how his uncle had looked different as he'd channelled the portal.

"The ring – what was it for? What did it do?" he asked.

"The Alzeiber is a magical ring that feeds off desperation, amongst other things. It's more of a weapon than anything else and a very dangerous one. Wylie knew only to use it when nothing else would work. From what he told me, it siphons magic through blood, but not without taking its toll," Old Ron answered.

Even after everything else Wylie had done to try and save him, he hadn't hesitated to sacrifice himself to the ring for Olin's sake. "You haven't found his body?"

"No. But if you're asking, does that mean you didn't take it? Does that mean there could —"

"He's gone. I know it," Olin answered. He remembered L vividly describing how the Lord Watcher had ruptured his uncle's brain to learn Olin's location.

A wave of silence passed over the room, seemingly the entire house, before Old Ron's next words. "I'm glad to see you, Olin, but I have to ask, so I know this is real. How are you alive?"

Olin shook his head. "Wylie sent me through a portal that landed me in Queen's Hill. He told me to find Cyrus."

Old Ron nodded. "Cyrus. And you found him?"

"Not at first," Olin answered. "I found someone else instead who . . . helped me find Cyrus. But once I did, I was shocked to see him with a watcher from Walera." He noticed the raised brows and wide eyes of disbelief in Old Ron's expression.

"How?"

Olin knew that, like everyone else, the question was more about how he could tell that the man he had seen with Cyrus was indeed a watcher. "I recognized the watcher's eyes," he said. "He was one of the two that came to the house. I didn't approach Cyrus as planned because I feared he wasn't who Wylie thought he was, not anymore."

"I don't believe that of Cyrus. If anything, he disliked the Orders as much as Wylie did."

"Well, I was proven wrong after all when I eventually confronted Cyrus – more like accused him in the presence of King Ranald. At that moment, the true Watchers of the Order in the palace revealed themselves. Cyrus was killed, and the king barely escaped death."

Ravinshore had heard about the attack on King Edmond's palace at the hands of the Order. Still, Olin told Old Ron and his family the whole story about how he had stumbled onto the information of the Order's plot to poison King Edmond. Then he told Old Ron about how the Order had discovered him and followed him back to Hunter's Grove and even to Queen's Hill, where he'd realized that the plot didn't end with Ravinshore. He spoke of his capture as though it had been nothing and mentioned Levyna finding him.

"You, you were the daughter of the palatine?" Sara asked.

"Yes, I was, and somehow I still am," Levyna answered. "My father Fredrick was King Ranald's right hand before the Order of the Red Flame murdered him. But now the king has made my mother, Fiona, the palatine instead after what happened to Cyrus."

"Levyna is many things, she's . . ." Olin trailed off. He glanced at her.

It's fine, you can tell them, she answered.

"She helped get the message of the threat back to Ravinshore when I could not. She's a traveller."

"A – a traveller?" Old Ron and his wife shared a glance, neither understanding what that meant.

"Yes, her magic is unique. It was how she was able to reach Ravinshore, which was where she found . . ."

Levyna's heart skipped as she felt the emotion in his voice as he trailed off, unwilling to mention his mother. Olin could deny it, but all Olin wanted to do was ask if she had been here. If they perhaps knew where she was. Levyna didn't need to travel into Olin's mind to feel how much the thought weighed on him.

"Found what?" Old Ron asked.

"She found me, actually," Levyna answered. "Gytha."

A furtive gasp escaped from Sara as she shifted her gaze to her husband, who glanced at her in return. Both eyed the little girl sitting next to their son in the corner.

"You saw . . . you saw Gytha?" Sara asked.

Olin didn't miss the pause that followed the mention of the name or the glance at the strange girl. Olin was sure she wasn't theirs by blood – he hadn't been gone long enough to miss that.

"She was here, wasn't she?" Olin asked, staring at both of them. "When?"

"Olin, we never saw Gytha. She never came here. The only reason we knew she had been in Ravinshore was the girl," Old Ron said.

Olin's face pinched as he glanced at the child. "Who is she?"

"A young woman from Ovien came two days ago and dropped her off. She said Gytha had asked her to, that the child had been Ilda's ward but was now ours to care for," Sara said.

"Ilda? Do you mean . . ."

"You might not have many memories of her. She was Wylie's friend before she suddenly left a decade ago. The girl's name is Ella. And the young woman who brought her said nothing more to us before she hurried away, nothing beyond the fact that the child neither hears nor speaks like common folk," Sara said.

"Where is she? Where is Gytha now?" Olin asked.

Levyna blinked at the words she knew he had meant to ask since they'd arrived.

"I'm afraid we don't know, Olin. Gytha left no word of her whereabouts, and we haven't seen her."

CHAPTER TEN

Though it wouldn't be impossible, it was hard to imagine
how Ravinshore could return to what it had been before.
Days had passed, and though a semblance of normalcy was
slowly creeping back in, no one was foolish enough to pretend
that the worst was behind them. They all knew that the threat
wasn't gone just because Thorn had disappeared. And even if
King Edmond was keen on listening to the Order's excuses,
Ariana was not so kind.

Ariana had suppressed her fear, but that left only rage for what had been done to her palace, what had been brought to her children's doorstep. She'd hardly slept since the Order's attack, and every night she visited her children's rooms and watched them before returning to her bed. The thought of what had almost been taken from her was no longer followed by fear and trepidation but slow seething rage and burning desire to return the fear of the throne and crown of the kingdom to the minds of those like Walera.

Ariana glanced at Edmond, who nodded at her to keep an open mind, as the doors to the throne room opened and two figures walked in. Ariana had only seen them a few times before since her husband had become the ruler of the kingdom. The Wardens of Black Castle were a man and a woman dressed in cloaks covering the length of their bodies from neck to ankle. Each had a unshakeable pleasantness to their face as they approached the throne.

"Your Majesty, the Wardens of Black Castle," Ole announced.

The wardens bowed simultaneously.

The Order of Walera might have been the most well-known organization in the kingdom, but they were hardly the most revered. The Order claimed it did what was needed to keep the kingdom safe, to weed out anyone that disturbed the peace, and they were allowed to make decisions relating to those goals without consulting anyone. Black Castle was for those who were less inclined to exist under the watch of Walera. It was a safety net for those who feared the Order. If they could make an argument for their concerns, they were allowed into the Castle, the only place, other than the palace, where the Order could not trespass.

Over the centuries, Black Castle had grown from a simple safe haven from the Order and had strengthened its roots in the kingdom due to the fact that its wardens weren't simply ordinary people wanting to be free from the Order but were powerful Grand Mages. Those who wore the cloaks, even without physical weapons, could use magic in any form of combat. Those that had seen the Castle said it was built like a fortress and that half the people inside were warriors and mages. Black Castle didn't simply hide from the Order, its loyalty was to the people of Ravinshore and the king. To some, the kingdom's hierarchy was first the Crown of Ravinshore, then the Order, and finally, Black Castle, even though the Castle abstained itself from the politics and games of power within the kingdom.

Black Castle had never expanded beyond its borders in over four hundred years. It had seen people come and go, wardens pass on batons, but the walls of the Castle hadn't changed beyond what they had always been. The Castle never accepted anyone who had committed a crime. If a sinner had done something wrong and feared the Order's penance, they knew better than to turn to the Castle – the fate they would meet if they tried would be worse than at the hands of watchers. And the Castle wouldn't condone deceit or any plot of tyranny against the kingdom. It was met by death at the gatehouse before the traitor had a chance to explain. They stayed out of the affairs of the kingdom unless those affairs found their way to its gates. This made many consider the Castle only when there seemed to be no other option.

The wardens standing before the throne wore a pleasant expressions that made Ariana nervous.

"Thank you for coming, wardens," Edmond said.

"Your Majesty, Your Grace. Black Castle was deeply saddened to hear the horrifying news of the attack. We are more than grateful that His Majesty, the queen, and the rest of the royal family is safe. If there is anything Black Castle can do to be of service to the kingdom, we would like to extend those services," the first warden, the woman, said.

"Your kindness is appreciated, warden. And that is indeed why I have asked to see you. Please, take your seats," Edmond said.

The wardens took the first two seats to the left of the throne.

"I know Black Castle is known to stay out of affairs of the court, but I feel this situation is worth an exception. I am interested in what Black Castle has to say about what Walera has done and what it thinks would be the best way to approach our next steps," Edmond said.

The wardens glanced at each other. "There is nothing the Castle can suggest that would be better than His Majesty's decision," the second warden, the man, said.

"That is the issue. I am undecided. My palace was invaded, my sovereignty threatened, I was poisoned, and my family was put at risk. Had I been anyone else but the ruler of this kingdom, I would be at the gates of Black Castle right now, but instead, I have called for its wardens," King Edmond began. "I have heard from Walera, and they claim they are prepared to yield to whatever I say. Whatever that means. I am to declare war against them or try and negotiate peace. The mastermind of the attack is either dead or has escaped the kingdom. Most of his accomplices are also dead, save for a few, who are locked in the dungeon. The Order has a new Lord Watcher, who claims he doesn't share Thorne's beliefs. That the watchers Thorne managed to convince have already been delivered into the palace, most of whom have perished in the process. I know that Black Castle walks opposite the Order, seldom meeting at the point where the safety of the citizens of this kingdom is concerned, but now that the Order has taken such drastic action, I am curious to know what the Castle has to say."

Ariana carefully watched the reactions of the wardens before they spoke. They didn't seem uncertain, which was almost worrying. They should be searching for how to respond, unsure what to say.

"It's true that the Castle does not consider the Order the most diligent in keeping the kingdom safe. But one would be a pure novice to ignore the fact that, in the six centuries of the Order's existence, Ravinshore has not seen a single day of remarkable conflict, nor indeed, has any of the three kingdoms. For the most part, the Order has managed to keep to its duty of protecting the kingdom, but now it appears that its poison has finally seeped out, and they have forgotten whose kingdom this is," the woman said. "A blind hunt for all the watchers in Ravinshore might do more harm than good due to how deeply the Order is rooted in the kingdom. It could lead to war."

"So, what do you suggest?" Queen Ariana said. "Surely Black Castle has something to offer beyond telling us what we already know."

"Yes, Your Grace, it does. Difficult as it may sound, the Castle thinks His Majesty should consider the Order's offer for peace. Now, that's not to say the crown is ignorant of what has happened, but it would allow His Majesty a chance to do what the Castle suggests."

"Which is?" Edmond asked.

It was the man who answered. "First, have Walera force each watcher who knew about Thorne's plot to surrender themselves. After, His Majesty can take the Order out of the hands of Walera."

"And what follows?" the king asked.

"Since it is not the Order's foundation Black Castle is against, but its methods of taking action, the Castle is prepared to take charge of the Order at His Majesty's command," the warden continued.

Ole's brows twitched at the words. Strange for sure, but it wasn't particularly the worst suggestion.

"Black Castle would take over the Order of Walera?" the king said.

"Should His Majesty command it, yes. Walera has lost sight of what is important, which has always been the Kingdom of Ravinshore, its people, and its king. The crown already knows that Black Castle has no interest in power beyond what the crown provides. Should the Castle be given the reins of the Order, it would what it was intended six hundred years ago: a protector."

* * *

Olin couldn't understand why his mother had brought the child to Ravinshore. She hadn't been to Wylie's house, she hadn't been to Old Ron's, but she had been in Ravinshore, that much he knew now. If she'd been here, then there was a chance that she still was. The only other place that would have Gytha's attention was the palace, the origin of her initial mission. To return to Queen's Hill without knowing whether she'd been there felt wrong. He also wished to know that the king was safe and that Olin's fight to save the kingdom had been worth it. But Olin and Levyna knew the reason they were standing in front of the palace gatehouse was he needed to know if Gytha had left any footprints to follow.

"And who did you say you are again?" Ole asked, standing a few yards away from the threshold of the main doors of the palace. Between him and the two strangers asking to meet with the queen was a pair of guardsmen on either side of the door.

"Levyna, sir. And he's Olin."

"And what business do you have with Queen Ariana?"

Levyna could hardly say that her spectre had been in the king's chambers when he'd been unconscious, which was how she'd met the queen. "She's not expecting us if that's what you are asking. I —"

"If the queen is not expecting you, then I suggest you make yourselves scarce. The palace is not receiving idle guests at this time, in case you haven't noticed. If you don't have something of value to your presence here or your desire for a meeting with the queen, then you should take your leave at once."

Do not, Levyna said to Olin. She could tell he was prepared to go off at the man, knowing full well that Ole had no idea who either of them was. Ole didn't realize that he was in the way of a young man who wasn't particularly keen on being refused answers.

"We are not here with idle intentions," Levyna answered. "I think perhaps you might understand if you let Her Majesty know that the one who warned her about Walera is here. I'm sure she remembers."

Ole frowned, looking from her to Olin and back, and then his eyes widened as the realization struck him. Queen Ariana had told him how she had been visited by the spectre of a young woman who had revealed the king's condition had been Walera's doing. She'd also mentioned that there had been a young man who had learned the truth and had been taken by the Order. Though they had already suspected Thorne and his suspicious, overbearing interest in the king, having it confirmed had helped them prepare. He hadn't caught the names of the boy and girl who had warned them.

"Would you be —" Ole stopped himself as he realized the answer to the question wasn't meant to be heard by just anyone, even King's Guards. "Come along," he said instead.

Levyna looked at Olin, and the pair walked through the doors, following the Court's Counsel through the main corridors of the palace.

"I am to understand that one of you is . . . a spectre."

"Well, a traveller, but yes. My spectre visited the queen on Olin's behalf and the Grand Sorceress Gytha's direction," Levyna answered.

Ole nodded.

"Is His Majesty alright now?" Olin asked.

"He's very much alive, and I understand that part of the reason for that is because of you."

"What about the Grand Sorceress? Gytha? Is she here?" Olin couldn't hold back the question any longer.

CHAPTER
ELEVEN

"**O**lin, is it?" King Edmond asked.

"Yes, Your Majesty, Olinander," Olin answered.

"And who are your parents?"

Olin swallowed hard. The answer to the question was no longer a mystery, yet it felt as though it was – he had very little memory of them, and his uncle had become more of a father to him than his own. "My father was Bathlom, son of Eirik Efingard —"

"Efingard? Was he a noble?" Edmond asked.

"No, Your Majesty, he was not. He was a hunter."

"You say was. Is he no more?"

"Yes, Your Majesty. He passed many years ago," Olin answered, holding back that he'd only just discovered how it had happened.

"And what of your mother?"

"Her name is Gytha, Your Majesty. She is a Grand Sorceress, and I believe you've met her."

Edmond's brows pulled upward, and he glanced at his wife, who seemed just as surprised as he was. "You are the son of the Grand Sorceress Gytha? The same one who helped save my life?"

"Yes, Your Majesty," Olin answered.

"I have to ask: is it all a coincidence? That you learned of Walera's threat to my life and your mother was the one who brought me back from the brink of death?"

Olin glanced at Queen Ariana, who seemed genuinely interested in the answer. "I believe it was a matter of fate, Your Majesty, as, before her visit to the palace, I had not set my eyes on my mother in over a decade and a half."

Edmond made a thoughtful sound at the young man's disclosure. "And where is she now?"

"I was hoping I would be able to learn that with my visit here, Your Majesty. But by all signs, it appears she found no reason to linger."

Levyna felt the ache in his voice that he was pretending to hide.

"You have no idea where she is?" Ariana asked.

"No, Your Grace, I do not." Olin shook his head, glancing down before looking up at the queen. "No one does."

"Well, for what it's worth, I'm grateful for her presence in Ravinshore – for saving my life. And I'm glad that you are alive despite the efforts of Thorne and the Red Flame. It truly was a brave thing you did – escaping the Orders to warn us of their plans. Not many people in the three kingdoms would have dared to stand against them. The Crown of Ravinshore is grateful for your help and is indebted to you. As it is to you, Levyna," Edmond said.

The pair bowed. "Thank you, Your Majesty," Olin said for them both.

* * *

As much as he wanted to, it wasn't his place to question the king concerning Walera's actions. However, it was hard to imagine that the Order would continue unscathed after its attempt on the king's life. But his mission to the palace had been just as brief but less urgent than the time before when he had sought an audience. If Gytha had been at the palace, there was no reason to believe she was still in Ravinshore.

It appeared few were in the mood to rejoice, and the air felt heavy with gloom and uncertainty, but Queen Ariana had demanded that they stay for a meal with her and the king and that had been final. Surrounding the table, in what seemed to be only a gathering for sustenance rather than for merriment, the heaviness of the Order of Walera's attack surrounded them.

The king picked up his brass chalice and drank from it without hesitation, at least none apparent to any watching eye. There was no hint on his face that the thought of his poisoning lingered with every muscle. No one could know that with every breath, the realization of his brush with death haunted him. A death he'd been oblivious to. It was a darkness the man who wore the crown and held the sceptre would never be free of.

On the opposite end of the simply prepared table, the queen cut through the meat on her plate, pacing her breathing to keep her sanity. It would be mad of her to imagine that the meat she cut was the heart of the man who had tainted the life of her husband and her children, carved out and set on her platter. Queen Ariana couldn't stifle the reality of her fear, so she gently filled her belly to feed the hunger for revenge that would be equal to, if not overcome, the panic that had wearied her heart.

Levyna might not have sat at the dining table with royalty before, but she was no stranger to feasting in the presence of nobility. Passive as her mourning of her father had become since she'd found Olin, who had helped channel her emotions and soothe her thoughts, she had far from banished or hidden away from the memories of her father. She broke a piece of soft bread and ate it, holding it in her mouth as she suddenly heard her father's sonorous laughter, a memory that seemed magnified a thousand times. She could hear him, smell the scent of his wool coat, and see him in one of the empty seats at the table until she was pulled away by a voice in her mind.

Hey.

She turned to Olin, brought back to reality as his eyes peered at her like he'd known she had momentarily left the table. Was she seeing ghosts now too? Being an aquamot, a dreamer, and a traveller was not enough.

She shook her head.

Levyna had heard of King Edmond's acquaintance with her father years ago when he'd been alive, and she hadn't missed the surprise in the king's expression when he'd heard that his mother had been named the new Palatine. It was a distraction she was more than grateful to defend in the hope of something to keep the dinner from becoming a gathering of ghosts.

Olin tore the flesh off the chicken bone in his hand, hardly conscious of the fact that a king sat at the table with him, even if his misadventures had played a part in the man still being alive. The Order's actions might have taken everything from him, but it had brought him to his mother. And yet she had disappeared again. The food turned tasteless as he remembered the last person who had forced him to eat, even when he'd thought he didn't need it, and the guilt reared its head all over again.

Did he really want to go to Duken and lose himself searching for someone who couldn't be bothered? Gytha was a Grand Sorceress, and her powers wouldn't be easily overcome. The thought that his mother could have been defeated and unable to return to them wasn't a thought they needed to consider. And if Gytha was well, and had chosen to leave, again, did Olin really want to hear another excuse about how guilt had held her away? What would happen if he turned Duken upside down and still didn't find her?

* * *

"I knew your mother for only a short time," Queen Ariana said to Olin as the pair strolled down the corridor towards an inner balcony after she had requested his company following dinner. "Before that, all I'd heard from Ole and the Maedrian sorceress Isabelle, who'd hoped to heal the king, there was one person out there who could do the impossible and save the kingdom. I knew Gytha for a few hours, in what I would admit to you is one of the most terrifying days of my life, and before then, I had prayed to the gods that Isabelle would find the one to save my husband. And then she came, she healed him and afterwards took charge when the palace was threatened like it was her duty, like she had been sworn to do so.

"I owe her more than I can possibly think of, even though I do not know her." Ariana stopped by the balcony and turned to Olin. "As I do not know her story, I cannot blindly defend her absence. But I will say this, as a mother who would do anything for my children and who met Gytha when my family was the most vulnerable, I know that sometimes it's almost impossible for words to express the depth of our devotion to our loved ones.

"If the Gytha that saved my husband's life is truly your mother, then I wouldn't be quick to doubt that even with an ounce of her powers, she would fight to think of you wherever she is," the queen said.

* * *

Later, Olin lay with his eyes wide open on a bed in a chamber in the palace. The circumstance of their presence in Ravinshore and the past week's events. He shoved aside the thrill and ebullience he would otherwise have been filled with at the fact that he was lying on a bed that had been prepared by a servant in a clean room with a bowl of water, a towel in a corner, and a candle burning on a stick on the table—all in a palace that had housed centuries of the kings and queens of Ravinshore.

In a different lifetime, one where he wasn't besieged by guilt and grief and loss, Olin would have been crawling the walls of the palace in his quest to see and feel as much of the history embedded within as he could. To say that he had dined with the king and queen of his kingdom as though he was some long-forgotten family or acquaintance was a dream even he wouldn't have conceived in the peak of his youthful imaginations. The king and queen would have found the sciff he had been as a boy more memorable than his current reserved self. Instead, he lay quietly, palms crossed behind his head, as he stared at the nothingness of the stone ceiling till he heard a tap on his door.

Olin's first instinct was to grab his sword, even though he was in a palace crawling with the King's Guards. He got up, gently pulled the sword from its sheath, picked up the candlestick, and walked to the door, opening it with his sword hand before hiding the sword behind his back. Olin's brows twitched as the door slowly opened to reveal the Court's Counsel.

"Counsel Ole? Is everything alright?"

"You must come at once. It's urgent."

* * *

Olin hadn't realized until he arrived that there was no need for his weapon. He wasn't concerned about being in danger himself; he was worried that Levyna would share his fate. As he walked through the doors following Ole, he was grateful that he could yell out to his pertes in his mind, and she would know to disappear if she needed to.

Waiting in the room for them were two figures covered in cloaks. They turned to him as Olin entered.

Ole stood by momentarily before he realized that his presence wasn't needed.

"You are Olinander," the man said.

"Yes, I am. And who are you?"

"The nameless but not faceless. We are Wardens of Black Castle," the woman said.

Olin's eyes widened at the realization. He had never seen the Wardens of the Back Castle before. It seemed like so long ago that he'd considered fleeing there. "The Wardens?" he said.

"Yes. We have been told you are Wylie's son," said the man.

"Nephew. He was my uncle, my father's brother," Olin corrected.

"Of course." The woman nodded. Her counterpart hadn't been confused. His mistake was intentional, one of the many things to confirm if the young man was who he said he was. "Your uncle was a friend to many of the wardens in the Castle and myself. He was a brave and loyal King's Guard. Beloved by his peers."

Olin frowned. "Either you didn't really know my uncle, or you're just trying to take the piss out of me. I can't tell, but I must say that I don't appreciate the subterfuge, even if it's coming from the Wardens of the Black Castle. There's a reason Wylie left the King's Guard before he died, and it wasn't because he was loved by his peers. So please, will you tell me what this is about?"

The wardens shared a glance. "We are here because His Majesty has asked us to say this to you before we return to the Castle. We understand that the Orders have hunted you, and while your life has been threatened, the lives of the ones you cared about have been taken. The Black Castle will open its doors to you should you decide to accept. You will be assured safety and will no longer have to run from the Order," the man said.

Olin ran his hand through his hair, looking from one to the other. It seemed unreal. To have both of the things he had hoped to achieve a few weeks ago be at the tip of his fingers. To be standing in the palace, receiving an invitation to Black Castle – he would have accepted in a heartbeat nine days ago before everything had changed.

But this wasn't nine days ago, and as tempting as the safety of Black Castle was, he wasn't seeking refuge so direly now. "Do I have a say in this?" he asked.

"Certainly, Olin. Black Castle never takes a person against their will," the woman said.

"And, needless to say, it most certainly never gives out an invitation. But the other warden added, " His Majesty has made us aware of what you have done and has asked personally that the Castle offer you a home for as long as you want it," the other warden added.

"Then I thank you, wardens, but I am unable to accept the Castle's offer," Olin answered. He watched them closely, but the pleasantness on the wardens' faces didn't change.

"Might we know why?" the man asked.

Olin looked at the room's empty chairs, the lit braziers and torches that allowed him to make sense of the features of the faces in front of him. "I am not naïve enough to think that the Order has completely forgotten about me, and wherever I choose to go after I leave, I will probably still have to watch my back. But I don't think that hiding away in Black Castle is the right thing for me to do anymore. You might not understand and probably think I'm foolish because I more or less told Wylie the same thing when he wanted us to go to Black Castle instead of coming to the palace that night I learned of Walera's treason. But there are things I must do, things I cannot leave behind. I don't see myself being comfortable in Black Castle with what I know about the Orders, including the Red Flame."

"And the things you cannot leave behind, are they worth living with constant eyes over your shoulders, not knowing if and when the Order will strike?" the woman asked.

Olin exhaled as he thought about the question. He compared his feelings to the last time his uncle had suggested they flee to Black Castle. He knew more about himself now, but these wardens were ignorant of that fact. "I'm not completely helpless, warden. I don't claim to be immune to danger, but I believe that, should the Order find me, it will not be the same experience as the last time," he answered.

The man nodded. "We do not think you are foolish, Olin. Rather the contrary. It takes bravery to choose to stand on your own even in the face of adversity."

"Your magic, it will help you," the woman said.

Olin stiffened.

"Do not think too little of it. And, perhaps more importantly, do not let it costume you. Considering who you were to Wylie and what you have done for the king, you should know that, regardless of your choice now, the gates of the Castle will be open for you, should you need sanctuary," she added.

"Thank you." Olin nodded and watched as the wardens did the same before pulling their hoods up and leaving the room.

* * *

As Olin walked back to his room, he found himself stopping at the front of the door to the chamber where Levyna slept. She was one of the reasons Black Castle couldn't have him. He stared at the door for a moment before returning to his chamber.

CHAPTER
TWELVE

D ust trailed the horses as they galloped through the street
and slowed to a halt in front of the palace gatehouse,
where the riders must be identified before the gates opened and
they could ride in. Their descent from their horses was hurried,
to be expected considering the urgency of their mission. The
guards took the horses as the riders hastened towards the palace's
main doors, which fell open at their approach. If the stern expression on their faces was not enough to convey the severity of

their mission, then the sounds of their boots hitting the cobblestone of the hallway floor as they hurried to the throne room called attention to it. Despite their haste, they were stopped at the throne room door and asked to relinquish their weapons. A condition neither man could argue as they surrendered their swords before the doors opened. They hurried inside, where they found the king standing by a table holding a large scroll.

"You're late!" King Ranald said to the two lieutenants of the army.

Heart pounding in their chests and breath steaming through the air, they stood tall in front of the king. One of the men answered, "We came as quickly as we could. Got the horses and rode here at once when we got your message, Your Majesty."

"At once, Your Majesty. Is anything the matter?" the second one added.

Ranald chuckled. "Have you been living in a hole for the past three days? How can you ask such a silly question?"

"I meant no offence, Your Majesty. Of course, we know what happened, which is one of the reasons we rode even faster."

"Well, nothing new has occurred, but something will happen soon, very soon. And I want to be prepared for it when the time comes. I wanted to know how it would happen and just how quickly you would be able to respond!" the king said.

The lieutenants glanced at each other, then back at the king. At the same moment, the doors opened again, and Damiran walked in, followed closely by the palatine.

"You're late as well! Both of you, all of you! What if something was happening? What if something had already happened?" The king's voice was nearing a scream.

Damiran glanced at Fiona, who wore a similar expression to the lieutenants waiting before the throne.

"Your Majesty, I believe you just sent for us," Damiran said.

"I did? Did you know that a moment's – even a moment's – hesitation is enough for the enemy to get to you!" King Ranald pinched his thumb and first finger together to show how small he considered a moment.

He paced a few steps to and from his chair and stood with his hands behind his back. Everyone waited silently to hear why the king summoned them to the throne room in the middle of the night.

"Your Majesty?" Fiona said, stepping towards the king.

"Please, Fiona," the king said. "Do not ask me if something is the matter because that would make me incredibly furious. You all sleep peacefully when at any moment, chaos could strike. I wanted to know how quickly you would get here if I called. If there had been another attempt by the Order, it would all have been over, and you would have arrived only in time to find what was left of me afterwards!"

"Your Majesty, the Order has received word of your response to the Indulgence, and they have agreed. The entire palace is guarded by sentries that are fully conscious. The Order cannot get past them. They would need an army even to try," Damiran said.

"Or they would need someone inside. Just one inside, and that's all it would take. Is it not? They had four last time. Who is to say they do not have one left? Or more?"

"You are right, Your Majesty," Fiona said, drawing the king's glassy, bloodshot gaze. "One can never be too careful. And you are only being careful. There is no fault in that. But I think what Damiran was trying to say is now even the Red Flame knows you will not be easily caught off guard. They know you are prepared, which naturally means they will be discouraged and, as a matter of fact, foolish, to try again," she added, glancing at Damiran and then back at the king, who had tilted his head up and puffed his chest to show confidence at the praise. "I also think Damiran meant well when he tried to tell you that the Red Flame's acceptance of your terms of the White Indulgence means they would not want to risk anything going wrong. So yes, Your Majesty, while you are right that the danger is far from over for anyone in this kingdom to take a peaceful slumber, we also know that the king is not helpless. And Your Majesty knows we will be here whenever you need us."

Her words made sense to him. King Ranald swallowed hard as he stared at her, then glanced at the others in the room and nodded. All of them had shown up quickly, and he had to believe they would respond even quicker should the time come. "I hope you are right," he said.

"Your Majesty, the Order will not find it as easy as they did the first time," Damiran said.

"Very well. I will see you all in the morning. Good night," King Ranald said.

The lieutenants bowed, turned, and left the room. They were followed by Damiran and Fiona, as the king would be the last to leave the room according to his new tradition.

Damiran called the lieutenants, and they stopped. "Did either of you notice the scroll?" he asked.

"Yes. It's a map of the kingdom."

Damiran nodded. There was hardly a need to ask why the king would have it open. "I don't think I need to say this, but no word of this shall make it out of the palace," he said.

The lieutenants glanced at each other. "The safety of His Majesty and the kingdom is our priority, Lord Damiran. We do not sit idly by open fires and gossip. Have a good night," the second lieutenant said.

* * *

The palatine and the king's adviser glanced at each other as they entered the room, no doubt wondering how much sleep the other had managed after the king's call for a vigil. The aldermen already occupied the throne room, each oblivious as to why the king had summoned them.

"Lady Fiona, perhaps —" Alderman Simoen began to say.

"It is Palatine Fiona," she corrected her voice firm.

Simoen swallowed, glanced at the aldermen next to him, and continued, "My apologies, Palatine Fiona. I was going to ask if you perhaps knew the reason why His Majesty has summoned us?"

"I don't know. And I don't think you should be quivering at the thought of being in the presence of the king. His Majesty can summon you whenever he desires," the palatine answered.

"No doubt he can, but it would help to know why beforehand, wouldn't you agree? We are not merely nobles. We are aldermen who have people to oversee and shires to keep in line," Aldermen Kon said.

Fiona glanced at Damiran sitting nearby, who shook his head as though he knew what her response was going to be.

"Alderman Kon, be grateful that the king cannot hear what you've just said. Your shires and villages belong to the King of Queen's Hill. You answer to the King of Queen's Hill. Whatever the reason for your sudden forgetfulness, Alderman, I suggest you conquer it before answering to His Majesty's Court."

Aldermen Kon's face grew red, but before he could respond, the doors opened, and the king walked in.

Everyone stood. An alderman gasped and glanced at the others. Damiran's brows pulled up as he looked from his cousin to Fiona, whose eyes were locked on King Ranald as he marched past. Confusion spread through the court as the king took his seat on the throne wearing a cuirass, gauntlets, and boots.

Ranald's eyes scanned the room, as always, and landed on his palatine at his left. His glassy eyes hinted at sleepless nights as he glanced over the rest of the court, rolling his shoulders to comfort himself in the armour.

"Aldermen, thank you for taking time out of your precious responsibilities to answer my call," he said, his eyes landing on

Kon. "I will make this as quick as possible. Perhaps you have heard that I have agreed to a White Indulgence with those who attempted to have me killed. I have, indeed, and while I intend to honour the meeting, I want you to know that you have from now till two days after the Indulgence to bring me the watchers in your shires."

The air burst with a chorus of confusion amongst the aldermen, who glanced at each other at the king's insane order.

Aldermen Kon shot to his feet. "Your Majesty that is . . ."

"It is what, Aldermen Kon?"

"It is an impossible task you have asked of us, Your Majesty. We cannot possibly know the identities or the whereabouts of Watchers of the Order in our shires. It's a rule of their duty to be unknown. Neither I nor anyone else who is not part of the Order knows the identity of any watcher, and I believe the same goes for the rest of the aldermen."

"Yes, Your Majesty, it is simply something that cannot be done," Alderman Simoen added.

"To tell me this is impossible is to announce that you are incapable, useless, and quite frankly not worth the title you bear. I will not hear that it cannot be done." King Ranald stared at the aldermen, who were all on the edges of their seats. "If you value your roles in my court, you will find me the watchers hiding in your shires and deliver them to me. If you cannot, believe me when I say that the last thing you will have to worry about is losing your titles and your lands. If you cannot find me what I need, then I will be forced to do so myself. I know they exist.

"And, as to the other reason, I have summoned you. I have come to realize that not all matters require my direct presence in this court. Because of that, my palatine will be granted the power to rule in my absence."

Fiona's mouth fell open as she turned to the king. He just nodded, vigour in his eyes as he gave the order. The words were simple enough, but it was as though she couldn't understand what he meant. Had The king transferred the full power of the court to her in his absence?

"Your Majesty, forgive me, but I do not quite understand what you mean," Fiona said.

"exactly as you have just heard. When I do not feel like my presence is crucial in this court, you take charge and make decisions and relay to me what they are. I don't know why I didn't think of this earlier. It's a fantastic idea, don't you think?" King Ranald turned away from his palatine, who was still unsure what to say, to his cousin. "I'm sure Damiran agrees and will be more than willing to help wherever you might need him, yes?"

Damiran's eyes widened for a moment before his face grew firm as he tried to mask the shock at his cousin's actions. A wall of emotions tumbled through his mind, and he barely managed to hold them back.

"Damiran?" the king asked.

"Your Majesty, as your adviser, I must seriously suggest you reconsider this declaration. The role of the king in the court is not something that can merely be transferred. Your power as the sovereign ruler in Queen's Hill, the crown's power, cannot be passed around like —"

"Oh, enough, Damiran. I've heard your advice, and as much as I appreciate it, it doesn't change what I have declared. Besides, I haven't said I'm abdicating my throne. I'm only saying that instead of personally sitting on the throne all the time, someone I trust will sometimes serve in my place. She remains the palatine. Still, the only difference is that now she can hold court when I don't need to be here. And I will hear afterwards of the decisions she has made," King Ranald said, leaving the entire court speechless. "Very well then, as you were. If there's nothing that needs my attention, I will leave the court to the palatine." He rose, and the court followed, getting to their feet as the King of the Queen's Hill, still wearing full armour, strode out of the throne room.

* * *

Levyna was almost certain that Duken should be their next destination, but Olin wasn't so sure.

Last night, Levyna pretended not to notice the footsteps outside her door. She hadn't mentioned it when they'd reunited the following morning. Instead, Levyna silently listened as Olin told her who he had met with and why.

She stared at him as he finished. "And what did you say to them?"

"I turned down their offer," Olin answered.

In the almost imperceptible moment it had taken him to give his response, Levyna's breath had caught in her throat, and her heart thudded. "Wh – what?"

"Yes, I can't. I can't simply go to Black Castle and hide away from the Orders, there's more to be done, and I don't think I can miss it. I told them there are things I won't abandon, things I can't do in Black Castle."

Levyna believed she knew what at least one of those things were: the reason they were in Ravinshore in the first place.

"What Queen Ariana told me last night – I want to believe that maybe part of it is true, but it's hard. I might not be heading to Duken to search now, but I don't want to lose the option completely. It will be my choice," Olin said.

"So you won't go to Black Castle? Even though you know, you'll be safer there than anywhere else?" The statement was forced out of her mouth because she had to be sure.

"I know I would be. And truthfully, Wylie wanted us to go to Black Castle after I discovered the Order's plans. We were heading out that night when the watchers found us. But I never really wanted to. Though, at the time, I guess it was a better option than trying to face the watchers. Yondi suggested it too. He wanted to go on my behalf, but that was just to tell the Castle what the Order had planned. Things are different now. The king is aware of the danger, and the Order's ultimate agenda is in the open. I know they are far from defeated, but I don't want to hide out in the Castle even now."

Levyna studied him. Olin's eyes looked calmer than the day before when he'd discovered that Gytha wasn't here and no one knew where she was. Whatever Queen Ariana had said to him seemed to settle his mind. Levyna could see it. She could still feel he was holding back – he didn't want to leave the fight against the Order after what he had lost. Now it was personal. His hunt for Gytha wasn't over, either. She could see his reasons clear in his thoughts.

The thudding in her chest calmed at his rejection of Black Castle's offer. As they walked along the palace corridor to bid their hosts goodbye, Levyna hoped she hid her reaction well enough, hoping that the relief she felt hadn't leaked over their bond. She also hoped he wouldn't be able to tell that, even though she'd argued for him to accept the offer of safety from the Castle, she hadn't ever wanted him to accept.

They would return to Queen's Hill. Then the journey would take them to Kelegro, where they would seek to know more about Levyna's dreams of the phoenix. The dreams had to be their focus now. She hadn't learned anything new since she'd first had the dream, save for its persistence in her thoughts and the fact that she sometimes saw it when she closed her eyes.

* * *

"How did it go?" Posdel asked Levyna once Olin stepped out of the house. They had returned to Queen's Hill not too long ago.

"He didn't find her if that's what you're asking. He didn't find his uncle's body, either."

"I could have told him that. He probably knew he wasn't going to."

Levyna stood by the window and watched as Olin moved out of sight on his errand for Posdel. She looked down and rubbed the arm he'd held when they'd travelled.

"He was at the house – where it happened. I could feel the ache as he saw what was left behind. When he found nothing, we went to his uncle's friend, who told him that Gytha had told someone to bring a child – a young girl – to his family, but they hadn't seen the sorceress herself."

Posdel took a step closer. "Who's the child?"

"From what they said, she belongs to an old friend of Wylie's uncle, a woman. Olin wasn't interested in learning more," Levyna said. Olin had asked the little girl if she knew Gytha if she knew who had brought her. She hadn't. "So, we left and headed to the palace."

Posdel's brow rose as he turned to her. "The palace?"

"The Ravinshore palace. We met the king and the queen, I suppose, for the second time, for me. Olin got the chance to tell his story, and the king was grateful. But no one in the palace knew where Gytha had gone."

"I don't suppose that was easy to accept," Posdel grunted as he looked away.

"It wasn't. But Queen Ariana said something to Olin that I think helped. I know he's not done looking, but maybe he won't feel so much anger now."

Posdel's gaze strayed into the distance before he responded. "I wouldn't blame him if he were angry. He has been through quite a lot, which he feels responsible for. Finding his mother and then losing her is a valid reason to feel anger. For her to just disappear without so much as a word, it must be troubling for a young man who already carries enough weight on his shoulders. A question he cannot answer settles the worries he's held before," Posdel said. "I believe her presence was a consolation he hadn't been expecting. He's not a helpless little boy that much he has shown, but whether a sciff or a warrior . . . some clouds don't disappear because one wishes they don't exist."

"You know, he was invited to stay at Black Castle," Levyna said, feeling the cold breeze of the morning blowing in the window.

"I heard him mention it back when there was still an urgency to revealing the Order's plan in Ravinshore."

"King Edmond had the wardens personally invite him."

Posdel sounded intrigued. "From what I know, it's a haven, walled away from the influence of the Order of Walera. He would be safe there."

"He would be," she said, reluctance at the back of her throat.

"But he returned here, so I'm guessing he made a choice," Posdel said, turning to Levyna, who continued to stare ahead. Her brows were furrowed, and he could see that she was stopping herself from speaking. "I don't need to be able to read minds to know what's in front of me."

Levyna looked at him with young and naïve eyes, studying his expression. She noticed that his thin hair lay scanty on his head. He met her eyes firmly, and she wondered what he meant.

"You care for him, and he cares for you. I don't think his need to find his mother or his pursuit of the Orders, despite their lessening threat, is the only reason why he turned away the offer of sanctuary. Despite the chaos, somehow, the two of you found each other."

"Our magic did."

He scoffed. "Pertes are rare; yes, they are pieces of one whose magics intertwine and magnify each other. What I didn't tell you is that not all pertes manifest the kind of understanding and union that their magic does. The minds that control the magic might be aligned, but that doesn't mean hearts will be too. There are numerous tales of powers matching but spirits remaining divided, stories of pertes destroying each other when one seeks to steal power from their partner. But you two.... you two have been kindred spirits from the beginning, and it doesn't take a mind reader to see that magic isn't the only thing you share."

Levyna looked away from the mage. It felt as though he could see her thoughts.

"You must credit yourselves. What you have is rare and special. Your magic, together, could very well be unstoppable. But don't belittle it and say that's where it ends. Not many are lucky enough to find actual warmth when the world is burning," Posdel said.

CHAPTER
THIRTEEN

Damiran stopped on his way past the main corridor in the palace as he caught sight of the dark green dress. He observed her for a moment. Even in the dark garments, she'd worn since the death of her husband. It was hard to deny Fiona's striking figure. He took a few steps in her direction, glancing down from the balcony to see what had caught her attention. A flock of bluebirds flitted through the garden, shepherded by a servant carrying two chicks in each of his hands. The servant was moving in gentle, calculated steps, following the flock.

"I wonder what his trick is," Damiran said as he stopped a few feet away from Fiona. They both stared at the garden.

"I would suspect a very clear mind," Fiona answered.

"Have you ever held one before?"

"Only a few times. Have you?"

"I have tried many times, especially when I was younger. I remember King Ranald and I running amok through the garden for months when the birds came out of hibernation. We wanted so badly to hold one but never could. They would puff and sting, and their stings were worse than being shot by a ragged spear. Is it true? What do they say about the feeling of holding one?"

"It feels like floating in the air or having a third eye. It's extremely intoxicating," Fiona said.

"And you managed it without magic?"

Fiona nodded. "Of course, I had no spells to cast, still don't. Even if I had, there's no certainty that one could successfully spell a creature like a bluebird, which itself is a spell. My daughter, Levyna, loves them. She holds them like no one else I have seen. She's managed to hold one in both the seasons the birds have been active in the last ten years," Fiona said.

Damiran nodded, thinking about how Fiona and her family must have lived before the Order's insanity had begun. "I haven't seen her around since my arrival."

"She's safe. Away from the palace and the attention," Fiona answered.

"Hm, of course. The attention has been concerning, wouldn't you say? Not to mention the king's recent announcements," Damiran said.

Fiona shook her head slightly. "Lord Damiran, you must know I had no idea His Majesty was going to do what he did. It caught me by surprise as much as it did you."

"It's hard to doubt that Palatine, with all I've seen. But even you must admit that many of his actions are questionable lately."

"Maybe, but it's not every day one is faced with the kind of revelation he went through. Even legendary warriors who have fought tens of men can be affected by nearly losing their life. Especially when the threat comes from those they trusted," Fiona said, glancing again to the garden as the shepherd froze when a male bluebird turned to face him with wings outstretched, making itself three times its size.

"But is he prepared to accept those potentially responsible for that attack? You were there when the aldermen were summoned when he asked them to do the impossible. Do you still think it's wise for the king to agree to a White Indulgence when he clearly doesn't trust the Red Flame?"

Fiona looked at Damiran. "What would you have him do instead? Would it be better if His Majesty rejected the Order's attempt at a peaceful resolution and let the hostility fester?"

"The king rules over the Order. The king rules over everything in the kingdom. But I'm not concerned about his power being in doubt. The king detests the Red Flame and its watchers, advising me that he moved forward with the Indulgence when he is brimming with rage and panic, and hinting at war doesn't seem like a well-thought plan, Fiona." Damiran straightened as he realized his impoliteness. "I apologize, Palatine Fiona."

Fiona waved her hand dismissively. "It's fine, Damiran. For once, we should speak as two people who used to be close, instead of opportune members of the king's court," she said.

"We haven't spoken as old friends for decades, but I appreciate the courtesy. As long as you keep the same courtesy and tell me that you agree that His Majesty's order to have the aldermen hunt for watchers in their shires is a bad idea."

"It would be simple-minded to think all will be well once the king sits down with the Order, Damiran. But I think it needs to happen so His Majesty can see for himself that he's still in control. As uncertain as the arrangement may seem, the king needs to overcome what happened. We have both seen the toll it's taking."

"On his mind, you mean?" Damiran whispered his tone as he turned away from the palatine to watch as the shepherd set the chicks down to join the flock.

"Yes. Whatever happens after the Indulgence, it will help him function in the presence of those that represent the disturbance to his peace. Facing that will help. I believe it will."

* * *

It was impossible for Olin not to think of Yondi as he took the path Yondi had shown him through the streets. Olin didn't know why he had asked to run the errand for Posdel – whether it was to gain a semblance of normalcy again or so that he would feel less guilt for taking the mage's apprentice away from him. Regardless of the reason, Olin walked past the rabble in the market as he looked to break away from the crowd, making his way towards a smith's shop.

Olin had the hood of his grey cape over his head as he turned the corner. He might have thwarted the Order's efforts, but he shouldn't be too reckless in public, so he kept a watch for danger as he walked. Ever since he had become a target of the Orders, instinct had become a natural part of him. Unlike back in Hunter's Grove, here, there weren't many faces that struck memories of familiarity. Hardly anyone paid attention to him, and those whose gazes he caught quickly looked away. This place wasn't the same as Ravinshore – the people of Queen's Hill looked like they were foreigners in their own lands, with their heavy robes and colourful tunics. Yondi had told him it was because of the weather, but Olin hadn't taken the explanation seriously because Ravinshore never dressed like that in winter either.

It was easy to pick out the mark of the mallet on the wooden sign of the shop he was looking for, as unlike in Ravinshore, Queen's Hill wasn't famous for its blacksmith and builders. Olin pushed the door open and stepped in. He was greeted by a wave of the heat from the forge burning in the corner of the shop. Standing at the forge, a blacksmith held a dagger in a pair of tongs, dipping the hot metal in the water. Olin watched the steam rise to cover the man's face as he lifted his head to see the visitor.

The smith had a blackened and wrinkled face, and Olin wondered if that was a mark of his job. Streaks of sweat lined the smith's forehead down to his moustache and thick beard. His serious expression looked like someone busy with work. Had the smith been a foot taller and his hair a shade lighter, he would have looked like Wylie.

"Can I help you?" the smith asked, pulling the metal he had just quenched out of the water.

"Yes I . . . I am here to pick up a silver wand," Olin answered.

The blacksmith looked at him, and Olin pulled down his hood. "I don't remember seeing you here before," the smith said.

"No, I haven't been. I'm only picking it up for someone.

Posdel Sejon, the mage."

"Of course, Yondi's Master," the smith said. "And who are you?" He set the dagger on the anvil and picked up a mallet.

"Only an acquaintance of his. Do you have the wand?" Olin asked as the smith swung, hitting the dagger with the mallet, the clanking sound reverberating around the room. Olin wondered how he could live with that constant noise without losing his mind. The heat wasn't as irritating as the sound. The coal-fuelled forge burned in the corner, and Olin watched as the fire danced and the coal turned red.

The smith took his time before dropping his mallet and picking up the dagger to examine it. He then placed it back down on the anvil next to his hammer. Finally, he turned to Olin, giving him a long stare before he turned and walked to the back of the shop, where he pulled down a thin box from a shelf.

Olin kept his eyes on the blacksmith but caught something pass by the window out of the corner of his eye. He glanced over but didn't see anything. Turning his head, Olin looked out the opposite window. Nothing, still. He returned his attention to the blacksmith, who had returned with the wand wrapped in a small brown piece of cloth. He opened the cloth to show it to him, and Olin tried to take it, but the smith pulled back.

"I believe there's something you're forgetting," the smith said.

Olin reached beneath his cape and brought out a small glass bottle of glowing liquid. He held it out for the blacksmith to see. The man nodded, and Olin exchanged it for the wand. Olin glanced at the windows again as he slid the wand into his satchel and turned to leave. He paused when he opened the door, but saw nothing strange, so he exited the shop.

It was in his head, no doubt. Olin made his way back to the streets, turning left towards the market. He imagined how much Yondi would have betting, chatting his ears off on the walk back to the house – he would undoubtedly have said something about the price the smith had asked for the wand.

Olin froze as a pair of armoured riders pushed through the street, and the crowd parted around them to avoid the horses' hooves. An old woman tripped and was nearly overrun before another person helped her up. Olin watched silently. Steps slowed to make sure the woman was well. His gaze trailed after the horsemen as they passed, heads bobbing as the beasts galloped into the distance towards the palace. When he turned to look back ahead, Olin caught sight of two figures staring furtively at him.

They were strange. They were the only people who kept his gaze. Olin scanned their clothes – while they wore tunics, trousers, and vests like many others, they also wore gauntlets around their arms. Their boots also looked familiar, like those he had seen when he had been face-down on the floor of a dungeon. He turned around briskly. Then someone grabbed his arm. Olin spun to meet the eyes of the person holding him. They bore the same intent as the ones watching across the street.

Olin could have escaped. But the touch on his arm wasn't ordinary. Olin stood frozen before he felt power warp the air, and he and the man touching him vanished from the market street. But unlike last time, Olin and his attacker only landed in the alley not far from the market, and Olin felt his body shudder as he stood face to face with the man that had grabbed him.

Olin raised his fists, prepared to set the man alight, but then his arms jerked behind his back and locked into place. The ghost watcher, who wore a laced black shirt and a red ribbon at the end of his left gauntlet, waved his hand as he muttered the words of a spell Olin couldn't hear. Olin struggled to gain control of his arms. He realized quickly that they were being held by the two figures who had been eying him from across the street. Olin could feel his hands, but it was as though they had been tied by a rope he couldn't see. One of the new watchers pulled a black dagger from his belt and lunged. Olin's only option was to vanish.

He couldn't take himself far with all the travel he'd done recently. The jumps had taken a toll on his strength, Olin knew. He emerged just behind the watcher with the dagger and rammed his head into the man's nape as hard as he could, sending the watcher tumbling forward. The first watcher charged at Olin, but Olin jumped again, vanishing and surfacing inches from the man's side, tripping the watcher with a kick to the knee as he moved past. He might not have broken a bone, but the watcher fell to the ground, groaning in pain.

There wasn't a moment to pause as the watcher with the knife spun around. Olin appeared swiftly at the man's side and rammed his knee hard into his flank, a move he'd learned long ago when his uncle had first started teaching him to hold his own. The watcher's grunt of agony had barely escaped his lips before Olin appeared next to the one picking himself off the floor and kicking the same knee he had attacked earlier to send the watcher once again crashing to the ground in frustration. Though his attacks weren't powerful, they could weaken much stronger opponents when used in swift bursts.

But the watcher with the dagger seemed to have finally caught on, and he sidestepped Olin's next attack and sliced Olin across the thigh as he raised his leg to kick.

Olin vanished, landing by the watcher with the broken knee, only to be brought to his knees as his legs were yanked from underneath him. Olin knew he would be dead if he stayed down, and he locked eyes with the sorcerer who'd attacked. If he couldn't break the spell holding him in place, there was only one other thing he could do.

With a moment's thought, Olin closed his eyes and focused on his hands. His concentration was broken when the first watcher punched him in the face, sending him headfirst into the dirt.

Olin tasted blood, but he knew it wasn't over. Watchers didn't stop at fist fights – this was only a touch of personal anger at how infuriating the sciff had been, no doubt. But before anyone else could attack, Olin's hands burst with flames, and at once, they were free, as if the invisible ropes had burned away. Olin used the watchers' surprise to turn the flames onto the watcher that had punched him. Then he blasted them onto the watcher with the black dagger that had tasted his blood. The watchers burnt like dry wood before either of them could scream, and Olin turned to the sorcerer, whose pinched expression hinted that he hadn't expected the flames.

Olin clenched his fist. The sorcerer conjured a shield to block the fire, then dropped his arms and tried to trap Olin's hands again, but Olin disappeared before he could. The sorcerer spun around when he felt Olin's hand around his neck.

As the fire coursed from his arms through his enemy's throat, Olinander heard the words of the watcher's final breath. "Ferie – adion et pu – putet adiona."

Olin staggered back as the watcher burst into flames. Looking around for witnesses, Olin quickly made himself scarce from the scene.

CHAPTER FOURTEEN

"**I**t's nothing to be worried about, really," Olin said.

"Your face says otherwise." Levyna felt her face pull into a frown as she glanced at Posdel and then back at Olin, who was handing the mage the wand he'd gone to fetch.

"I swear, I'm fine," Olin said. "It was just an accident. Nothing more to it."

Posdel took the wand, barely glancing at it before dropping it on the table. He moved to peer out the windows and then walked to the door, ensuring no one was lingering outside before shutting it.

"There's no one following me now. I made sure of that," Olin said.

"So there was someone following you before?" Levyna asked, picking up on the emphasis of his wording.

"I -- I didn't say that."

"I can't hear your thoughts like she can, but even I know something happened," Posdel said, eyes grave with the look of a man who had seen more than anyone else in the room. "Who was it?" he asked.

Please, Olin, you must tell us. You must tell me.

Olin stared. Levyna's eyes held only worry. He'd tried to keep himself from thinking about her while he'd fought off his attackers because he knew that the moment he did, she would know, and spectre or not, she would have come to his aid. He had hoped he could lie his way through the bruises across the side of his face and the cut on his lip, but the dirt in his hair, the burn on his cape, and the blood streaming down his thigh where he'd been slashed was harder to brush off. He glanced at Posdel, whose eyes were wide and alert, a total contrast to the man who had stumbled in reeking of ale the first day Olin had met him. Olin knew neither of them would let his vague excuses pass.

"Watchers. The Red Flame," he said.

Levyna gasped. Posdel slapped his palm on the wall. "How many?" he asked.

"Three," Olin said. "And they weren't wearing masks."

"So how did you know they were watchers, let alone Red Flame?" Posdel said.

"You mean besides the fact that they wanted him dead?" Levyna shot the mage a quizzical glance.

"I saw one of their hands. It had the Order's mark – the flame," Olin answered.

Posdel exhaled as his face hardened.

"Three of them? How did you manage to escape?" Levyna scanned his body. If she could listen to the erratic beating of her heart, she would have grabbed his arm and held him.

"I was smart and fast," Olin said. "I had to be. One of them had magic, and they pulled me from the street not long after I left the blacksmith's shop. I couldn't do anything. He had my hands trapped, but I guess my flames were stronger than his spell." He turned up his hands and looked at them, drawing the glances of Levyna and Posdel. "I managed to get free, and I turned them all to ash," he said.

"And you're sure that you're alright?" Levyna glanced at the bloodied slash on his thigh.

"This is as much as they managed. It was quite a weak attempt, and it would have been over much sooner if my hands hadn't been tied. I don't know if it's because they were ghost watchers, but they seemed less capable than those I've faced before," Olin said.

"Surely you aren't underestimating the Red Flame now, Olin, because that would be a very foolish thing to do," Posdel said, face stern.

"Of course not. How could I?"

"Because you seem like you believe that just because you managed to win against three watchers, the Red Flame itself is no longer a match for you."

"I would never be so naïve!"

"I don't think he means that," Levyna said as she turned to Posdel, who seemed to have been struck by Olin's statement.

Posdel stared at Olin a moment longer before he turned to Levyna. "Get me the bottle with the red rope on its neck," he said to her, pointing at the shelf. Then he pulled a chair over to sit across from Olin. "You, take off the burnt cape and sit."

Olin did as he was told, and the mage moved to examine his thigh. The cut wasn't too deep, but it had already blackened around the edges. Posdel poked at it, and the Olin grunted. "How do you feel?"

"Fine," Olin said as he dropped his cape to the floor.

"Did you notice what kind of blade it was?"

"Yes. It was unusual. A black blade and black hilt," Olin answered.

Posdel's face pinched, and he looked back down at the injury.

"What is it?" Levyna asked, noticing Posdel's reaction. She stood nearby, holding the small bottle with the red rope in her hand.

"Knives with black blades aren't wielded for the same purpose as other daggers. They are notoriously capable of concealing dark magic." He looked up at Olin's face. The young man was trying to seem unfazed at the news that he could have been poisoned again. "But whatever it is, you will fight it." Posdel reached out a hand towards Levyna, who gave him the bottle. Popping the cork, Posdel held the bottle beneath his nose to sniff before handing it to Olin. "Drink it all."

Olin took the bottle and blinked at the mage before taking a mouthful. Olin coughed, and his face contorted into a grimace. "Wh – what the devil is this?" He wiped the back of his hand across his mouth to keep himself from throwing up.

"You don't want to know, and I don't have the time to tell you, but it'll help your body use your magic to heal faster. Now drink," Posdel said.

Olin swallowed hard, closing his eyes to prepare himself before he downed the rest of the potion. He gulped and shuddered before opening his eyes and shaking his head. "That was horrible."

"And it might just save your life. Tell me exactly how you feel," Posdel said as Levyna took the empty bottle from Olin.

"You've asked me that already, and I told you I feel fine," Olin answered.

"Is he lying?" Posdel turned to Levyna.

"He feels terribly sore," she answered.

Olin scoffed. "Because I've just survived three men trying to kill me."

"He feels sore, and the cut stings, but nothing more." Levyna stared at him but spoke to Posdel. Olin shook his head in disbelief but fell silent as he held her gaze.

"There is a small wooden canister two places to the left of where the potion was. Fetch it," Posdel said to Levyna before ripping Olin's trousers to expose the wound on his thigh. Olin grunted in a mixture of shock and pain. Posdel studied the injury closer. "It has not festered since you sat."

"That's a good thing, isn't it?"

"It means we don't have to consider cutting off the leg," Posdel said, and Olin's mouth fell open. Levyna froze in place as her hand found the canister. She met Olin's eyes.

"Could it be that bad?" she asked with a quiver in her voice.

"It doesn't look like it." Posdel stretched his arm and snapped his fingers at Levyna, and she placed the canister in his hand. The mage opened it to reveal a black sticky substance.

Olin shook his head. "Please don't tell me I have to drink that too."

"Not unless you want to crap your guts out," Posdel said as he scooped a small amount of the contents onto his index finger and smeared it over the injury. "This is made in part with the ashes of an oro. It will do the work of the potion you drank outside. It too will use your magic to make you heal faster." The mage took another scoop and smeared it on the wound. When he was done, he looked up at Olin's face. "How about the lip?"

"What? No, no, this was a fist, not a blade," Olin said.

"Are you sure?" Levyna asked.

Olin tilted his head and gave her a wanting look.

"Fine. But you must tell us at once if you feel the slightest bit of discomfort or if anything changes, don't try to bully your way through it," Posdel said.

Olin nodded. "I won't. I know better."

"Do you?" Posdel asked.

"So, do we think he might be poisoned?" Levyna asked.

"Not necessarily. But the fact that it's a dark dagger makes the precautions wise. If there's anything to worry about, this will get ahead of it," Posdel said as he rose.

"Again, I feel fine," Olin said as their gaze settled on him.

"Is it safe to assume that the Red Flame isn't done with him?" Levyna asked, sitting on the chair Posdel had left behind.

"Now more than ever, yes," Posdel answered as he dropped the canister of ointment on the table.

There was a moment of quiet before Olin's voice broke the silence. "The last one that I . . . killed, the sorcerer, said something just before he died."

"What did he say?" Levyna asked.

"Feri . . . adion e pute adion?" Olin said.

"Ferie adion et pu putet adiona," Posdel corrected.

"What does it mean?" Levyna asked.

"It means 'you cannot burn what is already afire'," Posdel said, meeting their eyes as they turned to look at him.

* * *

The market of Fie Valley bustled with life as the day slowly crept towards its end, and the crowds hurried to get their hands on the best produce and goods from across the three kingdoms. While it didn't have the luxury of a diverse population like Duken's Harbor Market, which sold just about everything from the sea, river, and land, it was common knowledge that Fie Valley was considered the heart of the three kingdoms. When smiths, carvers, and crafters in Ravinshore wanted to sell their wares outside of their town and kingdom, they made the long trip to Fie Valley in Queen's Hill. The same went for the fishermen and cross-sea merchants in Duken and the tulip and oro farmers in the hills at the kingdom's centre. The market was always open, but once every ten days, Fie Valley burst into life to host the wandering and hungry souls.

The fire hissed as a vendor pulled the stick of meat off the red-hot grate. In front of the stand, his customer watched attentively as steam rose from the meat and already had a coin held, waiting before the meat was even done cooking. Nearby, a vendor selling sweets on sticks and another with freshly chopped fruits were only a small part of the long line of food vendors stretching across the middle of the market.

With a half-full basket in her hand, the red-haired woman hoarded her smile even as she walked past the fruits, sweets, and stick meats. She ignored the variety of alluring aromas that teased at her senses and the calls of the sellers, offering her tastes of their wares and promising no disappointment, only for a single coin. Her next stop was the blacksmith's stand, displaying an array of jewellery from necklaces to rings, bracelets and wands, broaches and hairpins – the last of which she chose at random and paid for without a fuss. As she did, she glanced around to make sure there was nothing odd.

The red-haired woman moved through the crowd until she reached the baker's shop. She chatted a bit with a middle-aged man who smiled widely at her as he wrapped her bread in a cold leaf, took her money, and handed the purchase over. She added the bread to her basket as she stepped out of the baker's shop. She stood for a moment, again scanning the street from the corner of her eye. Not finding anything, she continued walking away from the market and headed south of Fie Valley. She caught a glimpse of the patchwork roofs of her town.

The path should not have been so lonely, especially on a day like this, as people flocked to the market. She walked unbothered along the path, which followed a ditch ending in the thicket of tall trees at the edge of a forest. The desolate path didn't scare her. She wasn't the type to harbour fear. Usually, she was the fear that crept in in the silence. But she wasn't worried about the quiet – someone would join her soon.

With her basket tucked beneath her left arm, her right hand slid beneath the velvet mantle covering her white dress to grasp the hilt of a curved blade. Then she spun, hoping to catch sight of the figure she knew was trailing her.

But the woman with red hair was alone. Her brows furrowed. She spun back to face the thicket at the sound of a twig breaking and still saw no one. She still wasn't afraid, but the uncertainty was just as maddening. Standing still, she focused on steadying her breath and calming her senses so she could catch whatever it was if there was anything to be caught. Her kind wasn't prey.

The path remained empty and the air still as she finally resumed walking. She was a hunter and couldn't shake the eeriness lurking around her. Suddenly, she spun once again, and this time she caught her prey. A figure, a face, one that brought a strange sense of foreboding, one she couldn't afford.

The fear seeped in between dropping her basket and raising the blade towards the figure's neck. It seeped in from her heart as it raged and fluttered in her chest, realising what was happening. It wasn't as though she'd ever thought herself immortal, but she'd always been the one who brought death to others and had never faced it herself. Her green eyes had been the last sight of dozens of victims before they'd taken their final breath. Red hair and a perfect smile hid her true purpose, and though she had walked into rooms as the deadliest creature, she had walked out, appearing faultless and innocent. Her hands had held the blade and the needle; her hands had held the vile venoms; her hands had held the stuffed cloth over their faces. And her hands had squeezed the life out of those she had killed at the order of the Red Flame. Those same hands relinquished her basket and weapon, clasping around her throat as though to keep the fear from spilling along with the spurting blood from the slice across her jugular.

But she couldn't hide the fear. It rippled its way through her futile effort to save herself and surfaced in her green eyes as she fell to her knees, gaze fixed on the image of the hands that had brought her end. The hands that had disappeared beneath the figure's black cloak. The figure that had brought her the fear she'd never felt while she'd lived in Queen's Hill as a ghost hunting for the Red Flame.

For all the promises Red Flame had made her, they had never given her a glimpse into the future as to when the end would come. The woman with red hair surrendered her shaking hands to the still limbs of death as she fell backwards, eyes staring sightlessly at the shadow of her killer as her blood soaked the fabric of her mantle and seeped into the ground beneath her. She savoured it, staring at the ghost watcher as she died.

The figure loomed over her body and carved a circle inside a larger circle on her forehead with the same blade that had killed her. Turning away the cloaked figure picked up an apple that had fallen from the red-haired assassin's basket and bit into it as they left the scene, knowing well that this market day of Fie Valley wouldn't be forgotten.

* * *

"I feel fine. You don't need to keep glancing at me," Olin said to Posdel.

"As much as I would like to say the stare is because I'm concerned about you personally, I'm more worried about that young woman we've left at home. Because I've seen enough to know that you tend to run towards chaos, even if you shy away from it at first,'" Posdel said. Though Levyna had reminded them both that she wouldn't break if she was left alone for the few minutes, it took for them to fetch the horses for the journey to the ghost village of Kelegro.

Olin's face pinched, falling into step beside the mage. "Do you mean I asked for this? For all of this?"

Olin wasn't limping, Posdel noticed. It had been hours, and the wound hadn't gotten any worse. It had even begun to heal, albeit slower than it would have if Olin was at full strength or if they had a healer available. Olin said he didn't feel any pain and barely felt the injury anymore. Posdel didn't know whether or not he'd been lying so that he could come along.

"Maybe you didn't ask to be hunted by watchers, but you can't deny that you've been quite the mark for them. It's no fault of yours, of course, but I won't watch her deal with the consequences of your fight with the Order."

Olin shook his head. He was beginning to think that he might have actually liked the mage better when he'd simply thought the man was some drunk, washed-up legend with haunted memories who'd taken it out on his apprentice. The drunk part he'd seen with his own eyes, the legend part Yondi had told him, and the frustration he had just assumed from the first day he had stepped into the man's house. But it was hard to stick to that first impression. Whether it had been Yondi's death or everything that had followed, Posdel had sobered up enough to become even more insufferable. Insufferably right.

"I wouldn't knowingly do anything to bring harm towards Levyna. You know that. But I won't just sit back if the Order says it's not done with me or the kingdom. I will not cower."

They arrived at the stable, and the keeper turned towards them. Posdel stopped and turned to Olin. "Which is what I'm saying, Olin. You cannot see yourself cowering, even when you carry so much. It's brave. I cannot deny it. It's noble to fight, but if you declare yourself an enemy, you must accept the consequences. Some of those consequences won't be yours to pay. You cannot afford to be reckless."

"I'm not being reckless —"

"And you must be mindful of a lust for vengeance. It's a sneaky little demon. One may never see," Posdel said, turning away to face the stable keeper.

Olin ran his hand through his hair, brows furrowed as he thought about what the mage had said.

*

They arrived back at the house. Three horses were tied outside to keep them from wandering off. Olin was the first through the door, and the creaking of the hinges was the only sound that greeted him. The fire flickered weakly in the fireplace. He walked further in.

"Levyna?" Olin called her name out loud as he checked her chamber, but it was empty.

Levyna? he called silently this time.

Olin moved to Posdel's chamber but was met with the same silence. He couldn't see, hear, or even feel her anymore.

Olin stood at the door, eyes wide, brows quivering as he stared at Posdel walking through the door.

"What is it?" Posdel asked.

"Levyna is gone," Olin said.

CHAPTER
FIFTEEN

I f Levyna closed her eyes now, there was a chance she would see it again – the phoenix. She had seen the image, so many times it was etched into the back of her mind. She could perfectly see every detail of the creature from the dream, even though it wasn't real.

At least she thought it wasn't real. The last animal she'd dreamt about had been a pale horse that had turned out to be King Ranald's stallion, which had shortly died. But a phoenix hadn't been seen in Queen's Hill or anywhere in the three kingdoms for almost half a century. So it was less likely that she'd dreamt about the actual animal.

Levyna hoped the trip to Kelegro would give her answers because this dream felt different. Unlike the others, it had come back, again and again. Even when she'd dreamt about the palatine's ring, it had been only once. Once had been enough for her to learn that her father would fall victim to the Order's attempt to usurp the throne. And she had still done nothing. It had been nearly a fortnight since he'd died, and the guilt still lingered. Which was why she needed to know what the phoenix was. Who it was.

Posdel had told her how dreamers had been demonized in the past. Being plagued with the gift of seeing death wasn't something most would consider a gift. To many, dreamers were considered harbingers of death, even vessels of death. In the ancient days, it had been common for them to be attacked by those who either thought that the dreamers could have foreseen the death of their loved ones, had seen it and not told them about it, or knew a way to stop it but hadn't taken action. So, slowly dreamers fell into obscurity, and the gift curse became rare.

Levyna didn't know what she would do when she found out who or what the phoenix represented. Perhaps she could find a way to warn them if it still meant death. Maybe the knowledge could at least give let them the chance to say goodbye to those they cared about before the end. She didn't know if she could predict or prevent the actual death. She hadn't been able to stop her father.

As Levyna knelt to add more wood to the fire, she thought of her mother. She thought of how they both had seemed to have been granted a different course in life almost right after her father had passed and how it had been just enough to keep each of them distracted from becoming overwhelmed by grief. Perhaps there was some truth to the fact that each of them had taken up a form of service to her father's memory. Levyna was bound to hunt down the meaning of her new dream, hoping desperately to spare someone else the same fate her father had suffered, and her mother had found herself in the position her husband had left behind.

Levyna would visit her mother before they left for the ghost village so that Fiona wouldn't be worried if she visited Posdel's house to find them gone. She would do it as soon as Olin and the mage returned with the horses.

She left the fire and moved towards the table and her half-empty cup of water. Levyna stared at the cup and swirled her left hand gently over it, freezing the water. She waved her hand in the other direction, and the water melted. She smiled as she remembered the first time she'd realized she could do this and how excited her mother had been. Opening her palm over the cup, Levyna gently waved upwards, and the liquid followed her wave without touching her hand, rising from the cup and into a thin, moving stream following her middle finger. Levyna curled the rest of her fingers in so it would be just the one finger leading. It felt like the water was alive and responding as she touched it with the tip of her finger. A small smile crept onto her face; it seemed like ages since she'd done anything like this. Ever since she'd realized her other powers of travelling and dreaming, her aquamot powers had suffered. She'd almost forgotten how it felt to manipulate water.

At the sound of a knock at the door, the stream of water fell to the table with a splash. Levyna turned sharply to the door. Her heart skipped a beat as she realized she was alone here. She eyed the sword Olin had left by the chair; he hadn't said it out loud, but she knew it was, so she could find it easily if she needed to. Levyna took a step towards the door, listening for who it was. She felt nothing – no heightened emotions from whoever was there, unlike she had with the guard Vernon. She quickly found a chair and sat on it, closing her eyes and concentrating.

When she opened them, her spectre stood several yards away from the front of the house. She could see who was at the door, A man with hair the colour of midnight. He raised his hand and hesitated before he knocked on the door again. His other hand was holding a cane to support his weight. Levyna couldn't see the man's face and couldn't tell what was wrong with the stranger's leg, but the man's stance suggested it was a chore to keep upright. Levyna looked around – there was no one else, not even a horse. He must live nearby if he'd walked, she thought. Levyna wanted to get closer but stopped as the man made to turn away, only to stop himself and knock on the door once more, a little harder than his last attempts.

"Posdel, are you in there?" he called.

She opened her eyes, once again in her body inside the house and walked to unlatch the bolt on the door. She opened it to find the man half-turned, accepting defeat. Then the stranger noticed her. This close, Levyna could see his face; it was pale, and he looked like he had been away from the sun for too long. Black eyes bordered by thin bags and faint wrinkles peered back at her. A thick dark moustache sat over the man's lip, and he had a short, unremarkable beard.

The stranger regarded her briskly before he spoke. "You're not Posdel," he said.

"No, I'm not. He's not home at the moment."

"Of course." The man nodded once in understanding, holding the cane with both hands to support his weight. "You wouldn't happen to know when he might be back, do you?"

"He shouldn't be very long," Levyna answered.

The man sighed and looked away from her towards the side of the house. He didn't look particularly pleased with the idea of waiting. He raised the back of his hand to his face and brushed at his nostrils swiftly. It was apparent that he was considering his options.

"Maybe you would like to leave a message for him?" she asked.

The man turned. "Are you his apprentice?"

"Something of the sort."

"Uhm. Well, my business can't be condensed into a simple message," the man said. "It's a matter that requires a meeting in person."

Had the circumstances been different, perhaps she would have invited him in to wait. Levyna felt sympathetic for the man, but he was a stranger, and she couldn't be sure of his intentions. "Perhaps a name, then? When he returns, I'll tell him that you called and asked for him. Perhaps he can come to find you if you remain in town," she said.

The man's black eyes regarded her once more, this time moving Levyna a little closer to the edge of fear. "A name, of course," He nodded, glancing down at his feet and then looking back up. "Tell him his old friend Eusa came calling. He knows where I live."

"Certainly. I shall tell him the moment he returns."

Eusa nodded and offered the young woman a final glance before he thudded his cane and turned around slowly to begin his departure. Levyna hadn't begun to close the door when he glanced around again. "What did you say your name was?" he asked.

"I never said," she answered. "But it's Levyna."

He nodded with a small smile at the corner of his lips, "Levyna . . . that's a very precious name. A noble name," he said, meeting her gaze one more time before he turned and continued away slowly.

Levyna watched his precarious gait for a moment before closing the door and throwing the latch. She pressed her back against the door, but a moment later heard a loud groan and the thud of what sounded like someone collapsing to the ground. She pulled away from the door, turned around, and stared at it before she quickly unlatched the bolt and opened the door to find the man lying face-down on the dirt. She hesitated for a heartbeat, then noticed the man wasn't moving and sprung out of the house and knelt at his side.

"Eusa!" she said as she turned him over. He made no sound. His eyes were shut, and there was a bruise on his forehead from the fall. "Eusa!" She nudged at the man.

When his eyes flung open, they were no longer black. Levyna gasped as the stranger gripped her arms and quickly spoke a spell. The last thing Levyna did before everything went dark was to try to set her spectre free.

* * *

Damiran walked through the garden to the shaded gazebo surrounded by three guards. Despite winter on the horizon, the colour of the grass hadn't faded, and the trees leaves still shone green, though the breeze teased through them gently sending a few twirling to the ground. The tulips, orchids, roses and lilies never went out of season; they had been there for as long as he could remember. Most of his teenage years had been spent wandering the palace gardens. Those memories were still strong, despite the new polished seats and the shade held upright by masterfully crafted brass piers. He stopped a few inches short of approaching King Ranald's wife, Queen Katina until she waved at him to advance.

"Your Grace." He bowed.

"' Lord Damiran," she said, pointing at the seat across from her. Damiran made himself comfortable, and Queen Katina looked at her guards. "Leave us," she said. The guards bowed and stepped away from the shade together, only going far enough for the queen's conversation to be out of earshot without letting her out of sight.

Damiran eyed the last guard as he made himself scarce before he turned back to the queen.

"Did the king tell you that I urged him to bring you to the palace?" the queen asked.

Damiran's brow rose. "No, His Majesty did not share that with me," he answered.

"Well, I did. I told him he needed someone he could trust to have his back, someone who wouldn't betray him for any reason. Someone whose loyalty would be to him before anyone else. Someone who was blood," the queen said.

Damiran bowed. "I appreciate Your Grace's faith in me."

"Do you, really?"

"Your Grace?" Damiran's face pinched with a frown.

"Do you appreciate being back and being able to play a part in ruling the kingdom?"

"Of course, Your Grace, I do."

"Then why is it that you are here and Fiona is the one who has been made palatine, Lord Damiran?"

He swallowed hard. This was something he'd forced himself not to think about.

"Out of everyone, I would have expected you to have that honour. Instead, you are playing lieutenant. Why? It's hard enough worrying about the Order taking my husband's life, but now I have to watch him conspire with another woman. And you say you're grateful that I am the reason you are here?"

Damiran exhaled. "Your Grace, you must know that I was completely unaware of His Majesty's plan to make Lady Fiona the palatine. There was little I or anyone else could do to stop him. It's my opinion that His Majesty considers her presence on the day he survived the attempt on his life as a vital reason to trust her. No one else but him can justify it."

"You have known him all of your lives. How could you not have a voice in his decision?"

"His Majesty gave no room for it, Your Grace."

The queen exhaled deeply, visibly trying to hide her annoyance. "You are here, and I am here, yet she is the one whose ears he seeks and the voice he turns his ears towards. A woman who has recently become widowed and unattached now has my husband, the King of Queen's Hill, listening to her and doing whatever she says. And I am here." The queen's voice trembled as she finished talking.

Damiran tried to find the right words to comfort the queen but couldn't find them.

"And it gets even worse. She has made him agree to a meeting with the same Order that wants him dead, and he's all but given her the power of the crown. Lord Damiran, if all of this has happened under your nose, what is your usefulness?"

"Your Grace, I know how hard it is, but I think all of this is temporary. It will pass."

"What do you mean?"

"I mean, His Majesty feels indebted in some way to Lady Fiona, and all he has done is simply a way to show his gratitude. Also, and most importantly, the king's decisions have been affected by his panic and fear since the Order's attack. Once the air has cleared and he has dealt with the Order, I believe His Majesty will realize just how impetuous many of his decisions have been and will begin making swift corrections."

"And how can you be so sure of that?" the queen asked.

"Because I have already begun a plan to ensure this outcome, but I must be discrete. As you know, His Majesty is very . . . attentive at this point. I cannot be seen trying to force the king's hand. In fact, I do not intend to force it at all. My plan centres on simply steering the king towards realizing his errors."

"And when will this plan happen? When Fiona has wormed herself so deep into his thoughts that he cannot be saved? Or when she has slithered herself into his bed?" The queen struggled to hold back the ache in her voice.

"I promise, Your Grace, it won't be long at all. You've seen to it that I am here because you know I have the king's best interest at heart, as you say. You must trust that you weren't wrong," Damiran said.

The queen regarded him as the breeze teased the white fur around her neck. She nodded. "But, Lord Damiran, you must tell me what this plan of yours is soon. I want to know. I have had enough of being kept in the dark in my own palace," she said.

"Of course, Queen Katina, once I have it all properly in motion, you will be the first to know."

CHAPTER
SIXTEEN

"**S**he's gone! She's gone, she's gone!" Olin yelled as he spun back into Posdel's room. He quickly left, running into the other chamber, hoping he's simply missed her when he'd checked before, and he might suddenly find her sitting there now.

"What do you mean gone?" Posdel asked.

"Can't you see?" Olin waved his arms, gesturing to the empty house. "It's empty. She's not here!"

"Okay, settle down, Olin. Of course, I see she's not here, but surely, she can't be far. You can use your connection." Posdel waved his hand as though gesturing a thought into the sciff's head. "Call out to her with your thoughts, hear her, and sense where she is . . ."

Olin knocked over a chair as he hurried past Posdel, who stepped aside to let him pass, and simply watched as he ran outside the house and around back where he screamed her name, circling the house till he made his way back to the front. "She's not there. She's nowhere!" he cried. "I can't feel her near the house. I can't call to her." He grabbed handfuls of hair in frustration. "I can't hear anything! I can't sense anything. It's utter silence, Posdel. She's gone, and I don't know where!"

Posdel glanced around the room; everything was exactly how they'd left it. He clasped his right hand into a fist, feeling it tremble as he stared at Olin. There was enough loss between both of them. This simply couldn't be; it was impossible to accept. She couldn't be gone. Not when her mother, the Palatine of Queen's Hill, believed her daughter was here, safe under his watch.

Her mother.

"The palace," Posdel said suddenly. "The – the palace. She's probably with her mother. She's most likely gone to inform the palatine that we are setting out for Kelegro. She must have decided to do it earlier than she said she would, Olin, she —"

"If she's with her mother, why can't I sense her? If she's still in this kingdom, why can't I hear her voice in my head, Posdel? If she's not . . ." He couldn't bring himself to form the words. "Why does it feel like I'm back before I met her?"

No. He couldn't accept that. There was nothing to accept. There was an explanation for what had happened – where she could have gone.

"This is my fault. I should never have left her alone after the attack. I should have known the Red Flame would do this!" Olin kicked another chair into the wall.

His hands were beginning to steam as he balled them into fists. Posdel knew things could get worse very quickly if the boy didn't calm down. "Olin," he said.

"No, no. She can't be gone," Olin said, shaking his head slowly and his hands began to redden.

"Olin!" Posdel yelled, risking annihilation as he stepped forward to grab Olin by the shoulders. "Olin, look at me."

Olin focused his gaze on the mage, eyes glassy.

"You can't do this now. You absolutely must not go down this path now. It is not the time to start blaming yourself, not if you want to find Levyna. I know you can't sense her, but that will only make it harder, not impossible," he said. "Now, look around and tell me what you see." He left one hand on Olin's shoulder but stepped out of his line of sight.

"I don't know what you're trying to do," Olin said, despondent and anxious.

"Olin, focus. You must focus. Look around. Does anything look unusual?" he asked.

Olin took a stuttering breath, something that barely resembled normalcy, then wiped his forehead with the back of his hand and looked around briskly. He frowned. "It looks – it looks like she might have just opened the door and walked out on her own," he said.

"Exactly. Unlike your previous encounters with the Orders, either of them, the house looks exactly how we left it, and most importantly, Olin, there's no sign of blood. I would consider that a good thing."

Olin nodded, turned around and spotted the sword he'd left behind. It was still there, sheathed. He moved towards it. "The sword is untouched," he said as he picked it up. "The fire is still burning." He glanced at the mantelpiece. "The door is intact, and there are no signs of . . . no signs of a fight or a struggle. But her mantle is still here." Olin looked at Levyna's cape hanging on the wall.

"So, Levyna most likely either stepped outside or simply vanished. And it wasn't planned, or she would have taken her mantle." Posdel walked to a small closet. "The fact that the door was open means that she perhaps opened it for someone." He grabbed a thin box and flipped it open to remove the wand Olin had fetched earlier. "Now you and I know that Miss Levyna is anything but a simpleton. She wouldn't have opened the door to a stranger."

"No, she wouldn't unless she was completely sure she had to. She must have had a reason," Olin said, turning his gaze to the door, then back at Posdel, who was holding the wand like a thin stick between his hands.

"And, as she said, she's not completely helpless. She could have – would have – done something had she even thought she was in danger."

"She would have called out to me . . ." Olin's voice trailed off.

"Yes, that too. But she didn't, which means, Olin, that whatever happened up until she disappeared, she didn't know she was in danger," Posdel said.

Olin exhaled. He agreed with what the mage had said but didn't feel anything close to relief. He was doing everything in his power to keep the absolute worst thoughts out of his head. "So what now?" he asked.

"Now, we try to find out exactly what happened." Posdel looked down at the wand in his hand, drawing Olin's gaze to it.

"How are we going to manage that?" Olin said, struggling not to be angry that the mage hadn't led with that.

"With this," the mage said, holding the wand up. "I had hoped it would be much later before I had to use this, but time doesn't respect plans. This is made of Akearian steel from the ores of the Blind Pit. The details don't matter beyond the fact that it's enchanted, and while I can't merely cast a spell with my bare hands and summon threads to see what happened to Levyna, this can help me channel much more powerful magic. To start, get me something of hers."

Olin hurriedly grabbed her mantle and handed it over. Posdel held the cloth as if searching for something.

"Ha." Posdel plucked a long strand of black hair from the hood of the cape and returned the cloth to Olin, who held it with both hands, staring at it intently before he reluctantly set it on the only chair still standing. He looked back at the mage.

"Every creature of magic sheds a bit of its power with things like this. A strand of hair on its own isn't enough of a source of magic itself, but with the threads that connect life and magic, this strand is still linked to Levyna. So we are going to use it to see the last traces of Miss Levyna's energy in this environment," the mage said. "Stand back."

Olin took a couple of steps back as Posdel held the wand and hair in his hands and muttered words of enchantment.

"Aberiro uneisa disunte, gaairia oto," Posdel said, and threads from his hand faded into the wand, a glowing white stream that connected it to the strand of hair. He surrendered the hair to the thread as it was engulfed. Slowly, the glowing image of Levyna appeared, outlined in only enough details to make her recognizable. The form came alive, standing behind the door, throwing the latch, and standing in the open doorway.

"Is she . . .?"

"Talking to someone, yes," Posdel said.

"Who?"

His question remained unanswered. They watched as Levyna closed the door and sunk against it before suddenly opening it again and stepping out. Olin followed immediately, with Posdel a step behind, and they saw Levyna's form drop to her knees.

"Whoever came, it looks like she was trying to help them," Posdel said.

Olin watched carefully, up until the moment she collapsed to the side and the form faded. "What just happened?" he asked. "What just happened to her?" He looked at Posdel, who was frowning.

"She collapsed. But more than that, her energy went out. It's as though her essence was drained in a heartbeat. Most likely by whoever she tried to help."

"What does that mean? Who would have done that? Why would anybody do that?"

There was, thankfully, no blood. Posdel met Olin's anxious gaze. "There's no reason I can think of that is kind, Olin."

"Oh . . ." Olin gasped, falling to his knees and dropping his head.

"We must find Fiona and tell her that her daughter has been taken," Posdel said in the tone of a man who had realized his failure.

* * *

The horses halted at the gatehouse, though Olin looked prepared to charge past. The darkness of dusk loomed, held back by the torches lit on each side of the gate.

"You must let us through at once!" Olin yelled at the nearest guard standing atop the gate tower.

"Identify yourself!" the guard said. "What's your business in the palace at this hour?"

"We're the reason your king is still alive. Open this door and let us through!" Olin yelled again, not giving Posdel a chance to act as a voice of reason to his brash approach. Then they saw four archers draw arrows, two on each side of the tower.

"You have one chance to identify who you are and what your purpose is, or you will be fired upon!" the guard said in a commanding voice.

Infuriated, Olin's hands began to glow as his patience for the gatekeeper's actions ran out. They had no idea what they were standing in the way of, and he wasn't in the mood for arguing, not in the mood for anything that didn't lead directly to him finding Levyna.

"Olin, don't do anything rash," Posdel said. "They are only asking why we are here, as they should. They will understand if we simply explain." He looked at the gatehouse and called, "We are here to see the palatine!"

"Why this hour?"

"Because it's urgent – it's in regards to her daughter," the mage said.

Immediately, the guard ordered the archers to stand down as the gates opened, and Olin and Posdel rode through.

* * *

Fiona was looking forward to settling down for the night. Her handmaid had been instructed to prepare her bath after her late meeting with the king and Damiran regarding the upcoming Indulgence. As she walked towards her quarters, accompanied by her guard, her thoughts drifted toward the challenges of her new role. She thought of her husband and how Fredrik had managed to keep the stress of his position away from her and Levyna. Her daughter. Fiona suddenly felt the need to feel her in her arms, a thought that was interrupted by a pair of men marching towards her. She stopped, recognizing them at once.

Olin and Posdel.

And then she realized they were alone. Levyna wasn't with them, and they were here this late, and there was only one reason she could think of – something had happened. Fiona felt her heart thudding in her chest, the pace increasing with each step it took for the men to reach her.

"Lady Palatine," said one of the guards accompanying them.

Fiona stepped forward, staring at Olin, heart thudding in her chest and frayed nerves threatening to overcome her legs. She met his eyes and studied his expression, searching for something behind it. "What is it? What has happened?" she said.

As they'd ridden to the palace, a wayward part of Olin's mind had hoped that perhaps he and Posdel had seen wrong or hadn't understood and that this was all some misunderstanding. Olin had hoped Levyna had simply decided that she no longer wanted anything to do with them, with him and his self-provoked quest to save the kingdoms from the Orders as long as she was safe with her mother. But at Fiona's question, Olin felt the iota of hope he'd carried, the hope that perhaps they had worried about nothing and Levyna had merely missed her bed, her own home, her mother's company, evaporated.

"It's Levyna, Lady Fiona . . . she's missing," he finally said.

Fiona's heart dropped at the words, "Wh – What do you mean she's missing? How?"

Olin glanced at Posdel.

"We think she might have been taken," the mage said.

"Taken? By who? Why?"

"We don't yet know," Posdel said.

Fiona's legs felt like they would give way beneath her if she didn't move. She turned to Olin and slapped him across the face. "You! You promised! She trusted you. I trusted you. Both of you" — she stabbed her finger at Olin and then at Posdel — "you promised me you would keep her safe!"

"I am so sorry, Lady Fiona —" Posdel began but stopped as the palatine raised a hand in a call for silence. Glancing at Olin's red cheek, he fell silent.

Fiona wanted to explode with the cascade of emotions running through her. She wanted to hit Olin again, even if it wouldn't bring her relief. She couldn't process this, not when she was still grieving. "How did it happen?" she found herself asking.

"We were fetching horses for a trip tomorrow morning. Posdel and I left her in the house. We were barely gone half an hour,"

Olin said. "We came back and found her gone. Posdel traced her magic, and we found evidence she had been taken."

"And whoever it was left this behind," Posdel said.

Fiona's stared at what Posdel was holding, eyes wide and quivering. She couldn't believe it, not until she took it from him. It was small, but what it lacked in size, it more than made up for its attractiveness and rarity.

"It's a bluebird feather," Posdel said.

* * *

Nari sprung out of his bed and tumbled to the floor at the sound of the King's Guards bursting through the door. He shouted in confusion. He didn't know what he'd done, but before he could ask, a guard struck him across the side of the head with a baton and two more pinned his arms and dragged him away. He was marched down a corridor where the palatine was standing with her guard, Olin and Posdel. The guards roughly dropped him to the floor to his knees and pushed him into a bow.

Nari's eyes were flushed with fear and confusion as he looked up at Fiona and at the faces beside her. "My – My Lady Palatine," he said.

As soon as Fiona had seen the feather, she'd remembered. She had seen this servant shepherding the crown birds in the garden, a role no one else in the castle grounds or the kingdom could boast of. There was nothing remarkable about the palace servant except that he had magic and was one of the few people who could interact with the bluebirds. Bluebirds were considered the crown's possession in Queen's Hill due to the amount of magic they possessed, their striking appearance, and their rarity. It was forbidden for anyone else in the kingdom to possess one, and if one was found outside the palace, it was taken there immediately. However, new birds were rarely found, as they only appeared from their slumber once every decade.

Their magic meant they hardly ever shed feathers, and if they did, they wouldn't be found except by someone who could get close enough to grab it. Hence, the pool of people who could have taken her daughter, who had intentionally or unintentionally left behind one of the rarest feathers in the kingdom, was very small. And there was one right in front of her.

"Was it you?" Fiona asked.

"Was what me, My Lady?"

"Was it you who took my daughter – Levyna?" Fiona said, noting the look of shock and confusion on the shepherd's face.

He shook his head. "No! My Lady Palatine, of course not. It wasn't me. Why would I ever do something so foolish and insane and cruel? For what reason? I would never!"

"I don't know why you did. Maybe it wasn't you. Maybe you're working for someone else. Perhaps the same people who tried to take the king's life?"

Nari clasped his hands together and shook his head vigorously. "Lady Palatine, I beg you, please. You must believe me when I say that I have no knowledge of your daughter. I beg you. I have no business with the people who tried to take His Majesty's life, Lady Palatine. I know nothin' . . . I am no more than a gardener and a shepherd," he pleaded.

"Which is what has given you away." Fiona held the small feather in front of the shepherd's face. "This was left behind when she was taken. How many others can be around a bluebird, let alone get one to shed a feather?" she said as the gardener shook his head. "Do not lie to me now. This is my daughter. Believe me when I tell you that there is no end to what I will do to find out what has happened. To get her back."

"And I swear on my life, and that of my daughter, that I have not a single clue what has happened to your daughter, Palatine, I swear to you. This is a misunderstanding." Nari lowered himself to Fiona's feet as he sobbed.

Fiona stared down at him silently. She had been so certain it was him. The odds of a coincidence were as rare as someone owning a bluebird and just happening to cross paths with her daughter. Rare. But impossible?

"Should His Majesty hear that my daughter is missing and learn that I suspect you have something to do with it and that you could be connected to those who attacked him, you might not see the dawn. You can be certain you will never see that daughter of yours again if she exists," Fiona said. "Tell me now or seal your fate!"

A trembling Nari slowly lifted his head from the feet of the palatine, looking furtively to the side as sweat and tears streaked his face. He looked up slowly. He met Olin's burning gaze, and Olin's fists clenched at his side, then the shepherd turned to the palatine and sobbed.

"I have nothing to confess, Palatine. I have never in my life laid a single finger on your daughter, and I have sworn to it by my life and that of the one I cherish even more so than myself. Whatever my fate will be, that will not change. Surely His Majesty will have me beheaded should he think that I am part of the evil in the palace. If that is to be how it ends, I have nothing else to say than to beg you to let my daughter know that her father was not an evil man if and when you find your daughter."

CHAPTER
SEVENTEEN

K ing Ranald was still wearing his cuirass when he entered
the throne room late that evening. He glanced at the faces
waiting for him, and his feet halted as the memory struck him
of the last time he'd seen them together. Then he saw Fiona,
wearing a look of pure sadness, though she still bowed as he
walked to the throne.

"Lady Palatine," he said. "And Olin, is it not?"

"Yes, Your Majesty." Olin nodded.

"What has brought you here this late?" the king asked.

"Your Majesty, I must apologize for disturbing your rest, but this simply can't wait till morning," Fiona said.

"Tell me."

"It's my daughter, Your Majesty. Olin has brought news that she was taken from the mage's house, and they don't know where she is or who took her."

King Ranald stiffened. He turned to Olin and Posdel. "Is this true?"

The mage nodded. "Sadly so, Your Majesty, we were merely gone a short while, and she disappeared. There was no sign of a struggle, but I used a spell and discovered she had been knocked unconscious before she vanished.

"She's the dreamer, is she not?" King Ranald asked.

"Yes," Olin answered.

King Ranald looked at his palatine, a mother. "Is this the work of the Order? Has the Red Flame done this?"

Fiona shook her head. "We don't know. Olin says it doesn't look like it – the Order does not take, they merely kill."

"However, much of what the Order once was has changed. Their morals have become loose, given their grab for my throne and my life," King Ranald said.

There was silence as Fiona, Olin, and Posdel realized he was right – the Order had shown that they were capable of breaking the rules meant to bind them.

"In the spell I cast, it appeared that she opened the door to someone who pretended to need help. She wasn't attacked outright," Posdel said.

"I had no idea my guards were watchers in disguise until they came for my throat. An attack can be subtle," the king reminded them.

His argument was valid, except for what Olin had found near where she had disappeared. Fiona held out the feather in her hand. "This makes it difficult to believe it was the Order."

King Ranald glanced at her hand. "Is that what it looks like?"

"It's from a bluebird, and whoever took her left it behind."

"Do we know what it means?" the king asked.

"No, only whoever we're looking for might be close to the birds," Fiona said.

King Ranald exhaled and nodded. "Very well. Inform the garrison and have the lieutenants send men to search the town. They may find something if we're lucky, and it wasn't the Order. The garrison won't rest until every household has been questioned. They'll search the whole shire if they have to."

Fiona didn't object. If she had her way, she would turn the whole of Queen's Hill upside down to find her daughter at the chance that she was somewhere close, at the chance that she was still in the kingdom, at the chance that her baby was still alive.

The doors opened, and Damiran walked in, bowed to the king, and turned to Fiona. "I just heard," he said. "I am terribly sorry."

Fiona nodded, doing all she could to keep herself upright and her thoughts away from what could be happening to her daughter. She didn't need sympathy. What she needed was to find her daughter safe and bring her home.

"I have ordered the garrison to search every household and to widen the search as needed. If this wasn't the Order, as her mother believes, then whoever has her will know that the kingdom is looking for her – I am looking for her," the king said.

Olin and Posdel stepped out of the court as a messenger hurried to deliver the king's order to the garrison, leaving the king and his advisors in the room.

"Your Majesty, I understand the Indulgence is planned for tomorrow," Fiona said. "I fear that if I attend, I will hardly be of any use with what has happened. I cannot ask you to move the meeting to another date, but I would ask for your permission for my absence until my daughter has been found."

The king nodded. "Of course, I would not ask you to serve at a time like this. Damiran —" he turned to his cousin.

"Your Majesty?"

"You will send word to the Order first thing in the morning that the Indulgence is delayed. I will not hold it until the palatine is able to attend."

"Your Majesty, you don't need to delay the meeting for my sake. You will still have Lord Damiran by your side. There's no reason to put it off."

"My palatine's daughter, the young woman who also helped save my life, has gone missing. That's enough reason if I say it is."

* * *

Damiran glanced left and right briskly before he opened the door and stepped inside, closing it gently behind him. Ahead of him, the queen was sitting on a chair. She looked at him, and he gave a curt nod.

"Your Grace."

"I've been dying of anticipation. When you told me you already had a plan, I didn't know that it would be so swift or that it would take this form. You promised you would tell me before you made a move," the queen said.

"Yes, Your Grace, I did, and I still intend to do that when it is time."

"Is it not time yet? Your plan is already paying off. I will admit, I didn't think you would go this far, though I feel I need to ask you if the girl is still safe."

Damiran's face pulled into a frown, and he tilted his head. "Your Grace, I'm afraid I don't understand what you're talking about."

Queen Katina's stared at him. "Do you intend to play coy with me? You mentioned you had a plan, and now this has happened."

Damiran stepped forward. "Yes, I did say I had a plan, one that I have not yet brought to life and most certainly one that has nothing to do with the missing young woman."

A moment passed as the queen tried to decide if he was trying to fool her, perhaps denying it because he feared the king would learn what he'd done.

"You mean to say the current situation is not your doing?" she finally asked.

"Oh, it's not, Your Grace. It is not. Whatever has happened to the palatine's daughter has nothing to do with me," he said.

"Is that so?" Katina brushed her blonde hair away from her face. "Well, I have erred in my thoughts then. I felt betrayed that you didn't reveal your plan as you promised. I'm glad I was wrong. Nonetheless, it's a shame what has happened to Levyna. I cannot imagine what her mother is going through right now. It must be a terrible thing."

"It is. The palatine has asked to be excused from the Indulgence, and His Majesty has subsequently decided that the meeting should be delayed until she can attend."

Queen Katina nodded. "Oh, I see. That's quite the development."

"Yes, it is. And though I have had nothing to do with the situation, I certainly intend to ensure that His Majesty realizes how much of a service I can be to him while the palatine is preoccupied."

"Of course." A furtive smile grew in the corner of the queen's face. "And I think that would be incredibly thoughtful of you. You will do well to ensure that the king finds your advice indispensable."

"If you will excuse me, Your Grace, I must see that messages are delivered to the aldermen," Damiran said.

Katina nodded, and Damiran bowed before he turned and exited the old drawing room. She watched as the door closed after him and straightened herself. She didn't know whether or not he was sincere about his part in the girl's disappearance, and frankly, she didn't think that she wanted to know. Other than the fact that it would make her seem a fool. If he had ordered the girl taken, Katina at least hoped that he wouldn't harm her at all. The goal, after all, was to keep this new palatine from amassing yet more pity and gaining more power from the throne. The kingdom had enough to occupy it.

If Damiran wasn't behind this, then Katina owed whoever it was for their exquisite timing. She wasn't heartless enough not to feel terrible for the mother missing her child, as Katina couldn't imagine what would become of her if anything happened to either of her sons. She was not so evil that she would wish Levyna harmed in any way. But she wouldn't mind if they held onto her for a little while so that Katina's husband could be rid of Fiona's influence and regain his senses.

When she was sure Damiran was long gone, the queen set out for the palatine's quarters of the palace.

CHAPTER
EIGHTEEN

K ing Ranald spent the night thinking, eyes open and staring. He couldn't remain blind to what was happening.
He had been alert, been cautious of everything he ate and everyone around him. He had been watchful, true, but then this
setback had happened when he had been so close to getting
ahead of things for once. Why? Fiona couldn't see it, and no one
else could either. The young woman's fate was terrible, but it
was too much of a coincidence that it happened the day before

the Indulgence. There was no way the Red Flame wasn't behind it. They had spent years being steps ahead of the kingdom – of him – but he wouldn't allow himself to be fooled anymore. His palatine wouldn't agree, too busy worried about her daughter, but he wouldn't let them win. He wouldn't let the Order get a step ahead of him again.

To ensure his success, he cancelled the message that would be sent to the Order to delay the Indulgence. It needed to happen as planned. If the Red Flame had taken Levyna as a way to disrupt the Indulgence so they could attack again, he wouldn't grant them the privilege. They wouldn't be able to dream of attacking, unlike last time. He'd meant it when he'd said that they would pay. His palatine would understand why he needed to do this.

The next day, Ranald sat on his throne and watched the doors open. Damiran stood next to him as three Watchers of the Red Flame walked in, one after the other, spreading into a line before the throne. The watchers wore their uniforms, fully cloaked in dark leather armour, black shirts, and mahogany trousers. Masks covered their faces, leaving little to see, save for the colour of their eyes. None of the three wore the red tag on their gauntlet, the mark of a mage. Good. So they hadn't breached that agreement, at least.

If they had been truthful, they carried no weapons whatsoever. But that remained to be seen, and the king ordered them to strip so he could see that they hadn't snuck something past the guards.

"Your Majesty, being subjected to such ridicule was not part of the terms of this Indulgence," Eden said.

"Say what you will, but you are in my palace now, and the last time men like you stood before this throne, they tried to kill me. If you wish to continue with this Indulgence, then you must be willing to agree to my additional condition. Besides, there is no ridicule here when only men stand in this room," the king said.

Eden's face grew grim beneath his mask, but they had already come so far, and to back down would be failure. "We agree to the disrobing, as long as the king's company do the same," he said. He knew there was no way the king himself would disrobe.

"Fine, agreed," the king answered without even looking to the man in question to confirm whether or not he was willing to do it.

Damiran froze, gaze locked on King Ranald, but the king just waved at them to begin.

"Time is precious," he said. The watchers began to disrobe, but the king had to snap his fingers at Damiran to make him begin.

Moments passed before the four men proved they were unarmed, though the watchers kept their masks on. They dressed again and only then were the watchers allowed to approach the throne. The king remained seated, still wearing his complete armour, with his helmet on his lap.

"Your Majesty, this Indulgence has been called because the Order recognizes some of our recent actions have disregarded what the Red Flame represents and our role in this kingdom," Eden said.

"Some?" the king asked. "You say some of your actions? I won't accept that. If you want me to sit here and listen to you, then you must begin by explaining exactly what has brought us to this point."

Eden sighed – this was a little more frustrating than he had expected. "The Order's attempt on the life of His Majesty and the assassination of members of His Majesty's court in an attempt to take power and the throne. A despicable act orchestrated in a moment of complete madness by members of the Order who were unfortunately fooled into following another Order's deceiving Lord Watcher."

"So Red Flame let Walera dictate their actions. Is that what you're saying?" the king said.

"Red Flame was led by a spineless lord, Your Majesty. Liaton gave in like the fool he was, did as Walera's Lord Watcher ordered, and managed to seduce dozens of Watchers of the Red Flame into his mission to betray the kingdom. The Lord Watcher guiding us was a gutless little thing that couldn't hold his own and defend his king. And he has gotten what he deserved for his betrayal – a dagger to the heart from true Watchers of the Red Flame, who didn't hesitate to dispose of him once we learned the truth of his betrayal."

King Ranald leaned forward and stabbed a finger at the watcher. "Yet my palace was still attacked. Do you think you can get away with blaming it on one man? A dead one, for that matter."

Eden shook his head. "We would not think to take His Majesty for a fool. Liaton's death disrupted Walera's plans for their king, but there were those of the Red Flame who were already part of it. One of those watcher's throats, I slit myself in front of the Circle of Watchers of the Red Flame."

The king scoffed. "Am I supposed to be impressed? Am I supposed to show you gratitude?"

Eden stepped forward; he noticed the king's flinch. "His Majesty does not owe me, or the Order, anything – it is us who have strayed, led by the one we called our lord who did the unthinkable by ordering his minions after their king," the Lord Watcher said. "Red Flame stands to defend the throne and the kingdom of Queen's Hill against forces that seek to undermine its peace and bring chaos. That is what we are, the flame that burns those who stand in its way, and though it was led astray and failed terribly, that will never happen again."

Words, words, and more words, All the watcher had was pretty words coated in lies for the king's ears – to make him think they were on his side. King Ranald was certain, in the back of the watcher's mind, behind the mask he wouldn't remove. He was mocking him. Ranald was being mocked to his face while the others no doubt waited for their moment to attack. He could see it in their eyes. It burned red, a flame that was not loyal to him. The king searched the watchers standing before him for any hints at their plan, but all he could see was how they waited for a moment of weakness to pounce. He was certain of it. Even without blades in their hands, these killers could still attack, and they would.

"Your Majesty?"

Ranald jerked his head to the side. Damiran was staring at him. "Yes." he looked from his cousin back to the watchers standing unmoving, dark figures of death. Ranald imagined the very floors on which they stood would be charred – not from their flames but from the evil they emanated. Even in the throne room where the Order had been birthed, they wouldn't hesitate to betray the crown. "You have come to me with mere words that make no difference. What am I to do with those?"

"Your Majesty, if I may," Damiran spoke again.

The king regarded him before assenting with a wave.

"The watchers have explained how the Order has strayed from its purpose. Surely, they are words, but I believe they should still be considered. It shouldn't mean the Order will be spared completely from the consequences of their actions. The Oder is at fault, even if the evil came from the minds and hands of watchers who had been so corrupted. Whatever His Majesty's verdict is, it would be wise to consider —"

"So you think I should accept their story and pretend it never happened? Is that it?" the king asked.

"No – no, Your Majesty. I'm saying that the Order has come to the Indulgence in good faith, and you should consider their explanation."

"Why would I consider these words when there are no actions behind them?" King Ranald shouted, his voice echoing in the room. "They didn't use mere words to attack me and kill my palatine and my commander, did they know?" He rose from his seat, and Damiran dropped to one knee. The watchers followed suit after a moment. Ranald started breathing faster as he stared at them. He wanted to step down and move towards the watchers threateningly, but the king couldn't bring himself closer, so vulnerable. He still felt like prey in his palace.

"Perhaps there is something that can show His Majesty the Order is determined to prove itself before the crown?" Eden asked.

"Penance," the king said, earning a look of confusion across the faces of the watchers. "I want to see heads roll for what happened—Watchers' heads, to be precise. I want to see the heads of every single watcher that followed the traitor that led them astray. If I cannot have the heads of every watcher in Queen's Hill, then I should at least be able to have that. It is the only thing I will consider as a gesture of the Order's penance to show to me that it is prepared to fall to its knees before the throne." The king sat back on his throne. Slowly, everyone stood from their bow.

Eden glanced back at the watchers flanking him before he spoke. "Your Majesty. I would like nothing more than to follow your command, but sadly all of those who played a part have all met their ends – from the old Lord Watcher to the watcher I slayed with my own hands and, of course, the ones who were foolish enough to try in the presence of His Majesty —"

"They did not try in my presence, watcher. They nearly killed me!" the king corrected.

Eden bowed. "Of course, Your Majesty, I apologize for misspeaking. But, I mean to say, every watcher that betrayed us has already been dealt with. They are gone, Your Majesty."

"And is that not convenient?" King Ranald scoffed. "That there is no one left to be held accountable. That the traitors are all dead and the ones remaining are upright and loyal and want me to believe them so I can slumber in ignorance and they can finish what they started. Do you see where my problem lies? You could have watchers in my palace, people I see every day. How many are there?"

"My Lord . . ."

King Ranald shot to his feet again, and everyone but Damiran fell to one knee. "I am not your lord – I am your bloody king! How many watchers are roaming my palace right now as we speak?"

"There are no other watchers in this palace except for the three in front of you, Your Majesty," Eden said.

"Lies!"

"It is true, Your Majesty. There are none. The only ones hidden here were following Liaton and were killed in the attack."

Ranald stared at them all. Of course, they denied it. They would never tell him they still had eyes watching and ears listening, not if he merely asked. What had he expected? The king began pacing back and forth before his throne, not taking his eyes off the figures of death in front of him.

"If I cannot have those that played a part, then I will have those who knew and kept quiet. That's only fair. I will have all the heads of every Watcher of the Red Flame who knew about the plot and didn't come forward."

"Your Majesty —" Damiran stopped as his cousin raised his hand to quiet him without sparing him the courtesy of a glance.

King Ranald stood, staring at the watchers on their knees. Eden's gaze was fixed on him. "You are the Lord Watcher now, are you not?"

"Yes, I am. Your Majesty must understand. I plead that you reconsider. What you have asked is not something the Order can allow."

"Why? You came here to explain, but you came empty-handed, offering nothing to show for it."

"But we do offer something, Your Majesty – the loyalty of this Order to the throne of Queen's Hill on which you reign. My watchers and I are prepared to swear our allegiance should His Majesty accept that what has occurred was a terrible tragedy, a horrible betrayal, and something we will never allow to happen again," Eden said.

"Is that so?" King Ranald asked.

"Certainly," Eden said as his watchers echoed their agreement.

"Yes, Your Majesty."

"Rise." The king waved his arm as he returned to his seat.

Ranald had to decide. They were prepared to swear their loyalty to him – he could have that instead of the heads he wanted as payment for what the Order had done. He had wanted the Red Flame at his mercy, and now they were asking that he accept their allegiance so peace could reign, for the chaos to end finally. King Ranald looked at his hand, at the ring on his finger, the red adamantine crown marking him as the king and ruler of the kingdom of hills. He let the barrage of thoughts in his head settle onto what mattered the most – his authority. He rubbed at the band of the golden ring and looked up at the watcher.

"Very well." the king said. "I will bate my need for bloody revenge for now if you will swear your loyalty to me that nothing of this nature will ever again happen, and I shall consider tempering my wrath on the Order."

"I will swear, Your Majesty. We all will," Eden answered.

"Then approach, take off your mask, and swear to me." King Ranald held out his right hand bearing the ring.

A moment of stillness passed over the room as Eden remained where he was. Damiran watched, uncertain. Is this all it would take to resolve everything? That is if the Lord Watcher didn't go back on his word suddenly.

Then the stillness broke, and Eden walked with the gait of a warrior to the base of the throne, where he again kneeled. Damiran watched the king – not so long ago, he'd had a panic attack at the thought of being in the same room as a watcher, but now King Ranald looked calm in the proximity of not just any watcher but the Lord Watcher of the Red Flame.

Eden pulled down his hood and removed his mask, revealing his face to the king with no stirring reaction and meeting the king's eyes. Each man was wary of the thoughts that had consumed his mind before this meeting. "I swear my allegiance, and that of the Order of the Red Flame, to the King and Throne of Queen's Hill," Eden said.

The king kept his hand still as the Lord Watcher leaned in and placed a gentle kiss on the ring.

A moment passed as King Ranald withdrew his hand; Eden remained on his knees, waiting for the king's word. His fellow watchers waited, and Damiran waited. One more moment of wait, and then suddenly Eden's face pinched. His breath ceased, his throat began to close up, and he grabbed at his throat, struggling for air, fighting to breathe. The Lord Watcher pulled himself to his feet, staggering as he dropped the mask to the floor. By the time he managed to turn, catching Damiran's shocked gaze and meeting the eyes of his fellow watchers, his colour had turned deathly grey, and the veins of his neck had blackened along his neck.

The Third Watcher tried to help, but the Fifth held out an arm to stop him. Eden dropped to his knees after a couple of steps, horror in his eyes as his comrades stood and watched. He continued to claw at his throat for air that would never come. Finally, his efforts faltered, and he fell on his face, dead.

Loyalty to the throne, but not to him – Ranald. The ruler. All through his fancy words, Eden had been chipping away, hinting that the attack had been merely a scratch the king couldn't get past. Ranald hadn't missed the mockery in every word coming from the man's mouth, but he had suffered it, knowing he would get what he wanted. Had they been stupid enough to think he would simply let it go? Had they thought he wouldn't make someone pay? Had they thought he had been joking when he'd said he wanted heads to roll?

Damiran and the watchers looked on in horror as King Ranald rose and reached around the back of his throne, pulling an axe into his hands. He walked to the body of the dead watcher.

"I will not be made to cower in my kingdom! When I said heads will roll" — he lifted the axe — "they will!" He brought the axe down and chopped off Eden's neck, kicking it toward the remaining watchers. "This is my kingdom!"

CHAPTER
NINETEEN

S allen was colder than where he'd been the night before, and if the potter had been like everyone else, the chills would have crept into his bones. The way he held the horse's reins as it trotted through the street didn't change, even when the King's Guards approached from the distance. The wagon wheels behind him creaked rhythmically, punctuated by the sound of the bumps and holes on the road. The sun was drifting behind thick clouds, and a hint of fog rolled across, reminding them of winter, yet the streets were filled with people like every other day, albeit conscious of the armed men on horses patrolling the streets. Everyone was well aware of the reason for the presence of the King's Guards.

The potter slowed his horse as the riders focused on him and approached. Finally, he stopped the wagon altogether.

"Where from?" one of them asked.

"Me humble home," he answered, his foreigner's tongue jumping out at once.

"And where's that?"

"Small house over by Dead Stream," he said, nodding back in the direction he came from.

"And where're you headed?"

"To the market, sir, like I do every week," he answered.

The guards shared a glance before the next question came. "What do you have in the wagon?"

He looked back slowly and then turned ahead. "Just a bunch of pots, sir."

"Pots?" the guard asked while the other dismounted his horse and walked towards the wagon.

"Yes, sir, pots. I'm off to sell 'em, luck willing, I break even to make a profit," he said, eyes following the approaching guard. There was a moment's pause as the guard stared at him, glanced at his wagon covered by a grey blanket, then he grabbed the edge and uncovered it.

The guard relaxed at the sight of the vases carefully packed in the back of the cart – four in total. He touched one and felt the texture before he looked back up at the rider. "Thought you said pots?"

The potter tapped his head, a famous trait of foreigners to lament their fault in conversations. "Pots and vases, I make them all. Today I have vases to sell. Some other time it may be pots."

The guard replaced the cover of the wagon and walked to the front, staring at him intently. "Where are you from?"

"Edenborough, sir. Born and bred. Moved here a year ago."

"We're looking for a young woman gone missing from the next village, Pedina – chestnut hair, grey eyes, noble born. Could have been wearing a blue dress. Have you seen her?" the guard asked.

The potter's face pinched, and he shook his head. "No, sir, I must not. Never been to Pedina since I been to Queen's Hill."

"Has your house been searched?" the guard on the horse questioned.

"Yes, sir, it has. But you're welcome to look again," he said. That got them to relax, almost. If he'd had anything to hide, it was either terribly foolish or stupidly bold to invite them to check.

After a moment, the guards seemed to decide it would be pointless. The guard who'd checked the cart mounted on his horse.

"Can I ask, sir, who is she? The men that came to check me home didn't care to tell me, only that a young noble girl had gone missing."

"She's the daughter of the palatine, and His Majesty, the king himself, has ordered the search. Don't hold back if you know anything, and value your freedom. Otherwise, move along."

"Of course, sir," the potter said as he nudged his horse forward. He bowed as he passed the guards, keeping his face ahead.

The potter could feel the eyes of people around him watching as he headed to the market. The people were filled with apathy and resentment at being invaded all because the daughter of a noble had gone missing. Their faces didn't carry any special concern about why the king had ordered the search, but the potter could see that they would be talking about it for the rest of the day, at least. It didn't matter that she was from the other village. It didn't matter. They hadn't heard of her before. The king's word was out, and soon, every corner of the entire kingdom would know who she was.

As the potter's wagon rolled gently past the stony street, he eyed the cobbler who pushed the wooden windows of his little shop open to let in the daylight. Then he looked at a mother carrying her baby as she hurried across the street towards a small house. The potter passed the deserted carpenter shop and headed into the town's press, passing a tavern where a servant kicked an older, filthy beggar into the street. The potter hissed a warning at his horse as it nearly trampled the man. As he journeyed uphill, more windows on either side of the road opened for the first time, and people discarded buckets of water. His eyes caught on another beggar on the side of the road, and he wondered what he would find if he peeled up the sleeves around the man's arms.

* * *

"She's probably halfway to Duken with a ship waiting to take her and her lover across the sea to Maedro," a woman whispered not so discreetly to the vendor in front of her, another woman, who pinned the customer with an incredulous gaze as she packed potatoes. That was the wildest of the theories she'd heard about the missing girl, but she soon shrugged it off, almost certain it wouldn't be the last she heard of people's stories about what had happened to the palatine's daughter.

The potter stood in front of the shop, pretending not to listen to what the women were saying. Not that they would have cared – everyone was talking about it after all. The door to the shop opened to reveal a man, who pulled open a small drawstring pouch and showed it to him. The potter took the pouch, weighed it, and closed it up before burying it in his shirt and walking away. He'd just sold all the vases and had money to spare, so he walked a few shops over and picked out some melons, choosing two and carrying them to his wagon, eying the beggar across the street as he did.

Then the potter moved to the next stall, where the smell of fowl crap hit his nostrils. He looked over a small-sized bird and gave the seller a copper, generous of him but not his business. He added the bird to the other small things he'd procured in the back of the wagon. As he did, he watched as the beggar shook the cup in his hand to make the pebbles rattle. He furtively packed the things in the back of his wagon, not taking his eyes off the beggar.

Just then, another wagon tore down the street, wheels splashing through a puddle and spraying the beggar with muddy water. The potter was curious to know his reaction and wasn't surprised when the beggar glared at the wagon with a look in his eyes that would be underestimated by perhaps anybody else. But the potter could see it. It was something he was more than familiar with. His attention was drawn away from the beggar as a man walked up to the stall behind him and began to talk about what the king had done during White Indulgence, how the new Lord Watcher of the Red Flame was dead at the king's hand.

The king might have lost it.

There was going to be a war for sure.

One man said he was preparing to move his family to Duken. They would gladly stay there till the chaos passed. Others denied whispers of war.

The potter glanced at the men before he climbed on his wagon and headed back home, eying the beggar one last time as he passed on his way to the small house next to the Dead Stream.

* * *

The potter removed his purchases from the back of the wagon and returned the horse to the small barn at the back of the house before he made his way inside.

The girl's eyes flung open as the door did. The potter met her gaze as he removed his cape and satchel. He took the small pouch he'd gotten and walked to the corner of the room, where he opened a small chest next to a walking cane and tossed the pouch in with the contents, which were cushioned by an old red robe abandoned at the bottom of the trunk. Then he moved towards her, took her face in his hand, and examined her eyes. She peered back sheepishly, harmlessly. He patted her gently on the cheek – not a tease or a nudge to check if she would respond, simply praising the fact she was still there.

The potter walked back out of the house to fetch the melons and then chopped them into small pieces. As he did, he glanced across at the road, at the passers-by that looked like tiny objects in the distance. An arm stuck up and waved, and he reciprocated with a reflexive smile. It wasn't hard to imagine the traveller's topic of conversation. It was part of the reason why he was tempted to feel thrilled. Not that he'd done this for the fun of it, but knowing everyone was talking about it was a perk he hadn't expected. However, he had no real desire for the attention that came with it. What he sought was something far more than material praise.

The potter carried the plate of chopped melons into the house and handed it to the girl. "Eat," he said.

Her gaze dropped to the fruit, and she began to pick at it. He turned from her to the closed door leading deeper into the house. Raising his hand, he brushed his nostrils and ran his hands through his hair and exhaled as he walked to the door. When he reached it, he opened his palms and spread them apart, deasil for his right and widdershins for his left. Then, he turned the back of his hands together. As he pulled them apart again, threads spun from his hands, holding the handle of the door and the entire barrier shimmered along the threshold.

The potter turned the knob and opened the door, stepping inside a room with the windows spelled shut. Only some daylight filtered in, and he snapped his finger, lighting a small white flame on his index finger, allowing him to see the face of the one the whole kingdom was searching for.

Levyna lay on a bed, unconscious, wrists chained to the wall.

I am after something far more, the potter thought.

CHAPTER
TWENTY

"This has gone on long enough. We cannot continue to pretend we aren't thinking the same thing," Alderman Kon said.

He stood with his hands behind his back, a step away from pacing in front of the rest of the aldermen. This meeting had been inevitable. Kon had summoned them after the news broke of what the king had done at the White Indulgence. Had it been any other person to break faith, they wouldn't have made it out of the room alive, but he was the king, so no one had acted when he had poisoned and beheaded the Lord Watcher of the Red Flame. But that wouldn't be the end of it.

Alderman Simeon stepped forward. "First, he asked us to search our shires for a grain of rice in a sack of wheat, and now he has killed the Lord Watcher of Walera during a peaceful meeting. It is past time to acknowledge the king is not well, and his actions have gotten completely out of hand. He seems determined to incite a war within his kingdom." Simoen turned his palms up at the obviousness of the consequences of the king's actions.

"Is he determined, or is he blind?" said Alderman Royo, a bald man in a red robe. His voice was small but not frail.

Kon turned to him. "How can he be blind to the consequences of betraying an Indulgence to assassinate the Lord Watcher? He isn't blind. He's thirsty for blood. He wants a war. He has said it already."

"I don't think the king is in his right mind," Alderman Benedikt said. The rest of the aldermen turned their gazes on him, but not one spoke a word in argument because they all knew he had not strayed so far from the truth. "Forbidding arms in his presence, summoning us before daylight, wearing armour in the middle of his palace, even to his bed, and now this. You can see it in his eyes and the way he talks. It may have started with the attack, but that's not the only thing. He is more than simply fearful or cautious, he has something else in his eyes, and it's clear as day. The king's troubles are far more than just the Red Flame."

"Do not forget how he made Lady Fiona, who is still mourning the death of her husband, the palatine, and then gave her the crown's authority in his absence. This is not a sign of a sane mind," Kon added.

"I've heard he has two different servants taste his food before he touches it. Also that he no longer sleeps. He whispers all night in his chambers," Benedikt said.

"And I don't suppose that he's having a conversation with someone at those hours?" Simoen asked.

Benedikt turned to him. "The king locks himself alone in the room and doesn't allow servants or anyone else in. Not even his wife, the queen, I hear. When a man starts to whisper himself like that, we all know what we would call him. My father was a healer – I know what he would call that. The question is: can we continue to pretend?

"No, it's impossible to continue denying it," Kon answered.

"But we all also know, like Alderman Benedikt has said, that the king has been through something harrowing. It could very well just be that the stress of it all is taking over his mind. The Order's attack wasn't something to make light of," Royo said.

Kon scoffed. "Warriors come face to face with death all of the time, Alderman Royo, and they don't lose their minds and make a woman who doesn't know the first thing about the affairs of the kingdom the palatine. The king's decisions are evidence that he is no longer himself."

"Shouldn't we try to help then?" said Royo.

"Help? How? Look what he has just done!" Kon stepped forward, pointing out the window and gesturing to the rest of

Queen's Hill. "Do you want to be the one to hold the king's hand while watchers run your shire amok and murder you in your sleep? What would you do if he accuses you of being a ghost watcher and takes an axe to your neck? Are you prepared to continue denying the truth, risking the lives of the people of this kingdom?"

"I do not deny that the king's judgment has been questionable. I agree with that. All I am saying is that we should not be so quick to damn the man as we damn his actions. We all knew how King Ranald was before the Order's betrayal."

"And how exactly was that? What was he, before he was slow and unable to see the truth in front of him?" Kon said.

"No one here wants evil for the king or the kingdom, and we would be doing ourselves, and the people of Queen's Hill, a great disservice if we didn't consider that His Majesty could be leading us down a path that will bring us suffering.

"Alderman Kon is right."

The aldermen turned at once to the door where Damiran stood. They stared at him, and he scanned each of their faces as he approached. He stopped in the centre of the room, standing in front of Kon's seat. Royo sat to his left, and Simoen and Benedikt were to his right.

"Lord Damiran, to what do you owe your presence?" Kon asked.

"I'm here for the same reason you are – I have realized the gravity of the situation. The king's actions today opened my eyes."

Simoen crossed his arms. "You expect us to assume that you came here in agreement with us. The king is your cousin, and he brought you to Queen's Hill to support him, did he not, Lord Damiran? Don't take us for drooling babes. If your cousin asked you to learn our plans, you can feel free to tell him that we are too busy hunting for the ghosts he's sent us after to bother plotting against him."

"But that won't be necessary, Alderman Simoen, because I am not here to spy on you. Believe me when I say that I am here for the opposite. I'm afraid I have run out of excuses for my cousin," Damiran answered.

"How did you know we would be here?" Kon asked.

"I assumed that once you heard about what happened, you wouldn't merely sit back, and I was right. You're all too concerned about this kingdom to do nothing," Damiran said. "None of you were in the throne room, yet from the looks on your faces, it's as though you might as well have been. Watching His Majesty take an axe to the head of the dead watcher reminded me of something that made me tremble. It's something everyone in this room knows, something that's a part of our history, something that has always lurked in the shadow of the throne.

"You might recognize the name Mathea of Duken because it was his case that shook the three kingdoms the most. It was his affliction that called attention to it the most. His madness was the reason the very Orders exist across the three kingdoms. I don't think I am misspeaking now when I say that, though King Ranald is Queen's Hill blood, he is still a king in the three kingdoms, and the curse of the crown has sadly found his mind.

And the terrifying thing is that he has only just begun. The Red Flame's attempt on his life might have sparked it, but the fire has been lit, and I don't think it will be easy to quench," Damiran said.

"But what choice do we have, Lord Damiran? His Majesty is our king; we cannot cast him aside or ignore his commands. He is the crowned ruler of Queen's Hill," Royo said.

Damiran exhaled. "Before today, I had harboured an idea to help the king and the kingdom navigate the chaos sparked by the Red Flame."

"And what idea is that?" Kon asked.

"It's more of a who than a what. The only person I know whose presence would spark change is none other than His Majesty's brother, Prince Petr."

Simoen chuckled, and Benedikt made the sound of air sucking into his lungs.

"Prince Petr?" Kon said.

"I met with him almost right after I returned to Queen's Hill to tell him that his presence in the palace would go a long way to helping the king stabilize, but he wouldn't listen."

"Why?" Royo asked.

"You ask why?" Benedikt said. "Is it not obvious that he's still resentful of what his father did? Passing him over for the crown the way he did."

"I'm not sure if that's it," Damiran answered. "Remember, he's lived in the kingdom all this while and has made no effort to reach for the throne when he clearly could. Even when I approached him, all the prince said was that he believed his brother would do whatever was right because Ranald was the king. He did not sound resentful, merely uninterested in meddling with the affairs of the kingdom."

"Masking his acrimony in nobility and false contentment. Has history not seen that act before?" Kon asked.

"Indeed, it has," Benedikt said.

"If he was looking to gain the throne, would he not have jumped at my idea?" Damiran asked.

"Maybe he is waiting for it all to go to ruins so he can come and claim the remains," Benedikt said.

Damiran shook his head. "Aldermen, please hear me when I say we do not need to demonize someone who has done nothing."

"Which is precisely the point," Kon said. "He has done nothing but sit in silence all this while. He has pretended to be unaware of what has been happening, and you expect us to see him as some kind of hope for this kingdom?"

"Neither you nor I can claim to know the prince's true reason for his silence. I stand here in your midst, trying to help, and yet my path has also led me away from Queen's Hill and the throne, or have you forgotten?"

Benedikt scoffed. "How can we?"

"So a deserter campaign for another deserter," Kon said, staring Damiran in the eyes.

"It is not desertion when the choice is virtually taken away from you!" Damiran snapped.

The entire room fell silent as his words echoed. The quiet lasted for a moment as the men caught their breaths. Damiran exhaled and straightened himself, then ran his hand through his hair and turned towards Benedikt and Simeon.

"I am not here to claim saintliness or debate the conditions of my absence or Prince Petr's because I know what it has cost me. I am saying you should look past your opinion of the prince's silence and see the possibility that he could be what Queen's Hill needs right now. His presence in the palace will change things."

"What is he to do?" Simeon asked.

"At this point, I would say that it will need to go beyond advising the king. His Majesty's decisions are not to be trusted, and it's unlikely that he would be willing to heed the words or thoughts of his long-absent brother," Damiran said.

"If not an advisor, what will he be?" Alderman Royo asked. "The king already has a palatine."

"One who has no right to be there," Kon reminded them. "So we are to choose between having the prince who wanted nothing to do with us or nursing a king whose bell has been rung by the watchers so he can no longer hear the silence?"

"Are we not forgetting something? The Red Flame is the reason why all of this is happening in the first place. How will they be dealt with? Or are we to assume they will be someone else's concern?"

"And whose problem will they bloody be, if not ours, Alderman Simoen?" Kon asked.

"Prince Petr's, if that's to be the plan. We've been talking about fixing the wheels while forgetting the Order-sized hole in the wagon," Simoen answered.

"It's fair to say that none of us here are capable of fixing the problem of the Order on our own," Damiran answered. "But with the prince, there will be answers, surely."

"How can you be so confident?" Benedikt asked. "Do you know something we don't? Because you sound certain that Prince Petr can sweep away the Order with the flick of a finger if only he's brought into the walls of the palace."

Damiran looked at each of the aldermen. "No, I don't know anything about the prince's power. I don't think he will merely erase all our problems, and everything will be just fine. But his presence in the palace would undoubtedly serve as a message to Red Flame, especially if their quarrel is with King Ranald. If King Ranald is the reason for their grudge all along, then it might help if they no longer have to deal with him. Before the king killed him, the Lord Watcher said Walera had tricked his predecessor into betraying the kingdom. We, of course, don't know how true this is, but if it is true, and the watchers who believed Walera's lies have perished, then the Red Flame has no issue with the throne. Except that now, King Ranald has made them his enemies, and his absence would only soothe relations between the kingdom and Order."

"We're saying all of this with the assumption that the prince will agree to return to the palace. What happens if he has too much ego or is too determined to let his brother lead the kingdom to ruin while he stands aside and watches?" Alderman Kon asked.

"We make him realize that the whole kingdom will know that it was his choice this time," Benedikt said.

"So, when the Prince arrives at the palace, what happens to King Ranald?" Roy asked, his gaze moving from Benedikt to Damiran.

CHAPTER TWENTY-ONE

I t felt like death. Levyna had often assumed she knew what death would feel like – an eternal silence that would grab her, leaving her destitute, even without the benefit of her thoughts. What if this was some penance for her power – the harbinger of death, the dreamer. She had never before imagined what the consequence would be, but this seemed apt. But who had decided what crime she had committed?

It felt like desolation. Levyna was conscious, and yet at the same time, she was not. She couldn't feel her surroundings as much as she used to. Before she'd even open her eyes most mornings, it had been as if pieces of her were already floating above her body, and once she'd willed it, those pieced could coalesce, and she could exist completely outside of her own body. She'd been able to do that whenever she'd wanted, leaving and appearing across the ocean in a fraction of a heartbeat. And if she wanted to, she could wander into the dreams of another's consciousness. All because she was connected to everything around her. But now she felt nothing. She felt no one.

Not even Olin. Usually, even if she couldn't hear his thoughts, she would at least be able to feel his emotions. And, if somehow even that was out of her reach, she should still be able to feel his consciousness. Or at least tell if he was close or far. She should be able to talk to him. But now she couldn't sense him at all, her other half, her pertes, and it was terrifying. Olin wasn't simply silent. He was gone. As though he had never been there in the first place. As if her being trapped here wasn't enough to make her panic, the oblivion and fear at what had happened to Olin made it worse.

She didn't jolt awake. It was more gradual.

Levyna's eyes opened slowly to see only blurry darkness. There was a taste of awful bitterness in the back of her throat as she swallowed, closed her eyes, and tried to make sense of where she was when she opened them again. The blurriness faded away towards the edges of her vision till she could see, but it was only bits and pieces that the meagre light allowed. Most of the room was in shadow. What little light there was came from a hole, a crack underneath a window. It was daytime. She was in a room, not a particularly large one, and most likely not one she was familiar with. The bed was right across the door; the small window was at the foot of the bed.

Levyna tried to move, but her body was so heavy that all she could manage was a flimsy stir. Her back ached. She was trapped inside her body. Just then, she heard the sound of footsteps approaching before the door opened. She was startled but could barely move her head, let alone the rest of her body, to escape. Her panic slowly turned into curiosity when she saw the person at the door.

It was a young woman, the same age as Levyna, if not a bit older. She had dirty blonde hair and extremely pale skin. Levyna remembered where she had seen skin like that – the old man who had taken her. But this young woman looked nothing like the feeble man that had come knocking on Posdel's door. Right away, Levyna felt something eerie about her. She was holding a candle in her hand and staring at Levyna, eyeing her loose tunic shirt, trousers, bare feet, and the hair left in disarray around her neck. Levyna frowned as she noticed a scar on the girl's throat. But even that scar wasn't as curious as her ghostly white eyes.

Levyna and the girl stared at each other for a seemingly unending moment. Levyna wasn't sure what to say in this situation, and when she finally decided, she realized she had to claw her voice from her belly, a laborious and terrifying chore. For her to be cut off from her body was one thing, but being unable to speak was a different kind of fear. She pushed past the fear, mouthing the words and swallowing a few times before she managed to crack the web around her throat and whisper.

"He – Help me . . ." she said. Falling silent again, she watched for the odd girl's reaction. Nothing. So she tried again.

"Help me . . ." she said again, struggling to gesture and failing to lift her head or move any part of her body more than a twitch. After the third time of voicing her plea, Levyna frowned. Was this a statue in front of her?

"Who . . . are you?" she asked instead. Still, the girl didn't answer. Then Levyna's heart skipped a beat as a new set of footsteps approached, and a face she recognized entered the room.

"I'm afraid she can't tell you," Eusa said. Unlike the last time she had seen him, he was sharper and standing comfortably without the help of a cane.

Levyna's breath stopped as the man leaned towards her and raised his hand, and snapped his finger, calling a flame to provide more light to the room. As though she needed a reminder he had magic.

"Who are you, then?"

"I told you my name, have I not?" he said.

Levyna flinched as he reached for her right hand, looked at the chain around her wrist, and then did the same for her left hand. "What have you done to me? Why am I here?" she asked.

Eusa was quiet for a moment as he finished examining the chains, and when he looked up and met her eyes, she saw that his eyes were now a shade of green instead of the black they had been. He searched her gaze. Then he shook his head as if he'd heard her thoughts.

"I have no perverted intentions for you," he said.

Levyna didn't know if that was reassuring. She gave a tug, trying to pull her arms away from him but was dreadfully incapable. She soon realized why he was holding her hands as she saw a thread of enchantment appear between them, tying them together from his arms. It felt like a stab, and it hurt. But it wasn't just the physical pain alone that took her. Levyna fell against the bed, her eyes rolled to the back of her head, and everything went dark.

* * *

When she opened her eyes again, the girl was sitting on a chair by the door. It was still open. Levyna tried to move again but could still barely raise her arm. Nothing had changed since the last time she'd been conscious – if she could call it that – if anything, it was worse. She still couldn't feel where she was, couldn't get away, couldn't hear or reach out to Olin.

Levyna closed her eyes again, trying to focus like she'd been taught when she'd first learned to control her magic. Her magic. She was a dreamer, a traveller, but before she'd known all of those things, she'd been an aquamot. Levyna flung her eyes open and glanced around till she saw the bowl sitting on a table in the corner of the room. There was a chance it held water. She tried to direct all of her energy towards it, filtering out the fear and the confusion but got nothing.

Levyna opened her eyes, exhaling out the frustration before trying once more. Again nothing. Always in the past, even when she'd been too distracted to think of or use her magic, Levyna had still felt the stir of power when she'd been around water.

She'd always been able to sense it come to life the moment she approached it, willing it to move with the smallest of efforts. The blankness she got now was yet another layer to her frustration.

"Why are you here?" she asked the ghost-eyed girl. Her voice was hardly above a whisper, and all she received was more staring. It wasn't enough to be trapped by a man she didn't know, for a purpose she couldn't guess, but the mystery of this girl was going to drive her insane with frustration if the uselessness of her own body didn't do that first.

Levyna studied the girl. Her pale skin, the white eyes, the scar at the throat. Levyna couldn't remember ever hearing, seeing, or learning anything about someone who looked like her. Levyna looked closer, hoping that perhaps she could notice a clue or at least find a way to start a conversation. But Levyna didn't see anything in how she sat quietly with her hands crossed. Like a guard.

A guard.

A watcher? Levyna thought. Could it be? Was this the work of the Red Flame? If so, why? Were these watchers? It was less likely, considering her past encounters with the Red Flame had hardly ever involved such mystery and usually included more blood. Had she been taken because of what she and Olin had done? Was it because she had interfered with the attempt at assassinating the king? Did this have something to do with her mother? Normal watchers wore the same uniform, always ready for battle, but if these were ghost watchers, they would look like normal people, regular folk. Only their eyes would probably have death etched in them, Levyna thought.

"Are you a watcher?" Levyna asked.

"She's not," came the voice from outside the door.

Levyna glanced at Eusa and twitched. The man stood, cleaning his hands with a rag as he stared at her.

"And are you? Have you captured me for the Red Flame?"

Eusa's nose flared, and he brought his hand to his face to brush his nostrils. The man spat on the floor. "She's not a watcher, and neither am I. You couldn't be more wrong to assume you're here to serve the Red Flame."

"Then why am I here? Why am I in chains, trapped inside my own body, and locked out of my head if this is not some plan of the Red Flame? If you don't plan to kill me, who are you, and what have I done to you?" Levyna asked.

Eusa sighed. "Perhaps I should apologize," he said, stepping forward. "It's not my intention to take your life. You should know that."

"It doesn't feel like that," Levyna answered.

"Yes, I can see that. But this is necessary. You have something I need, and this is the only way to get it."

Levyna frowned. "What? I have nothing of yours in my possession. What could you possibly want from me?"

"Your magic. Or, to be more clear, your powers," Eusa said, straightening his neck.

She didn't understand. "My – my powers?"

"Yes, Levyna. Your powers." Eusa waved at the girl to get up and took the chair to sit beside the bed. "You know what you are, do you not?"

Levyna held off from answering. She didn't know what he knew. She was many things. The only power that was as public was her aquamot abilities. But there were many aquamots in Queen's Hill. She stared at him, waiting for him to give her more information.

He chuckled. "Don't try to hide or lie. It's pointless."

"I'm an aquamot," she said.

"That's the bottom of your barrel, wouldn't you say?"

He knows.

"I don't know what you're talking about."

"I told you, it's pointless to lie. I know," Eusa said. "And you must know too. You must have been told how rare it is for someone of your kind to exist: a dreamer and a traveller. I believe that there has never been anyone like you before. To have one of those powers is rare enough. To have both, it's impossible. You are a myth. A fairy tale people whisper of. And you're just the thing I needed."

So there was no point in denying it. "How do you know?" she asked.

"Do you know how hard it is to find someone whose powers shine like a flame at the top of hills? It's not that hard if you know what you're looking for," Eusa said. "I will admit that I wasn't looking for a traveller when I realized you existed. I was only searching for someone whose powers could make my goal easier, and then I stumbled on you. It was purely a coincidence, you see. I had to give up something I wanted to do that day, but it turned out to be worth it."

"What are you talking about?"

"I knew you were there when I stood at Posdel's door. I knew you had manifested behind me."

"How?"

"Let's say I know things. However, that would perhaps be too vague. But, just like you carry rare gifts, I would say that I'm something of that sort too."

Levyna sucked in a breath. "You're a . . ."

"Not a dreamer or traveller, something else, something considered . . . abominable. Should never have existed." He brushed his nostrils with the back of his hand and shrugged. "But here I am. Ha. Here I am." His eyes were wide.

"What are you?" she asked.

He turned his gaze on her. His eyes clouded with anger at the judgment he could see in her. He remained unresponsive till he suddenly frowned and stood.

"I don't need to tell you what I am," he said. "It doesn't matter what I am. It only matters what you are and what you will help me achieve."

"You keep saying all these things, yet tell me nothing. If you're going to hold me here in chains and tell me that you don't have any depraved plans and don't wish to take my life but merely want my powers, then you must tell me what you are and what your plan is."

"I don't have to tell you anything, Levyna. I know I've said I don't plan to kill you, but don't tell me what I must do."

"Surely you must —" she caught herself. "You realize that it's the least you can do. I can feel my thoughts decaying from what you did to me. I'm not just trapped in this room, you're holding my magic hostage, and I'm withering away. I want to know why."

Eusa turned to the pale girl, then glanced back at Levyna, weighing her argument in his head. "If you must know, Levyna. As I said before, I'm not a watcher, and neither is she or shall I say not anymore. You're not here to fulfil a plan for the Red Flame – quite the opposite." He brushed his hand against his nostrils again. "You are going to help me kill all of the Watchers of the Red Flame."

CHAPTER
TWENTY-TWO

"**W**e should have done something!" the Third Watcher said.

"It was wise not to, Gossie. The king would never listen to what the Order had to say. He merely wanted to make a statement. Trying to get in his way would have been foolish," the Fifth Watcher said.

"So you did nothing," said Sixth. "You did nothing, and now the Order is seen as weak. The kingdom thinks we wave nattered by the king."

"But we have not been," Fifth answered

"Eden is dead! He was the Lord Watcher of the Order, and just like that, he's dead, and there have been no consequences. How does that not say the Order's grit has been stifled?" Fourth said.

"Because it has not been. One thing that came of the Indulgence is we know more than ever that King Ranald must go. Perhaps his court will try to hide it, but it's clear he's on the brink. And a man like that is as unpredictable as he is vulnerable," Fifth said. "The Crown of Queen's Hill won't last long on that man's head, even if Red Flame doesn't raise a finger. He's poised to destroy himself already."

"Don't tell us that we have to wait," Sixth said.

The Fifth Watcher turned to the Third, who stood with his back to the rest of the group as he stared out the window in deep thought. His words would be nothing but suggestions for the new Lord Watcher, and since Eden was dead, that right was passed down to the highest-ranking watcher in the circle, Gossie. Slowly the others fell silent and looked at Gossie as well.

Gossie exhaled and turned around. "I detest the mere thought of waiting. But perhaps that is what we must do, till the perfect time to strike."

The Sixth Watcher frowned. "And when shall that be?"

"When Eden's plan declares itself," Gossie answered.

"Eden is dead. Unless he shared his plans with you, how will we know when that will be? How do we even know he put it in place before he died?" Fourth asked.

"I know the plan has been put in motion. He shared it with me, which is why I am forced to urge patience." Gossie looked to the Fifth Watcher. "Eden's plan will progress shortly, and when it is done, King Ranald will get what has been coming to him." He exhaled deeply, slowly balling his hands into a fist. "He had an axe waiting behind his throne during a White Indulgence. Who's to say what else he had prepared?"

"You could have killed him right then and there if you'd been allowed to, but we couldn't know what he had planned. We most likely wouldn't have made it out alive."

"Does the sacrifice to the Order not come first?" Sixth asked.

"Do not choose this time to question my loyalty, watcher, do not!" Gossie said, and the Sixth Watcher's nose flared before he lowered his head. "I wanted nothing more than to boil the blood in his body after what he did, I still do, but that would have cheapened Eden's sacrifice. It takes more than brutality to be a watcher. Worse is the mystery of the agony when we strike at a time when it's least expected. He feels powerful now, but he made a mistake in letting us go, and if, for some reason, Eden's plan fails, I will walk into that palace and kill Ranald myself, even if it means that Queen's Hill will face war."

"So what do we do while the king lets the head of a watcher rot on a spike in front of his palace?" Sixth said.

"We prepare for what's to come after Ranald is dead. It will be only a matter of days, not long at all. Don't show your rage.

Instead, use it to sharpen your knives and arrowheads for the aftermath. There will be those who will stop us when the time comes, and you must use your anger to defeat them all so the Red Flame can take what it deserves. If we must serve Queen's Hill, it must first bow to us," Gossie said. "Once King Ranald is out of the way, it will be simple to take control."

"What about the palatine and the king's adviser?" Fifth asked.

"Just as with the aldermen – we leave them alive as long as they don't grow a sudden sense of duty towards the king. For now, we wait to see if either will be a problem," Gossie answered. "Ranald doesn't realize that he can never win a war against the Red Flame. He will only end up burning the kingdom to ash."

"With how he's been acting, he might not care," Fourth said.

"If he doesn't, you can be sure that his aldermen still do. Even if Ranald somehow manages to survive, they know they cannot run from the Order – the flame will find them no matter what hole they hide in. If they have any wisdom at all, they will turn their backs on him quickly," Gossie answered.

"Will you tell us?" Sixth asked.

"Tell you what?" Gossie said, tone taking the shaper edges of his new role as Lord Watcher.

"Eden's plan or, I suppose I should say, your plan."

Gossie stared at the watcher for a moment before he walked forward and placed his hands on the Lord Watcher's throne. He had pictured himself in this position many times since he'd became a watcher – having the Order of the Red Flame answer to him. Of course, he hadn't known it would happen so fast, hadn't even been sure he would ever get the chance. Normally Lord Watchers didn't fall like flies as they had the last fortnight. It was unthinkable for the Third Watcher in the circle, the third lieutenant of the Lord Watcher, to become the commander of the greatest force in the entire kingdom. And yet, this unpredictable series of events had led him to where he stood.

This morning, he had simply been the Lord Watcher's right hand. Now he held the power of the most revered and silent commanders in the history of Queen's Hill. He paused to take it in. Then he looked up from the throne to the faces of the other watchers.

"You will find out soon enough, but I will tell you that it's perhaps the single greatest weapon the Order has ever wielded," Gossie said.

Fourth and Sixth glanced at each other but remained silent.

"And you're certain there's nothing we need do to ensure its success?" Fifth asked.

Gossie shook his head. "Nothing to be done with any urgency, watchers, but if you must, begin to spread the word to the ghosts in the kingdom. Tell them to prepare."

"I suppose it goes without saying that we need not be concerned about King Ranald's command for his aldermen to hunt down watchers in their shires?" Fourth asked.

"No alderman in Queen's Hill or anywhere else in the three kingdoms would be foolish enough even to consider it," Sixth answered.

The Fifth Watcher frowned and lowered his head. Gossie noticed and looked at the man sharply. "Do you think otherwise?" he asked.

The watcher looked up. "I . . . I don't believe that any of the aldermen would be foolish enough to dare, but perhaps . . ."

"Perhaps what, watcher?" Gossie asked.

Fifth exhaled, reached into his gauntlet and brought out a small piece of cloth, spreading it across the table. "There have been three so far."

"Three what?" Sixth asked.

"Three ghosts dead in the past week alone," Fifth answered.

"What? How is that even possible?" said Fourth.

"I don't know. But it has been happening."

"You're saying someone is killing our ghost watchers?" Gossie asked.

"That is what it seems like, and this" — he pointed at the piece of cloth — "this is what they've been leaving behind," Fifth said.

"A piece of cloth?" Fourth picked it up.

"No, the mark. It has been carved on the flesh of every one of the ghosts," Fifth answered.

Gossie stretched out his hand, and they passed the piece of cloth to him. He stared at it. Two circles – a small circle set inside a larger one. "What does it mean?"

"It's not common, but it looks like something I've seen before, in the books of an old Yetrik temple," Fifth said. "And if I remember correctly, a circle enclosed in a larger circle was a symbol of a life inside a life: motherhood."

"And do we know anyone who has donned this mark in the last decade?" Gossie asked.

"I brought it so I could gain your approval to spread the word. If someone has, they cannot hide for long," Fifth answered.

"Are watchers being hunted by a cult of mothers?" Sixth asked.

"How did they even find the ghosts?" Fourth added.

"It's beyond me. But the first kill happened before King Ranald declared the hunt, and no one knows yet that they were watchers, certainly not the king, or he'd be bragging about it right now," Fifth answered.

"Perhaps that would not be the worst thing, after all," Gossie said.

Fifth frowned. "How so?"

"King Ranald could be crazy enough to want to meet whoever it is, and should he invite them, it would be as easy as waiting for prey to rear its head," Gossie answered. "But before we set it up, find out all you can about who this is, including why they targeted the dead ghosts. If they're half as careful as they have been, it will take some doing. But they have made themselves an adversary of the Red Flame. They must know they have signed their death warrants."

The Fifth Watcher nodded and looked to the other two before he removed his gauntlet and placed it on the table. He gave a final nod to the new Lord Watcher.

CHAPTER
TWENTY-THREE

Eusa returned, took the chair from the girl again, and sat in his place next to Levyna. She had some idea of what he was about to do as he took her hand. In the few hours he'd been gone, she'd tried to think about why he might want to kill the Red Flame. The pale-eyed young woman had simply sat and watched without saying a word. Levyna thought she was creepy.

"Can't she talk?" Levyna asked her captor.

Eusa didn't need to glance back at the girl, sitting with her back to the wall, to know who the question was about. "No, she doesn't. Not anymore. But you know, most of the time, words are very overrated," he said.

"Is that why you won't tell me who you are – you believe your words are overrated?" she asked him.

Eusa's brows pinched, and he stared at her.

"I want to know who you are."

"What do you mean?" he asked.

"I can see you."

Shock washed over his face.

"I might not have all of my powers, but my eyes still work, and I can see the shimmering around your face. I don't know a lot about magic, but if I were to guess, I would say you're hiding your real face with some kind of spell."

Eusa's brows remained furrowed as he leaned backwards. He looked at the chains – she had barely moved since the last time he'd checked. She couldn't use her powers, and yet her magic wasn't completely dead. There was more to the palatine's daughter than he'd expected, and from the way she sounded, it seemed it was a surprise to her too that she'd been able to do that. He regarded her in silence for a long moment, pondering.

"What do you think I'd do if you showed me who you really are?" she asked. "If you won't tell me, then at least let me see your true face. I have no power to escape now. And, if what you've said about killing all of the watchers in Queen's Hill is true, then you won't be setting me free anytime soon," she added.

Eusa blinked and looked away at the wall. She hoped it was because her words were getting to him. If she could get some real answers, then she could find a way to escape or at least a way to call out for help. "Does the reason you've hidden your face have something to do with your vendetta against the Red Flame?" she asked. "Or are you worried I'll tell everyone who you are if I ever make it out of here?"

"Stop talking."

"You don't plan to set me free ever, do you? But you've also said you don't want to kill me. There's no one for me to tell if I'm not free," she said.

"Shut it."

"Who are you, Eusa? What are you?" Levyna asked again and partly regretted it as Eusa shot to his feet.

"I said shut up!" he screamed.

Levyna fell quiet, eyes wide. Then she trembled as Eusa took off the spell, and she saw what it hid. Most of the skin of his face was covered in burns, save for his eyes. There wasn't a piece of clear skin. His hair, his true hair, was a lighter shade of brown and was wretchedly thin over his head. His scalp was covered in burns too, and his hair grew in patches and looked like it would be easy to pluck out. His brows were complexly gone, with no evidence of ever existing. The bridge of his nose was crooked, and his nostrils seemed to have been mostly melted together, leaving too-small holes for him to breathe through. If he ever had facial hair, it was all gone. His upper lip was pulled upwards towards his face, angling it to the right side, and his chin was chipped badly. She couldn't believe he was still living

Levyna hadn't known what she'd thought she would find under the spell, but it certainly hadn't been this horror. If she could move her hands and legs properly, she would have cowered. Instead, she stared at him, speechless, as he breathed heavily, leaning over her.

"Is this what you were desperate to see?" he asked her.

Levyna blinked. "Yes." She wasn't sure she lied. "Thank you." She didn't know why she said that either. "Will you tell me what happened?" she asked.

If his brows had been there, they would be pinched in a frown, but his eyes showed his surprise at her response. He brought his hand – which was just as scarred as his face – to his nose and brushed his nostrils again, staring at her as though wondering if the sight had broken her.

"I don't think you were born this way, which means something happened. What was it?"

"You can guess," he said.

"A fire?"

"A fire caused by the Red Flame," Eusa said. He slowly sank into his chair and resumed the spell, hiding his burns and looking away towards the foot of the bed. "It has been almost a decade now, and they have all forgotten about it, not just the watchers and the Order, but the entire village, the entire kingdom. No one remembers. I had kept the truth about what I was hidden for almost twenty years – no one knew me, but they had heard of me. There had been rumours, but they had always died down before. There was no way anyone could prove it, no way to know who I was until my son was born, and the midwife noticed him changing in her hands. She'd been so sure of it, but I told her she had been mistaken, that she must have imagined it. I should have known that would be the beginning of the end – the birth of my son. I should have realized, done something to protect . . .

"When I was five years old, I was peeling a grape. Trying to, at least, until my father took it from me and made it look easy with his bigger hands. I remember staring at his hands and wishing that I had hands like his. I barely felt the change, but suddenly my father dropped the grape and grabbed me and ran into the house. I didn't know why until he grabbed my hands, and I realized they looked exactly like his. I was thrilled, but he was terrified. He closed the windows and the doors as quickly as he could and told me to change back. I wanted to argue, but he wouldn't let me. Then, I saw the fear in his eyes, and before I knew it, my hands were my own again. As far as I know, that was the first time I ever shifted."

"You are . . . a shifter?" Levyna asked.

"One of a very small number. Most have been hunted into extinction," Eusa said. "The Order of the Red Flame managed to convince the former king that shifters were born of dark magic and were a danger to the kingdom. They and most of the kingdom believed – still believe – that shifters were impure and should not exist. So while the people cast out the shifters they knew, the Red Flame made them disappear, one after the other. I doubt you would have heard of it – the legends have been erased with time, but shifters were once some of the most powerful people in Queen's Hill.

"My father warned me never to reveal who I truly was to anyone. I heeded his words until I was a teenager, and then I wanted to prove to a couple of foreigners that I had magic. It was just meant to be fun, but I shifted, taking the shape of one of them. They were shocked and terrified. I ran away. I returned to my father, and that night, we left Queen's Hill for Duken. A decade later, after my father died, I came back." He huffed and brushed his nose again. "No one remembered who I was, so I found myself a village and settled in. I met my wife, Miraila, and we married. Then she got pregnant, and we had a son – a beautiful boy who didn't wait till he was five years old but instead shifted in front of the midwife.

"I thought all would be well when she left smiling. I thought I had been able to convince her that she was old and had seen wrong. I thought she believed me and would simply return to her home, and we would never hear of it again. At the very least, I thought she would want to protect my son, a baby – a secret like that would spell doom for my child. If I'd been even half as cautious as my father had been with me, I would have left that very night with my family the moment the midwife left. If I had known the truth about her, I would have killed her with my own hands. But I was unwise. I chose to trust because I didn't want to uproot my family the way I had been. I was naïve." He ground his jaw and shook his head. "Something that would become the greatest sin of my life."

"What happened to them?" Levyna asked.

"Oh, it happened that night. Dusk came while my wife and newborn son slept on the bed. I opened my eyes at the sound of a crack. Before I could get up, a figure attacked stabbed me and left me for dead. I was forced to listen to the sound of my wife struggling before she, too, went silent. I watched her body fall limp. They didn't take my son away. I watched with my own eyes as they put the blade through his chest and dropped him on the floor like he was a piece of rag. And then they knocked over the candle – the flame spread. I couldn't move, lying empty as the fire consumed everything. Including me."

"But you survived."

Eusa turned to her, quiet as if he was trying to understand what she meant by survival. "Only because I heard my son's screams. Or at least that was what I thought I heard. I opened my eyes and saw the entire house on fire, in flames, with me inside of it. Only then did I realize I couldn't feel it – the fire, as it burned me. I managed to crawl out of the house, skin peeling off me, unable to help while I watched my house burn with my wife and newborn inside. Of course, no one came. I laid on the ground for hours after the flames turned to ash before I realized that there was no more reason for me to stay. I left with one promise in my heart that day – I would return to Queen's Hill and, with my own hands, kill every single watcher I found and then burn the Den of the Flame to the ground.

"The first was that midwife. She was a ghost watcher, put in place to find the 'bad' newborns, just as the Red Flame had ordered. I killed her first, for my son who she'd held in her hands, brought to this world and then betrayed. The coldness was there in her eyes all along. I gutted her, and it still didn't feel like I'd done enough."

"I'm sorry about what happened to your family. I can only imagine the kind of pain you're in, but I do know what it feels like to have the Red Flame take your loved ones away from you. They killed my father," Levyna said.

"I'm aware, Levyna."

Her brows perked. "You are?"

"Yes, I know."

"So you know that I'm the last person who would want anything to do with the Red Flame, who would want anything beyond their end?"

"Yes."

"So why won't you set me free so I can help you?"

Eusa brushed his nostrils and shook his head. "What I need from you isn't something you will willingly give if you have the choice. Knowing I'm fighting the Red Flame might help you understand, but it doesn't mean that you can relinquish your powers, the essence of all of your magic, to me. You simply cannot, no matter how convinced you think you are. You cannot."

"How will you know if you don't give me a chance?"

"Because I don't have the time to test and trust and try to make you an accomplice, Miss Levyna!" Eusa said.

She frowned again. This was the first time he'd referred to her respectfully, and it seemed as though he'd said it without thinking. "How did you know?"

246

"Know what?"

"What I am – a traveller, a dreamer. You said it was by chance. How?"

"Do you remember the watcher that killed your father? The guard."

"Vernon?"

"Yes."

"What about him?"

"He had a partner, did he not? Not one that helped him in his evil work for the Red Flame, but one that was there that day your friend set him on fire."

Levyna was trying to bring back the memory.

"It was me. I was his partner. I was waiting for the right time to kill him, but you beat me to it. It was my first time in the place, and I couldn't imagine my luck when you showed yourself. The way you looked at him, I wasn't sure at first, and then . . . You know how you can feel something of someone, well I have something similar. I can tell what most people are thinking, but I simply couldn't for you and your friend. I was curious, you see. But then again, it takes one to know one, wouldn't you agree?"

"Are you saying you're a traveller?"

"I'm a kind of traveller, Levyna. I told you I'm a shifter, something thought to be an abomination, but another of my powers is being able to possess those with simple minds."

"What do you mean?" she asked before Eusa took her hands and drained even more of her magic.

Then, without warning, as Levyna lay, eyes narrowed into slits, motionless and helpless, Eusa suddenly dropped to the floor. Immediately, the pale girl jerked awake and walked over to them. Levyna wasn't sure if she was seeing things, but it looked like the shimmer she'd seen on Eusa was now on the young woman.

Then Levyna could only watch as the girl cracked her neck and proceeded to drag Eusa's body out of the room. She struggled to keep her eyes open as she followed the girl's movement through the open door. The girl left it open, so Levyna could see her leave Eusa in the main chamber. She then started to dress, pulling on boots and a black hooded cape and slipping knives into a belt.

Then the girl looked at Levyna, and Levyna thought she heard her say, "I'll be back soon," just before the door closed, the frame shimmered with enchanted light, and Levyna drifted off into unconsciousness.

CHAPTER
TWENTY-FOUR

L evyna had been gone for hours, and still, they knew nothing; he still knew nothing. Olin sat at the table, eyes wide
as they had been since she'd gone missing. They hadn't learned
anything new since then. The search ordered by the king had
found nothing – no one had seen her, either alone or in the
company of anyone else. No one had any information about
the missing daughter of the palatine who'd been with a stranger

from Ravinshore and a mage with a knack for choosing ale and wine over reality.

Olin couldn't help but blame himself. He had thought about it all night as he'd watched Fiona struggle to hold herself upright before retiring to her quarters, no doubt sleepless just like him. He'd seen it in her eyes, how she held him responsible for what had happened. It didn't matter that they had thought she would be safer in the house, considering his attack on the streets. Olin clasped his hands into tight fists around his head. His mind was quiet.

He'd wanted this quiet only a few days ago. Levyna's thoughts weren't annoying, but they were there – he could hear her every time she wanted to talk to him or tried to reach him. He could sense her mood as if it were a part of him. Even though it seemed they'd only just met, he was already used to it. It had felt natural – at least until Gytha had disappeared, and thoughts of her had flooded his mind, and Levyna hadn't stopped trying to get him to talk to her. Even when she wasn't opening her mouth, he could hear her there, like a soft, gentle knock on a door in their minds. And when she wasn't knocking, he could sense her presence, and he knew he wasn't alone. He had found it annoying and had been short with her. He had wished for absolute silence as he tried to find his mother and figure out what it was about him that made those he cared about fall away like flies.

Olin had shouted at her and tried to push her away, thinking it was what he wanted, and then she had appeared in Ravinshore and . . . Every step of the way, all she had ever wanted to do was help . . . help him. Even as she grieved for her father, she tried to help him, a sciff from Ravinshore who only brought trouble, and all he had done was try to ignore her. He'd wanted their connection to disappear. It wasn't until she'd found him at Wylie's house and he'd felt their connection again that he'd been selfishly glad she was still there. He'd been glad she was with him, and then … .

Olin slapped his head harder, shaking it as if to make the thoughts of the worst happening go away. If it did, it would surely end him. If Levyna suffered because of something he had caused, he would never forgive himself. If yet another person became a victim of his inability to avoid trouble, he would never recover. He hadn't recovered from Wylie. He hadn't recovered from Yondi. And though he'd known Levyna only a little longer than he'd known Yondi – and not anything close to how long he'd known his uncle – what he felt when it came to her was nothing like how he'd felt about the two of them.

Olin was pulled out of his thoughts by the sound of glass breaking. He lifted his head to see Posdel staring down at the pieces on the floor as though his glare could carve out the truth of where Levyna had gone. Olin glanced at the pieces, then back at Posdel. The mage wasn't clumsy unless he was wasted. Olin frowned.

"Are you serious?" Olin asked.

Posdel looked at him.

"Levyna is missing, and you're just getting drunk?"

The mage stared at him, swallowed hard and turned slowly away from the glass. Olin sprung to his feet and grabbed him by the shoulder. "What's the matter with you? She's gone, and this is the best you can do?"

"Leave me, Olin," Posdel said.

"She trusted you and me. She was taken from your house! And all you can do is find the nearest bloody bottle to drown yourself in?"

"As supposed to what, Master Olin?" Posdel said, glancing at the young man before he yanked his arm away from Olin's grip, And turned away.

Olin couldn't believe this. He watched Posdel steer himself towards his bed chamber. "So this is all there is to you after all? A drunken old fool, useful to absolutely no one? I could never figure out what convinced Yondi that you were anything other than this. You stood by and watched as he died because you couldn't have cared any less" — Posdel turned sharply — "and I was a fool to think staying here and having Levyna stay here was the right thing to do. Because you clearly cannot be bothered about anyone enough to —"

"You watch your mouth, young man!" Posdel appeared in front of Olin faster than a man halfway to tipping over should. He stood inches away. "Watch it, or watch me bury your face on the floor right now! Don't speak of what you don't know."

"And what don't I know? That you pretend to be wise and shrewd, yet somehow you let your apprentice, a boy you were responsible for, fall to the Red Flame!"

"Do you not think it haunts me?" Posdel yelled louder than Olin. "Every single moment I am here, that I am alive, I remember he is gone, that he was killed while I was sleeping on my bed thinking he was safe in the hands of someone he trusted – do you not think I am tortured by the memories of what I could have done differently? My heart is in pieces! He is gone, and I don't know why I'm still standing!"

Olin blinked, speechless for a moment. "Yet you choose to drink when another person in your care has gone missing, Posdel! What does that say about you?" he asked.

Posdel raised his hands and released a pulse that sent Olin flying at the wall. Shocked and upset, Olin pushed himself up, hands balled into fists and glowing. He grabbed the chair next to him, and it burst into flames. Then Olin threw the chair at Posdel, who knocked it to the side and was about to release another pulse just as Olin gathered himself to lunge when a voice cut through their fight.

"Will you two stop it!"

The pair froze. Posdel straightened, and Olin's hands stopped burning. Fiona stood in the open door.

"What has come over you?"

* * *

Olin tossed the charred furniture outside and turned to face the palatine. She looked prepared to slap him again, looking between the two of them.

"My daughter has been missing since yesterday, and this is what you're wasting time on?" Fiona asked.

Neither of them had the right words to answer.

"Olin is a boy, but Posdel, what about you? Are you not supposed to be the adult? How is this supposed to help get her back?"

Posdel exhaled, wiping his face with his hand as he shook his head. "I apologize, Palatine."

"I don't need your apology. I have no use for it!" Fiona yelled. "What I want is my daughter. I am already disappointed in you, in myself for being so careless with her, and now . . ." She pinched the bridge of her nose as she shook her head slowly.

Olin and Posdel glanced at each other as Fiona settled on a chair. Neither of them knew what to say. Olin ran his hands through his hair, hating himself.

"Her father died, and I was terrified she would hate me or retreat into herself for ignoring her dreams. Levyna was always so friendly with others in the palace, the noble maidens and young men. She didn't lack options for company, but I always knew when my daughter wanted to be alone. And she spent so much time alone, mourning her father and huddling in bed, I was close to losing my mind at the thought of having her pull away. And then she dreamt of you," Fiona said, looking up at Olin. "She dreamt of you, and it was as though something yanked her out of her grief. I was still terrified, but my daughter had something to push her to move forward. She didn't know who you were, but she hunted you down. She spoke of you as though you were a memory she'd just recovered from her past. And then she found you, and your road led here." Fiona turned to Posdel. "I always know when my daughter doesn't want to be somewhere, but since what happened at the palace, I hadn't seen her look so comfortable anywhere like she was here at your home.

"She wanted to be here, and I allowed it because I thought she would be safe. I believed you would keep her safe and away from the danger at the palace. Levyna wanted to be here because of you, Olin." She turned back to him and saw that Olin was fighting tears. "Ever since the two of you found each other, every other conversation I have with my daughter has been about you, a boy from Ravinshore she hadn't known a fortnight ago. She spoke of you like she had known you for a lifetime. She never shut up about your connection, and now you tell me that you cannot . . . you cannot find her? If anyone should be able to find my Levyna, should it not be her pertes?"

"I swear to you, Palatine Fiona, I cannot sense her. It's so quiet in my head that it terrifies me. I have no idea where she could be. If I did, I would be scouring and digging with my bare hands, but I don't," Olin answered. "I cannot sense her."

Fiona sighed, turning to Posdel, who looked utterly remorseful. "And you too, you have no idea how to trace her? No one who can help?"

Posdel hesitantly shook his head. "There's only one person I can think of that might be powerful enough," he said.

CHAPTER
TWENTY-FIVE

G ytha knew it was him the moment she heard the ship
ripping apart. She knew what Thorne must have done
and what would now happen to the ship. Only moments ago,
she'd handed the now-healed child to its mother. Within the
blink of an eye, everyone in the cabin was thrown against the
hull as the ship trembled. Then water quickly began to fill the
hull.

Gytha burst into motion, rushing to the deck – what was now the other half of the ship. There she found the bodies of the boatswain and another man. Thorne was nowhere in sight. He'd managed to escape, most likely taking a portal off the ship. They were certainly close enough to land for it. Gytha looked towards Edenborough in the distance, then back at the sinking ship. She had a choice to make – help as many as she could, or go after the man that had threatened her son's life.

There was no way she could save a ship this size from sinking. Not when it had already been ripped into two pieces and was halfway sunk in the water. If she wanted to do the impossible, she would have to think quickly. She headed back below deck.

"Everyone, come this way and stay together!" she shouted, waving them towards a section of the ship that hadn't gone under.

"We should find a way to get off!" a voice said.

"We should jump!" another yelled as he clung to the hull

"Perhaps the sea will be merciful!" said another in a trembling voice

"Do whatever you want, but if you wish to survive, do as I have told you – huddle together now and hold on to someone else!" Gytha shouted above the noise.

Gytha looked at the woman whose baby she had just saved. The mother was clutching her child, struggling to keep herself vertical amidst the chaos. People were still screaming over top of each other, their voices loud, but she could hear other voices coming faintly from the rest of the ship as it slowly perished to the sea. Outside this room, people were fighting the waves of the water overtaking the vessel. They didn't want to die, didn't want to drown. The voices began to fade as the people died anyway, their screams falling into the background among the plethora of other sounds of the ship, tearing apart and wood and metal to be swallowed by the sea.

Even though they didn't know what she was going to do, most of the passengers began to move toward the woman with the child, especially those that had seen Gytha's magic. They were not in the position to question a rescue.

Some believed they could survive the sea and turned away. One of them was a man who began to prepare, pulling off his cape and taking hold of a wooden board that had once been part of the cabin's floor but was now on the side of the ship. The man wasn't alone, as another looked ready to fling himself into the water rather than stay in the ship. Two others, who were either too shocked to move or paralysed with indecision, also stayed. The Grand Sorceress had about a dozen people clustered around the woman with the child – men, women and children who had listened to her.

"Whatever you do, don't let go of the person you're holding. Hold each other tight! And keep your eyes closed," she said, and the group pressed even together. Gytha opened her hands wide, standing merely a foot in front of the group of passengers.

"Ariento-peri levavi ad assentum," she said, and at once, a large light sizzled in the cloud above them. Threads of enchantment eased out of Gytha's hands as she lowered the cloud, enveloping the group. Then Gytha took the hands of the woman with the child, joining everyone else who already held her. Gytha met the eyes of the woman, and if ever she had forgotten what fear for one's child looked like, the Grand Sorceress was reminded in the tearful eyes and quivery brows and lips of the mother holding her child.

"Everything is going to be okay," Gytha said, nodding before she closed her eyes and the group vanished.

The man holding the board stood there in shock, stupefied. The second man screamed as he stumbled towards the place the group had stood, hoping to catch them, but only managed to grab a floating scarf that had fallen off its owner as they vanished. Hardly a moment later, the water burst into the cabin, consuming the two incisive men before washing away the rest, including the man with the board.

In a matter of minutes, all that was left of the ship called the Flea was debris floating to the surface as the hull descended into the sea. None of the debris carried survivors.

* * *

"Where do you think she's from?" a young boy asked another.

"Maybe from Duken or Queen Hill," his friend said.

"I've been to Queen's Hill before, there're a lot of people there, and it's true that many of them have magic and can do incredible things," the boy said.

"And what did you see when in Queen's Hill that makes you believe in magic?" His friend glanced at him out of the corner of his eye as each boy pried at corn with their teeth.

They were sitting at a table in front of a closed stall, watching a house that had seen many visitors and gotten many gifts. Its occupant was the source of many different stories.

"I saw a man walk on air once," the boy said.

"You mean he vanished and appeared?"

"No, I mean he walked several yards with nothing but air underneath his feet."

His friend stopped chewing and looked at him. "You lie."

"No, I don't. It's what I saw with my own eyes. It happened in a place called Sollen or Sillen. I don't really remember the name. But I remember very well what I saw that day, and I've never forgotten it. That's why I think she must be from Queen's Hill."

They sat and watched as yet another person approached the house, asking if they could see the woman that had saved all those people from the sunken ship. They were once again turned away. There were stories about what she'd done – the truth was she'd made all fourteen people and herself disappear and then appear at the shore in the harbour of Edenborough. But the truth wasn't ever that simple. There were different tales about how she'd managed it. Some said she'd controlled the weather, and some were sure that she'd kept the water at bay because she was an aquamot. Others said she'd rescued them one after the other from drowning in the sea, and others even said that she'd used her powers to manipulate time, allowing her to rescue everyone quickly. There had been countless ideas since the woman had appeared with the survivors, but all agreed on one thing – that the mysterious sorceress had saved fourteen lives from the wreckage of the Flea.

There were also stories about what kind of sorceress she was and where she had come from. Those who had heard her speak said her tongue sounded like it was from the three kingdoms but wasn't deep enough for them to know if she was an easterner or had come from the north or Duken. Many thought she must have been part of a King's Guard because of how strong she was. There were those who thought she was a watcher of one of the three Orders. Everyone in Gatli town and the whole of Edenborough had an opinion about the mysterious woman who had saved fourteen lives from a doomed ship in the middle of the sea.

The boys watched as the man was turned away, but he left his gift behind, and as he walked down the street, he started talking. Though they couldn't hear his words, they could tell from the man's gestures that it was about the woman.

* * *

Gytha opened her eyes to see silk draped over her head. She closed her eyes again. They felt too heavy, but a few moments later, she opened them, and this time a face stood over her. She frowned.

"You're awake," the voice said, shocked. "You're really awake!" It was a young girl, a teenager, whose eyes were wide at seeing Gytha conscious. "She's awake!" the girl yelled as she darted away from Gytha and out of the room.

Gytha kept blinking, trying to keep her eyes open. She heard the sound of footsteps, more than one, rushing into the chamber.

"You mean she's —" One of the women following the girl stopped short as she realized the sorceress's eyes were open. "You're truly awake."

Gytha hadn't even been able to muster the words for a response when the woman threw her arms around her in an embrace. Even when she let go, she took Gytha's hand. Gytha looked from the woman to the girl. Behind the girl stood another woman, watching them.

"Thank you for waking up, thank you so much," the woman said. "Do you – do you remember who I am?"

"I do," Gytha answered. "How is your baby?"

The woman smiled wildly and nudged the other woman to fetch the child. "See for yourself," she said as she showed Gytha the healthy child. "She is well. She is perfectly well," the mother answered with an almost painful smile on her face.

Gytha nodded and then remembered what had happened to the ship. "And . . . how is every one that —"

"Everyone you saved is alive and well. All of them. They've been calling at the house, asking to see you. It has been a great chore keeping them at bay, though they probably mean no harm and just want to show their gratitude. They haven't stopped coming, and they've been leaving all sorts of gifts for you."

"You have two horses and one pony," the girl blurted, unable to control herself.

Her mother glanced at the girl and shook her head. "As I said, you have a lot of people trying to show gratitude. Had we allowed it, some wouldn't have left you alone." The mother handed her baby over to the next woman.

"You are very, very popular. People are talking about you," the young girl commented.

"Where are we?" Gytha asked, face carefully neutral.

"Gatli, in Edenborough," the woman said.

Gytha swallowed hard. She'd got them home, of course. "And how long have I been asleep?"

The woman looked at her teenage daughter, then back at Gytha before she spoke, "This is the first time in five days you've opened your eyes."

CHAPTER
TWENTY-SIX

E usa, still possessing the young woman's body, stood in the corner, pressed against the side of a pub, watching in silence as the buzzing of the street dwindled as the day ended. Eusa had been using the young woman to follow the man since early in the evening, all the way from the streets of the market.

He made the woman watch for almost an hour, studying every motion of the cup as the beggar jiggled for passers-by, every reaction he made whenever someone passed him by and every reaction when they offered him coins. The Orders had many ghosts, but only a handful of people had been on this level. They were the most dangerous.

Watching through the eyes of the possessed young woman, Eusa noted who the beggar paid the most attention to and waited to see if there were any that would cause him to stir or break character, but nothing gave. Eusa was just about to return home when he saw a young boy walk towards the watcher, drop something in the cup and turn around, hurrying away. Because Eusa was watching, he caught the moment the beggar dug the coin out of his cup and jerked his gaze in the boy's direction. A few moments later, the beggar slid the coin into his clothes and got to his feet a little too sharply for someone who was supposed to be destitute. Eusa urged the woman's body to follow him through the street. Finally, the beggar opened the door to a pub and entered.

Eusa followed, sitting in the corner of the room and watching everyone that crossed the beggar's path. The only person who said a word to him was the young server tending the pub as she took his coin and served him drinks. The beggar didn't interact with anyone else throughout the evening as Eusa watched and waited. He waited up until the moment the beggar stumbled outside, and Eusa followed in the shadows as the beggar walked totteringly down the street, occasionally stopping to belch, inches away from falling over. Perhaps that was why he missed how quickly the beggar turned the corner and disappeared into an alley.

Eusa followed around the same corner, then stopped and frowned at the realization that there was no one there. Then he turned sharply and was knocked backwards by a punch to his face. He remained on his feet as the ghost watcher attacked again with a kick that Eusa managed to evade. Then the watcher pulled a knife and swung. Even possessing the young woman's body, Eusa was fast and managed to escape each stab and slash. He stayed on the defensive until he found an opening and pulled out his dagger to make it a fair fight.

The watcher faked a stab to the right, then spun to land a punch on the left side of Eusa's face, knocking him back. Eusa wouldn't give him a chance for a third hit and pulled out a second knife as he spun away, then stabbed the watcher, who wasn't quick enough to block it. The first knife lodged in his arm, and Eusa used the distraction to slash him across the belly with his second knife. Eusa yanked the blade from the watcher's arm, and the man groaned in pain as he tried to use his other hand to slash Eusa across the chest, but Eusa stepped away, spinning as he slashed the watcher's other arm.

Eusa didn't give the man time to recover, slashing him from behind before meeting a feeble attempt at a stab. He escaped and retaliated by burying his second blade in the side of the man's neck. The watcher gasped as he raised his hand to the wound. Eusa pulled out the blade and rammed it into the watcher's chest, then watched the light fade from the ghost's eyes. All Eusa thought about was his son.

The beggar dropped to the floor, relinquishing his blade. Eusa stood over the watcher's body, then reached down and ripped open the man's tunic, exposing his chest. Then he flipped the knife to his right hand to carve the mark in the skin. The large circle is for his wife and mother of his son, and the smaller circle is for their child.

Afterwards, Eusa wiped the knife on the dead watcher's body and then searched it. He found a pocket full of coppers and silvers but couldn't find the coin that had startled the watcher earlier on the street, the one the child had given him. Eusa searched everywhere on the watcher's body before he decided it wasn't there, which meant he must have left it behind. And the beggar had only stopped at the pub.

* * *

Eusa returned the girl's body to the house, closing the door behind them before he opened the door to the main chamber and took back his own body sitting on the chair in the room. Opening his own eyes, Eusa sucked in a breath of air hard. The young woman staggered backwards and then collapsed. He rose and helped her to sit on the chair as he stripped her of the knives, the belt, and the cloak. He also took off the boots and placed them gently by the chair next to the wall. Eusa glanced at the woman's split lip from the punch the watcher had landed, then moved to hang the cloak on the wall. She would feel sore from the battle – it was her skills he had used. That and what was left of her memory. He brushed his nostrils with the back of his hand.

Four dead, and it was hardly enough. He needed to kill more of them. He needed dozens and scores of Red Flame to fall at his hands or the hands of those he controlled. He was convinced he knew where to turn his search. He knew how the watchers communicated at least one way: with the passage of coins – coins only a watcher would recognize, like the coin given to that beggar. Eusa would return to that pub in the morning and see the barkeep that had taken the coin. If he could, he'd also find the boy that had brought the coin. It would be simple enough to enter his head and learn where he got it.

Eusa lit a lamp and stared at the flame as the wick burned, seeing and hearing things in the fire that he couldn't make himself forget. Things that would never make him stop wanting peril for the Red Flame, its watchers, and anyone else who'd had a hand in his family's death. Whoever they were.

Holding the lamp in hand, he unlocked the door he had spelled shut. Eusa opened it to find that his captive hadn't moved since he'd been there a few hours ago. She opened her eyes at the light.

"What did you do?" she asked.

The girl asked a lot of questions, that much was evident, but she wasn't insufferable to the point that he would consider going back on his word about keeping her alive. All he needed was her power – if she survived what he had to do, then he had no reason to kill her. She was the only person in all of Queen's Hill who knew what his true face looked like, so he wasn't worried that someone else would recognize him if she ever spoke. It wouldn't be a problem, even if he hadn't had the power to change the way he looked at will.

"I went to kill someone. A watcher that was pretending to be a beggar," he answered.

The man spoke so casually of taking a watcher's life as though it was a light chore. "But you didn't . . ." Levyna thought about what she had seen before he'd left, what she had heard.

Eusa placed the lamp by the table next to the bed and sat on the chair he'd left not so long ago. "I told you that we're sort of alike.

You are a traveller – you leave your body and walk around. I do the same. Only I end up in someone else's body instead. I believe it's because of how alike we were that I was able to know what you are."

"You possess people's bodies?"

"If you have to put it like that, yes. I do. But this is the first time I've done it for a purpose greater than mere pleasure or satisfaction. I'm using my powers to get close to the Den of the Red Flame so I can end it all. And my power now is only a fraction of what it will be once I have your powers as well. When I combine yours with mine, I'll be able to do incredible things, and I will make sure that every single watcher pays for what happened to my family."

"And you truly believe you can bring down the entire Order alone?" Levyna asked.

"I know I can. With your powers, I can."

"How do you intend to do it?"

"Do what?"

"Take my powers," she said, hoping to hide the tremble in her voice.

Eusa brushed his nostrils and sniffled. "Well, if you must know, I cannot merely siphon it out of you, though that would be much easier. Right now, I can take only so much to keep you faded and weakened for when I can possess your body. And when I'm able to do that, I will need to wait till the essence of my magic absorbs yours completely, and then I will have no need for you, and you'll be free to go."

"Your – your magic is going to absorb mine?" Levyna asked, panic increasingly evident with every syllable.

"Yes. It already is now, but when I'm in your body, it will happen at a much faster pace, and then I will be able to finish my mission." Eusa raised his hand and snapped his finger. A white flame lit at the tip. "I wasn't born with the power of flames, but I possessed a man with this power, and before I knew it, I'd stayed in his body long enough to absorb his essence. Now here I am."

"But you don't need to absorb my powers. I don't care about the Order after what they did to my father. I could help you if only you would —"

Eusa shook his head. "You say that because you're worried about what will happen when you no longer have your powers, but I'm not interested in a partner. I have no use for one. I only need your power, so the Order can get what's coming to them. Don't try to make me see reason. It will only make me mad, and you don't want to know what will happen when I'm angry," Eusa said.

Eusa suddenly grabbed her arm, and she panicked. He felt a jolt and flinched back, falling out of the chair. He quickly returned to his feet, face contorted and nostrils flaring as he stared at her. What had she done?

"You!" he said sharply, murder in his eyes as he breathed heavily. He stepped forward and struck her across the face hard, twice. Levyna let out a cry. "I told you not to make me angry, and you try to be cunning!"

Eusa grabbed her arms again, clawing his fingernails into her flesh as he held her tight. Once again, the thread spun from his arms and ran into hers. Levyna squirmed and gasped as he began to absorb her magic, this time looking to drain her for a much longer time. She couldn't do anything foolish if she couldn't think at all.

CHAPTER
TWENTY-SEVEN

I f anyone should know where Levyna was, it was him. Fiona's words kept going over and over in his mind, and if Olin hadn't been sleepless before, he most certainly was now. Whoever had taken Levyna hadn't simply vanished. They were somewhere – most likely still in Queen's Hill or the three kingdoms, but he couldn't think of where. He'd considered the Den of the Red Flame several times, but if Red Flame was responsible, they wouldn't have taken her alive. He'd been taken only because they had questions for him; he'd been a threat to their plans. Unless the Order had taken her as a way to get at him, it most likely wasn't the work of the Red Flame. Questions went round and round his head as the sun set on the second evening of Levyna's disappearance.

Fiona had returned to the palace after her timely intervention of the blame-induced fight between him and Posdel. Posdel had said the only other person who might be able to track Levyna would be Gytha. But his mother had also disappeared without a trace. It felt to Olin as though he couldn't escape his questions, and no matter how he tried, he couldn't figure out where she'd gone.

He'd left the house not long after Fiona had gone. Against Posdel's caution, Olin had gone to the bank of the Black River, to a familiar spot. He slid down the slope and stood on the bank, watching how the sunset reflected over the small, narrow part of the river.

This was where he had first landed in the kingdom, where an eternally curious and optimistic mage's apprentice had found him face-down in the mud. Olin had been here only once since then, with Levyna, very briefly to spend a moment in remembrance of the stranger who'd become his friend and helped him without hesitation. Now Olin didn't care about the danger he still faced in light of the Red Flame's recent attempt on his life. He sat on a small rock and just stared at the water. He had no idea what to do.

It wasn't the same, but he thought this must have been what Levyna had felt when he'd ignored her. Olin ran his hands through his hair and pulled at his scalp in frustration. He dropped his head between his legs, elbows resting on his knees.

He closed his eyes and called in his thoughts, Where are you?

* * *

Eusa had said that he could absorb her powers through touch. Levyna had to think quickly. What if she could do the same? Perhaps she could try if their powers were as similar as he'd claimed. So while he spoke, instead of focusing on trying to manipulate water in the room or force herself out of her body, she attempted to do what he'd done to her. Completely unsure of anything beyond the fact that she needed to try something, she directed all of her energy into her hands as he made contact with her arm. It felt somewhat familiar – a little like what she'd felt when she'd first touched Olin, at least until her captor was thrown backwards.

Levyna didn't know what she'd done, but she'd felt some residual power. And now something had changed. She couldn't feel all of her magic, but she could sense something, as though a crack had appeared in the wall wrapped around her mind. It wasn't enough to escape. It was momentary. She didn't bother wasting the chance trying to travel. There was only one thing she wanted to do in the heartbeat of a window she had – reach out to the one person who would hear her, wherever he may be.

Olin! she called.

* * *

Olin jerked his head up, wide-eyed at the sound of his name. Levyna!

"Levyna!" he yelled loudly as he jumped to his feet. He looked sharply left and right before he realized where it had come from. Olin rushed up the small slope and ran towards Posdel's house.

I'm coming, Levyna! Hold on. He said as he sprinted through the fields like he was running on air. He ignored the pain in his thigh. He couldn't just portal back – he felt he'd need that strength when the time came.

Olin barrelled through the door, almost breaking it down, and Posdel snapped awake as he entered.

"Olin?"

"I know where she is! I – I know where Levyna is!" he yelled.

Posdel's let out a quick breath and moved to the shelf, grabbing the arcane wand and turning to the sciff. "Let's go," he said, face a mixture of rage and excitement.

* * *

Eusa slammed the door shut so hard that it rattled the whole house and sent dust raining down. He'd been naïve enough to think that she wouldn't try anything. He'd let himself get carried away by her questions and had forgotten he had no interest in bonding. She'd seen his face and hadn't been repulsed, and he had allowed her to get to him because of it. She had turned him weak, distracted, and then had taken advantage of it.

He brushed his nostrils with the back of his hand twice as he paced the living chamber back and forth, trying to calm himself down. He'd said he wouldn't kill her, but things could change. Yet he would gain nothing from her death. He didn't need to take her life – unless she belonged to the Red Flame – it was just her powers, her magic, that mattered to him. He had an enemy, and it wasn't the palatine's daughter. His enemy was those who had taken everything from him, from his family and the people like him.

Eusa moved to the corner of the room and knelt in front of the chest. He opened it and dug out the red robe – what was left of the robe that had belonged to his son, covered in holes from the fire that had consumed everything else. Eusa clutched the robe to his chest, and, as he sat on the floor, he lowered his head and sniffed it again, searching somewhere beneath the decade-old smell of flame and death for the tiny scent of his freshly born child.

* * *

Olin and Posdel appeared in front of the house. Olin stared at it.

"Is this it?" Posdel asked, looking around briskly. It wasn't Pedina, but it was close.

"Yes, it is," Olin answered.

"Can you sense her inside?"

Olin didn't bother to glance at the mage as he answered. "I don't need to. I know Levyna is in there," he said as he marched towards the front door. Posdel followed him. Olin raised his hands, preparing to burn or break down the door, but Posdel stopped him.

"Wait."

"Why?"

"If she's there, you don't want to hurt her by chance," Posdel said.

Olin dropped one hand and knocked on the door instead.

Eusa opened his eyes and shot to his feet. He dropped the robe as he stared at the door. The knocker wasn't friendly; he knew that much. He reached for the cane and unlocked the door.

Olin's rage dissipated a bit as the door opened, and he saw a gravely old woman with white hair holding herself upright with a cane. The woman blinked at them. He and Posdel stood in a momentarily awkward silence before Olin said, "Where is she?"

"Who are you, and who are you asking for?" the old woman asked.

Olin had no patience. He stepped in, brushing the woman aside and almost knocking her to the ground as he started to look around. "Where is she?" he asked again.

"You have the wrong house, lad." The old woman's gaze turned to Posdel, who didn't look any less convinced.

"She's here. I know she's here," Olin said as he moved from the living room to the first chamber. He opened the door and found it empty, so he moved to the other and stared at the closed door with his heart barrelling in his chest. He held the knob and opened it. Olin almost felt his legs give out, and he frowned. He didn't understand. It was empty. She wasn't there.

"I . . ." He ran to the kitchen but saw nothing there either. "She was here." He shook his head. "She – she is here! I know it!"

"Perhaps he's lost his mind?" the old woman said.

Olin stepped angrily towards her. "I haven't lost my mind. I know what I know!" he said.

"Olin —" Posdel said.

"No! She's here!" Olin shouted. "She is. I know she is!" He turned around and faced the house again. His breath heavy and his heart was beating wildly.

Posdel looked from Olin to the seemingly harmless old lady and then back at the house. His eyes caught on the boots in the corner by the chair, and he gripped hard at the wand in his hand. "Olin."

Olin turned around just as Eusa stabbed Posdel with the cane.

Posdel stepped backwards and pointed the wand at Eusa, who quickly knocked it away and kicked Posdel in the chest, sending him tumbling. Olin directed a burst of flames from his hands, but the man snapped his fingers and raised flames of his own to thwart the attack. A small table caught fire between them. Olin grabbed a chair, broke it against the wall and picked up the pieces one by one to set them on fire and fling them at Eusa, who deflected the first one, but the second got past his shield and ripped into his gut.

Eusa dropped to the ground, and Olin rushed forward, grabbing and throwing him against the wall. Eusa crashed to the ground, and his hand caught his son's robe; he grabbed it just as Olin descended on him with a fist to his face. Eusa shifted back to the old woman's form, but Olin didn't hesitate. He punched her.

"Where is she!" he yelled.

Eusa, still in the form of the aged lady, trembled as Olin punched him again.

"Olin," Posdel said.

"Tell me where she is!"

"Olin!"

Olin kept punching, punctuating his hits with the questions. Eusa's face grew bloody. He didn't speak. Olin punched again, and this time Eusa shifted to his true self with his scarred and burned face, and Olin froze as he caught sight of it. He looked over the man's body, at the scars from where his skin had melted – it was almost enough for him to let go of the man, but Olin didn't.

Posdel held his bleeding belly with his hand where he'd crashed against the door as he watched Olin return to punching the man. "Olin!"

Olin hit once more with murder in his eyes. In Eusa's final moments, he saw a look in his attacker's eyes, one he was all too familiar with. Then Eusa let out her last breath, and Olin was left standing over the body.

"Olinander!" Posdel yelled.

Olin's fist stopped midway as he jerked his head in Posdel's direction.

"He's dead."

Olin turned back to the body. Blood was all over his fist. The body was still. Olin blinked hard as he let go. He raised his hands and looked at them, at the blood, at the body, and then at Posdel, who was slowly bleeding from his wound. Then Olin realized what he'd done – the man was dead, and he hadn't told them where Levyna was.

"No! No – no!" Olin screamed as he grabbed the dead body and started to shake it as though he could bring him back.

"Olin," Posdel called, but Olin didn't respond. "Olin!" he said again.

"He's dead." Olin turned back to Posdel. "I killed him, he – he —"

"Olin, you need to come here and help me up now. Come on," Posdel said.

Olin shook his head. He'd murdered their only hope for finding Levyna in a blind rage.

"Olin, look at me!" Posdel said again, and Olin finally turned. "You must come here and help me up. We need to find her. If you say she was here, then there's a chance she still is."

Olin latched onto the words, and he quickly moved to help Posdel onto his feet, struggling to banish the memory of all the stab wounds he'd seen before.

"The wand," Posdel said, pointing at the wand Eusa had knocked away from his hand. Olin spun and picked it up, handing it over to Posdel, who gripped it hard as they stepped towards the last door Olin had opened. "Close it," the mage said.

"What? It's empty, Posdel. She's not there!" Olin answered.

"Just do as I bloody say!" Posdel ordered, voice echoing the pain in his gut.

Olin closed the door and watched as the mage took a step forward.

"Periloles levaidi," Posdel said, waving the wand clockwise and then, "Eriotum," he said as he waved it in the other direction. The frame of the door shimmered brightly in front of their eyes, and Olin glanced at Posdel, who nodded at the door. "Come on."

Olin's heart was in his mouth as he grabbed the knob for the third time and opened the door, and this time the room wasn't empty. A young woman was lying on the bed, and Olin crashed into the room and took her face in his hands.

"Levyna – Levyna," he said as he nudged her. She didn't make a sound or move. He looked back at Posdel and then back at Levyna as the light from the lantern cast sullen shadows. Olin grabbed at the chains that held her and yanked them from the wall at once. He pried at the cuff around each wrist and broke them into pieces, setting her free. Olin took Levyna's face again and gently tapped on her cheeks.

"Levyna, hear me. I'm here, Levyna," he begged. Olin's heart was nudging at the wall of his chest with the silence before she groaned, and he sighed. "It's Olin. It's me."

"Olin . . ." She opened her eyes, closed them, and then opened them again to see Olin's face.

Olin chuckled nervously and smiled. "Yes, it's me."

She blinked. "Olin," she said again. "Someone – else," she said.

"Wh – what? Someone? Who?"

Olin looked at Posdel in confusion just as a knife came to Posdel's throat.

CHAPTER
TWENTY-EIGHT

He didn't wait to find out who it was. Olin vanished from beside Levyna and appeared behind the woman holding the knife to Posdel's throat. Before anyone else could twitch, he had snapped the young woman's neck. The body dropped to the floor, and Posdel turned around. He shared a long glance with Olin before looking at the body on the floor. Olin turned her over so they could see her face clearly.

"I had wondered where her body went," Posdel said, looking down at Moreen, dead for the second time. He saw the scar on her throat from the fatal knife wound. Her eyes were completely bleached. Posdel exhaled at the agonizing truth of what had happened to her. She hadn't even been granted the privilege of dying properly.

Olin would have cared about Moreen and would have been lost in the memories of what she'd done, but he had something more important to worry about. He also didn't think about the fact that he'd been the one to take her life. Somehow, it didn't seem right for him to pass judgment on what she'd done to Yondi.

Olin quickly returned to where Levyna was trying to sit herself up. He helped her and met her eyes in the low light. They stared at each other for what seemed like an unending moment before Posdel groaned from where he held himself upright on the door's threshold, reminding them of his injury.

Levyna smiled before she closed her eyes again.

* * *

"He was killing watchers," Levyna said. "He wanted the Order gone, wanted the Red Flame to pay for what they'd done to his family."

"And what did that have to do with you?" Fiona asked as she sat next to her daughter's bed in the palatine's quarters of the palace.

"He wanted my powers. He was going to use my magic to fight the Red Flame."

"How?" Fiona frowned, then she shook her head. "You know, don't answer that. It doesn't matter anymore. He was a deluded man, confused, and he was going to hurt you. I'm so glad you're okay," she said as she held her daughter's hand.

Fiona had been beside herself with relief and had nearly collapsed at the sight of Levyna when Olin had brought her back. Fiona had fought tears as she helped Levyna clean up before bed. She had been gone less than two days, but it had felt like a decade to the mother.

Fiona had asked more than a dozen times if she'd been hurt in any way, and Levyna had repeated the same answer. Nothing more than bruises from the chains and on her face from the one time Eusa had gotten angry.

Fiona noticed her daughter's pensive expression. "What is it, my dear? What is on your mind?"

"Mother, you must forgive Olin and Posdel."

Fiona exhaled and looked away. Levyna clutched her hand tighter.

"It's truly neither of their faults what happened. There was no way they could have known who Eusa was and what he had planned," Levyna said.

"You were under the mage's watch. He promised he would keep you safe and Olin . . . he was utterly useless, was he not?"

"And they both wanted me to be safe, which was why I stayed back at the house after the Red Flame attacked Olin."

Fiona turned to her daughter with furrowed brows. "What happened with the Red Flame?"

Levyna swallowed and pursed her lips, wondering if talking would do more harm than good for her argument. Fiona's persistent stare told her that she wouldn't get away with not answering. "He was attacked, but he managed to get away."

Fiona gasped.

"But we needed horses, and they didn't want to risk me encountering the watchers. I promised I would be able to take care of myself, and that was the only reason they left me alone. Besides, it was my fault Eusa could get as close as he did – I opened the door and ran after him when I thought he'd fallen. If I'd just stayed inside, he wouldn't have been able to get past the spell on the house."

Fiona pushed away the image of Olin coming face-to-face with watchers, with death, once again, and had immediately risked everything to chase after Levyna right after. "I'm still unable to see anything beyond how they failed to keep you safe."

"But Eusa was in the palace. Did you know that?"

"What?"

"He was the other guard with Vernon the day we discovered he'd murdered father. Eusa had taken the form of Vernon's partner. That was how he knew I was a traveller," Levyna answered.

If the shifter had been in the palace, that could explain how he'd gotten his hands on the feather of a bluebird. Fiona tightened her grip around her daughter's arm slightly, thinking about how she'd been oblivious to the danger.

"I know you want me to be safe, Mother, but I promise Olin does as well, and not being able to sense me wasn't his fault either."

Fiona exhaled and looked at her daughter, taking her in. She was alive. That was all that mattered. "You must rest now."

"Mother . . ."

"Rest, Levyna. You've been through a lot. We will talk when you wake." Fiona stood and kissed her daughter on the head before she turned and walked out of the room, looking back at her baby before she closed the door behind her.

* * *

Five days. Gytha could hardly believe that she had been asleep that long. Then again, she had more or less used all of her energy and stretched her essence to the limit moving fourteen souls across the sea. Had she been anyone else, she would either still be unconscious or never again recover enough to bring her essence back to life. That, or she would be dead. And those fourteen people would be at the bottom of the sea. But Gytha hadn't done it for the gratitude – perhaps she had felt guilty. Thorne had only attacked the ship to stop her from following him, to slow her down. But now that she was awake, she needed more than ever to finish it. She needed to find Thorne and ensure that the Lord Watcher was gone for good.

"Will you tell us your name?" the young girl asked.

Gytha looked up from the bowl of soup in her hand to her audience of two – the young girl and her mother. "It's Gytha," she answered.

"Gytha? As in Gythamina?" the girl asked.

The sorceress smiled and nodded slowly. "Yes, though no one has called me Gythamina in over two decades," she answered.

"It's a very beautiful name. I like it," the girl said. "Where are you from? Is it Duken?"

The girl's mother shook her head and nudged at her shoulder. "Mira, your questions won't allow her to finish her food or rest. Go on, give her some time," she said. The girl looked like she was about to say that Gytha had gotten five days of rest already, but after another sharp look from her mother, she walked out of the room, smile slightly faded.

Gytha was left alone with Selina. "She means well, but she can get very carried away."

Gytha nodded and placed the bowl on the table in front of her. "I know what it's like," she answered.

"Are you sure there isn't more we can do? Perhaps something you need?"

"No, nothing at all. You have done more than enough, keeping a stranger in your home for five days. I am indeed grateful," Gytha said.

Selina shook her head. "No. It's I who am grateful – you saved my baby's life, and then you saved all of our lives. That's a debt

I don't think anyone can ever repay. What my family and I have done is nothing in comparison."

"Not many would see it that way."

"Well, many here do. If you step onto the street, you'll hear a story about yourself. You chose to save many when you could have just saved yourself. Now, there aren't many who would do that," Selina said.

A moment of quiet passed in the room before Gytha spoke. There had been something on her mind. "Can I ask you something?"

"Yes, of course."

"I did not look . . . like this when we were on the ship, did I?"

"You don't remember? Of course, most people weren't in their right minds at that moment. But you did. I mean, you looked different when you healed my Ina. I remember being confused for a moment when you looked . . . younger, and you told me everything was going to be fine. But no one cares about that," Selina answered.

Gytha nodded and gave a small smile. Somewhere between when she'd rushed onto the deck and when she'd returned to the cabin, she had changed from being an old grey-haired woman to someone much younger. No one cares about that. At least she didn't have to worry about being confused for a shifter and drawing unwanted attention.

The baby cried in the other room, and Gytha thought about her child. It had been five days, and she was only supposed to have been gone two. She needed to return to Queen's Hill. But first, Thorne.

"Selina, again, I appreciate all that you have done for me, but I must leave."

Selina's face turned sour. "Of course. You had a family and a life before all this. We got carried away, excited that you were here and hadn't even thought about who must be worried about you." She shook her head and ran a hand down her hair. "Would you at least wait till my husband returns in the morning – he wouldn't forgive me if he couldn't express his gratitude in person. I'm at least that selfish."

"I would like to leave before dawn."

"I hope he's back by then," Selina answered. "I also hope you know you're welcome to stay for as long as you want and can come by whenever you feel the need."

"Thank you, Selina."

"We'll begin to pack your gifts. It won't be hard to find a wagon to help —"

"I won't be needing them, please. You can have them. And your daughter can have the pony. I have a feeling she might like it," Gytha said. "I will only be needing a horse."

Selina's mouth gaped. "No, please, we cannot take them."

"I insist," Gytha said.

CHAPTER
TWENTY-NINE

Damiran glanced at Alderman Kon while they waited for Prince Petr to show. Kon sighed deeply, and Damiran could guess a few reasons why the man needed to brace himself for the meeting, and all of them revolved around the king. Then Petr appeared at the threshold of the door. He paused to regard the men waiting for him before he walked into the room accompanied by his mutt.

"Your Highness." The alderman bowed, and the Damiran followed.

"Lord Damiran," the prince said, and then he looked at the alderman. "Alderman Kon. I would say that it is a pleasure to see you, but considering the timing of your visit, I suspect you don't have cheerful news."

The alderman and the king's adviser shared a look again. "It's a sensitive matter, Your Highness," Damiran said.

"And why do I have a feeling I know exactly what it is about?" the prince asked.

"Because you probably do," said Alderman Kon.

The prince walked to the room's tallest chair and sat, gesturing for his guests to do the same.

"If you've come to ask me if I've changed my mind since last we talked, Lord Damiran, then you've wasted a trip."

"Prince Petr, if I may." The alderman spoke before the Damiran could answer. "Lord Damiran has told myself and the rest of the aldermen of his effort to convince you to return to the palace. He also told us your response. But we believe you might reconsider intervening given the recent events."

"Queen's Hill has a king, Alderman Kon."

"Yes, it does, Price Petr, but the way things are now, the way things have shifted . . . something that may have once been a solution has now become the cause of our problems."

"Remember that is your king you speak of."

"Yes, Prince Petr, but you have to understand that if we don't speak now, the consequences of silence will be far worse. It could be dire. With every day that passes, His Majesty steers away from reason, and it is more than concerning. Perhaps his past orders can be rationalized, but his actions now – there are no words. They are intended to drive the kingdom into chaos."

"You said we needed to trust the king – you said you trusted the king. But Your Highness, do you truly believe that killing and beheading the Lord Watcher, in the throne room, in the middle of a White Indulgence called to avoid a conflict with the Order, is a sane course of action?" Damiran asked. "People are growing terrified, and rightly so. The Order might have begun the conflict, but King Ranald is quickly losing the support and trust of his people if he hasn't already. No one wants war against an Order of watchers who will kill without questions. We don't know how many they are or who they are, and that scares people."

"So the king has made a statement against the Order that some don't like. How is that a cause for concern?" the prince asked.

"Because it's more than just the one act, Prince Petr. It's more than a statement. It is everything, things that haven't made it out of the palace, things that . . ." Alderman Kon stopped himself short of finishing the statement.

"Things that what?" the prince asked, his face intent on the alderman.

"His Majesty's actions reminded me of a certain king of Duken six centuries ago," Damiran said, looking right at his cousin. "It's heavy to say, Your Highness, but just as the alderman mentioned, if we, who are closest to the throne, choose to remain silent, then we are saying we agree with the consequences that will come afterwards. His Majesty is, quite frankly, acting as though he's not himself. He trusts and takes the advice of no one and does not follow reason. With every day that passes, he inches towards war with the Order and, by consequence, his people, and he doesn't seem to even care."

"Because he wants the Red Flame gone, is that not it?"

Alderman Kon shook his head. "It might very well go beyond the Order, Prince Petr. It may have begun with the Red Flame, but it has festered. He wants the Order gone. Enough that he will behead any of his aldermen who fail to bring him the watchers from their shire. And even if the head of each and every Red Flame watcher is piled up in the courtyard and set on fire as the king . . . as the king has described vividly – even then, it wouldn't guarantee that His Majesty will end it there. The Order might have tried to take the throne, but if the king continues to behead watchers in his throne room and continues to call for the head of the Red Flame, it's only a matter of time, a very short time, before something breaks."

Prince Petr rose from his chair, hands behind his back as he walked towards the fire, slowly heating the room from the fireplace.

"We know you have your reasons and your reservations, Prince Petr, but can you push that aside for the needs of the kingdom? The people of Queen's Hill cannot afford to leave things to chance with His Majesty anymore. We fear the worst. I fear the worst,'" Alderman Kon said.

"Do not think I am so naïve that I cannot see what you mean, Alderman Kon. I may not have power, but that doesn't mean I don't understand your allusion to becoming the villain who abandoned his people. I do not desire any harm, conflict, or chaos in this kingdom, and my decision not to interfere won't change that. My father made a choice years ago, one that Queen's Hill accepted. I have not contested it. I am content."

"So you shall just watch?" Damiran asked.

"The only reason I can possibly consider stepping foot in the palace now is if Ranald himself asks for my presence. Or something befalls the king, something more than mere supposition and panic from those who are meant to help keep the kingdom together," the prince answered, turning away from the fire slowly to face his guests. "You mentioned the king from Duken and his curse of the crown. I assure you that whatever King Ranald has done is nothing compared to Mathea's madness. Don't be so quick to spread the worst-case scenario, cousin," he said. "If the king is in a precarious state, and is making questionable decisions, then it's your job, and that of the palatine, to help the king remain true to what is best for the kingdom."

"Prince Petr, considering the king's state of mind, it will be difficult to make him understand that he needs your presence. His Majesty has become quite indifferent about many things," Damiran said.

"I'm not negotiating, Lord Damiran. Unless either of those things happens, I have no business in the palace." Petr shook his head. The king's advisor and the alderman glanced at each other.

* * *

Kon was seething at what had become of the meeting. He'd known all along that it would turn out like this and yet had allowed himself to try anyway. But all they'd done was tease a man's ego who wouldn't be moved unless the king came crawling for help. Or died. Kon spat on the ground, riding between his two guards back to his shire. It was late, but they'd wanted darkness for the meeting. They couldn't be sure who was watching, not when the Red Flame was on everyone's lips.

Kon kept thinking of how the prince had spoken, throwing everything they'd said back at their faces with his fancy polished words. Prince Petr was too high and mighty to be controlled by an alderman and a king's advisor – he was full of pride. That had to be it. That was the only explanation Kon could think of. Kon imagined the prince on the throne, taking reign over the kingdom. If he was insufferable now, there would be no stopping him when he gained the crown. He would remind them that they had come to him and begged him to take power. If Ranald was mad, if that madness followed the crown, then Queen's Hill could be even worse off with his brother. Kon wished badly that he could have spoken his mind. He blamed Damiran for coming up with this insane idea.

The guard ahead slowed.

"What is it?" Kon asked.

"Torches, someone approaching."

"Do we know who it is?" said Kon as the other guard moved ahead from the rear.

"Hard to tell. What do you want to do, Alderman Kon?" the guard said.

They were almost home, and he had no business with the Red Flame. There was nothing to be worried about. "We keep going," he said.

The guards, each holding a torch, forged ahead and led the way. They made it a few yards before the lights in the distance disappeared. The alderman's entourage stopped abruptly, but before they could figure out what had happened, one guard groaned and fell off his horse.

"Ambu —"

The other guard's warning was cut off by the whistling of the arrow piercing the air. It hit the guard's face, and he fell. Alderman Kon pulled his horse around and urged it into a gallop in the opposite direction, keeping his head low to avoid the arrows.

But he couldn't do the same for his horse. It was hit from behind after only a few yards, and the beast crashed to the ground, throwing Kon to the ground. Kon pulled his leg out from underneath the horse and scrambled to his feet, then began to run, utterly oblivious to where he was headed in the darkness. He didn't get far before he felt a sharp, piercing pain at his back, sucking the air out of his lungs. He dropped to his knees, groaning as he raised his hand to feel the head of the arrow sticking out of his chest. Any hope of fighting was snuffed out as a second arrow ripped into his throat.

CHAPTER THIRTY

Levyna knew who it was before they knocked on the door. At the sound, she felt a tiny flutter of excitement. She nodded at the maid, who opened the door to let Olin into the bed-chamber.

He took a few cautious steps before stopping and staring at her. She was awake; she was alive. "You look better," he said.

"Thank you, I feel much better, too," she said. "I'm not sure if all my magic is back, but I can sense the way I used to. And it's a huge relief."

Olin nodded. Levyna may have recovered, but the same couldn't be said of him. Olin's eyes were flushed, and despite his fresh clothes, he still looked dishevelled. He stood a distance away, looking.

"Are you going to come closer?" Levyna asked.

Olin lowered his head before moving towards her bed. The bed-chamber was by far the largest Olin had ever been in. He stopped by her bedside, where he could study her up close. It seemed that a night in her bed had returned the colour to her face – a complete contrast to how pale she had been in his hands the evening before.

Levyna frowned as she looked at him. He was nearly as pale as the girl had been. "Olin, are you alright?" she asked.

"I feel fine. Shouldn't I be the one asking you that?"

"We've already agreed I'm well, and I'm only still in bed because Mother would have an apoplexy if I left the room before noon. What I'm keen to know is . . ."

"You know I can hear what you were thinking it," he said, eyes on her.

"Well, then. You look as though you haven't slept in days."

"How could I? You'd been taken, nowhere to be found, and it was my fault."

Levyna's face pinched. "Oh, you must stop that at once, Olin! I can handle Mother thinking she needs to hold you and Posdel responsible, but I cannot have you blaming yourself for what we both know was certainly not your fault," Levyna said.

"Your mother is right – I was supposed to be there. If I had been, he wouldn't have been able to take you."

"Will you stop already? I have had enough of everyone thinking I'm some helpless little child who cannot take care of herself. You must stop it at once! I might have made a mistake when I tried to help Eusa, but no one, not even you, could have guessed at his vile intentions. What happened was my mistake. I got it wrong. It doesn't mean I'm an imbecile who cannot be left on her own for a moment." Levyna's voice trembled as she spoke.

"I would never think of you that way. You know that. But it's hard not to imagine what could have been different if I'd been there. Maybe I wouldn't have been able to stop him, but I could have tried, and at least I would have known you were alive, would have known how to look for you, and then maybe you wouldn't have had to spend so long chained by that madman."

Levyna sighed. "He wasn't a madman."

"He took you, kept you paralysed in enchanted chains while he siphoned your magic."

She shook her head slowly. "He wasn't mad."

Olin stepped towards her. Hands turned up. "He possessed someone who should have been dead. He kept her alive just to use her, Levyna."

"I know, I know. But he . . . I know everything he did was horrible and unspeakable, and I was terrified of what he would do, but Eusa wasn't mad. He was a man who lost his wife and newborn son to the Red Flame, who was burned alive himself. He wanted revenge. He wanted the Order to pay. He might have chosen the wrong ways to get what he wanted, but how else could he have fought against the Order? He was in pain, but he wasn't mad."

Olin frowned, stepped away, and raised his hand to pull at his hair as he shook his head. "I can't believe you. You're defending a man that kidnapped you? He was going to kill you!"

"He wasn't going to kill me."

"He was a killer!"

"And so are you!"

Time froze to a heartbeat as her words rang through the air. They stared at each other, Olin's face pinched. "Wh – what?"

Levyna's brows raised at the realization of what she had just said. "Olin . . ."

"Did you . . . is that what —"

Levyna shook her head. "Olin, I didn't mean it that way."

"That's what you . . . think of me?" He took a step backwards, face contorted into a frown of confusion and heartbreak.

"It's not, Olin. It's not." She continued to shake her head as she climbed out of bed, hoping to reach him.

"I should . . . go."

"No."

"Stay away," he said as he turned and ran before she could try to catch him.

"Olin. Olin!" Levyna called after him futility as the door slammed shut. It echoed the trembling in her voice.

* * *

Olin had managed to get Levyna and the injured Posdel to the palace after they'd rescued Levyna. After, Olin and Posdel hadn't felt any urgency to leave. A healer had attended Posdel, and they had been given rooms in the guest quarters of the palace castle. Levyna hadn't visited yet and hadn't seen Posdel since she'd been at his house – not counting seeing him injured and bleeding when they'd rescued her. She knew now he was out of danger.

"As comforting as it is to see you are well, I cannot help but think that there's another reason for your visit," Posdel said. He was sitting in front of a window, looking down over the hill. Beyond, they could see the side of the mountain slowly surrendering its colour to the approaching winter.

Levyna stood nearby, quiet. She was wearing a dress covered by a simple robe. She looked down at the floor.

"It's about Olin, is it not?" Posdel said.

Levyna nodded. "He came to see me, and our words grew heavy and I . . ."

"What happened?"

"I said something to him that I absolutely didn't mean. Something cruel and unfair, and I'm afraid he doesn't wish to talk to or see me again," Levyna answered.

"What did you say?"

"I . . . I might have called him a killer," she answered, taking her time before she looked back up to meet the mage's face.

Posdel let out a deep exhale and nodded. He glanced out the window as a bird flew past.

"Of course, I didn't mean it, not that way, but he called Eusa a killer, and he said I was defending the man when I was only trying to make him understand that Eusa did what he did because he was after revenge for his family, against Red Flame, and that he wasn't just a madman. But Olin wouldn't listen, and he was so angry and . . ."

Posdel turned back to her. "I don't know what is happening, but I fear it is more than simply the anger and fear of your absence. Olin, he . . . When he fought Eusa, he used his bare hands – it wasn't the fact that he chose his fists. It was that he hit the man and hit and hit and would not stop hitting. I called to him several times, and it was like he couldn't hear me, like he wasn't there, not . . . himself. He didn't stop hitting until the man was dead. Dead by his hands, and when he finally turned to me, his eyes . . . I had been stabbed, I was dying too, I could very well have been seeing things that weren't there, but I was sure Olin had this rage in his eyes, like beating that man to death had been nothing. Of course, he realized quickly what he had done, and he grew sober. But even then, it was only because he thought he had killed the only person that knew where you were. He didn't feel remorse for the death itself," Posdel said. "To kill a man with a weapon, to defend yourself, is one thing, but to take a man's life with your fists – let alone a man possessing another's body – that's something different."

"He has not slept in days —"

"Earlier, before we found you, he confronted me, almost burnt the house down because he thought I didn't care enough about you because I had a drink. He has been terribly on edge for the past couple of days."

"What do you think is happening?" Levyna asked.

"I would be lying if I said I knew for sure. I had assumed he was getting over Yondi's death, but he brought it up and practically threw it in my face when we fought. I don't think it would be wrong to say the deaths still haunt him – his uncle and Yondi, and perhaps even his mother's disappearance as well. Your abduction certainly primed the fire, and there were times when I thought he looked completely unlike who he had been a fortnight ago. There are all of that . . . and then there's his magic."

Levyna's brows dipped. "His magic?"

"Yes. Olin's magic is different. It took time to manifest, and you have helped him find it, but there's no absolute way that a person's magic must form, which is why control is the most important. I suspect we've only seen a fraction of Olin's power, and he could be at risk of letting it consume him if he cannot think clearly.

"There's a veil between the essence of the mind and the essence of magic. If it fractures and the magic takes over, it can be fatal," Posdel said, staring at Levyna. "History tells tales of people with magic who have lost themselves, and I hope he doesn't become one of them."

Levyna shook her head. "He cannot. He will not. I will never let him."

"I know you mean well, but there is only so much you can do."

"And that much I will do, even if he won't see me, perhaps someone else can reach him."

CHAPTER
THIRTY-ONE

Edenborough bustled with the life of a city that served as a bridge connecting two continents. South was Maedro, and north, across the sea, lay the three kingdoms. Edenborough was twice the size of Duken, and it was quite easy for one to get lost or confused if they didn't know where to turn. However, for Gytha, it wasn't her first time in the kingdom – she had journeyed here several times in the decade since her exile in Duken. Exile had been all she'd known the last time she'd been. Now, she couldn't shake the feeling that the five days she had lost to unconsciousness had taken something from her. Whatever she had missed, it wasn't going to be a second shot at Thorne.

The meat seller brought the machete down on the pork hand, splitting it in two before he started slicing it into pieces for the buyer in front of him. He packed the meat and handed it to the man who dropped the silver and continued alone.

"Hands and ham only, which would you prefer?"

"Neither," Gytha answered.

The seller looked up sharply, and his eyes widened when he recognized her. He released the machete and took one step away from the stall. "Gytha."

"Hello, Beleron. It's nice to see you too," the Grand Sorceress said.

Beleron scanned her from feet to crown. She was wearing a long black mantle over her dress, and her hair fell to her shoulders. "What are you doing here?"

"I need your help."

"You – my help?"

"Yes. Is there somewhere we can talk?"

The meat seller looked around to be sure they were alone, then nudged the boy next to him. "Watch it. I'll be back in a moment." He stepped away from the stall and led the way towards a storage shed. It was empty of people. "What can I possibly help you with, Gytha?"

"I want to find someone. They would have come to Edenborough about six days ago now," she said.

Beleron sighed. "Six days? That's a long time. How am I supposed to find them? Who even are you looking for?"

"His name is Thorne, and he's not a good man. He came to Edenborough escaping from Ravinshore. I was hunting him down on the ship that sank."

His eyes went wide. "You were on the ship? You were on the Flea when it sank? Wait, are you the legendary sorceress that people have been talking about for the past six days? The one who saved those people? Of course, you are! Why didn't I realize? Who else could it possibly be?"

"And Thorne was the one that caused the ship to wreck. He must have known I was following him."

"What has he done to you? Why is he still alive?"

"That's not a story I want to recount in a market shed, Beleron. I need to track him down."

"Of course. But wait, why would you need me? You can find him yourself if you want to. I know you can."

Though she did trust him, Gytha hesitated, revealing how much her little stunt across the sea had drained her. "I have come to you for help. Are you going to or not?"

He regarded her for a moment before he exhaled. "You know I will, but what you're asking is very difficult, searching for a man I don't know who's had six days to lose himself in the city." He spread his hands. "Are you sure he's still here? Are you even sure he made it off the ship?"

"I know he made it off, he's a cockroach, and if I turn over every stone in Edenborough and he's not here, I will move to the next kingdom. I will find him."

Beleron shook his head. "I wouldn't want to be anywhere near that kind of man," he said. "Very well. Let me pack up the stall. Then we'll head home."

"Thank you." Gytha nodded as the meat seller headed back to his stall. She hesitated for a moment, then stepped to follow. But froze. She frowned and turned around sharply to see a familiar face. "Levyna?"

"Hello, Gytha," Levyna said, her spectre portraying the relief of seeing the woman.

"What are you doing here? How did you find me?"

"I'm a traveller, remember?"

Gytha nodded. "Of course. Why are you here? Is everything okay? Is Olin okay?" She reached up to touch Levyna's shoulder.

Levyna looked down and shook her head slowly. "He is alive. He is healthy."

"But what? What is it?"

"He's not okay, Gytha. Olin is troubled," Levyna answered.

"What do you mean, troubled?" Gytha asked. Her eyes were fixed on every detail of Levyna's expression.

"I would have found you sooner, but it has been a very challenging few days. Olin is going through something, and I don't know how to help him. Posdel thinks it could be the trauma of losing so many people, or because he believes you left him again, or his magic."

"Oh, no . . . Olin. He thinks I left. Of course, he thinks I left – it has been days since . . . Wait, what did you say about his magic?"

"He's not himself. He's not sleeping. He's being curt. Posdel fears his magic could be consuming him."

Gytha's hands dropped as she stared at the spectre.

"Your son needs your help, Gytha."

* * *

Beleron returned to the shed with a satchel across his body just as the Gytha stepped out. Her face looked different, full of concern. "Gytha? Has something gone wrong?"

"There has been a change of plan, Beleron. I need you to find me a demican."

"Why?"

"I need to get to Queen's Hill immediately," Gytha said.

* * *

Demicans was the local term for a mover – a person with the magic to transport someone or something across great distances.

Demicans could either create a portal or could simply use their essence to travel.

Beleron knocked hard on the door of the cottage. They heard voices coming from inside. He raised his hand to knock again, and the door opened to the face of a young woman. The lass looked between him and Gytha as the sound of tittering and laughter came from behind her.

"What do you want?" she asked.

"The mover, where is he?" Beleron asked.

"He's not here," the woman answered, closing the door, but Beleron pushed it open and walked in. The men and women inside draped over each other, and the furniture instantly sobered.

The girl staggered backwards. "What's wrong with you?" she said, clutching her robe tighter. She was the most dressed person in the room.

"Where is the mover?" Beleron asked again, studying the random shocked faces.

"He's not here, I told you!"

Beleron looked back at her. "Lie to me one more time, and you will regret it," he said.

"Okay, okay . . ." a voice came from the corner of the room behind a zaftig woman whose dress revealed more than half of her breasts. "No need for violence, please." The man, a particularly short figure with a head of red hair and a thick ginger beard stepped out slowly. He was wearing what looked like a skirt, or maybe a woman's blouse, around his waist and held a bottle in his hand.

"Are you the mover?" Beleron asked.

"That depends. To whom am I speaking?"

Gytha glanced at Beleron, and the much bigger man got the message, grabbing the dwarf and carrying him outside despite his flailing.

"Put me down!" the dwarf said in protest before Beleron set him down and closed the door.

"I need you to take me to Queen's Hill immediately," Gytha said.

"Such insolence." The dwarf dusted his hairy chest and skirt as though something had been ruffled. "You could have at least teased a man before you rough-handled him." He glanced up at Beleron, eyeing the larger man in a sultry manner. Beleron frowned.

"Did you hear me?" Gytha asked.

"Yes, I heard you, lady," the dwarf answered.

"Good, we must leave at once," Gytha said.

The dwarf shook his head. "Uh . . . I don't think so."

"Why?"

"Because I cannot go to the kingdom of hills, that's why."

Gytha exhaled.

Beleron frowned. "And what can't you go there?"

"Because I'm a demican, not a bloody demon, and besides, I cannot afford to set foot in Queen's Hill due to political reasons."

"Wha – what political reasons?" Beleron said, looking like he wanted to rip the man's head off, if not for his absurd excuses, then for his lackadaisical attitude.

Gytha merely sighed, thinking about the circumstances that had brought her here. She'd been drained of her magic and had to stoop to dragging a dwarf out of a whorehouse to beg him to take her to her son.

"I cannot discuss it. All I know is there's no way I'm going anywhere near that kingdom, not if I care for this precious body of mine. And I do very much care."

"Fine, Duken then. Can you get me to Duken?"

"Now, that I can do. It will only cost you ten silver."

"What? No mover charges that much, scoundrel!" Beleron said.

"Feel free to go find yourself someone else. Call the extra five silver an inconvenience fee for what you've put my party and me through. If you can't pay, be gone," the dwarf said.

Beleron turned to Gytha, but she knew she didn't have much of an option. This was the fourth mover they had asked. The others had either been absent or had been in no position to cross the sea.

"It's fine. I will pay. But I insist we leave at once," the sorceress said.

"Very well, shall I put some clothes on or would you rather I take you bare?" the mover said.

Gytha exhaled deeply. Beleron nodded and waved at the man to get his clothes. The dwarf had no idea how fortunate he was that Gytha was in such a hurry.

The dwarf returned moments later, dressed in a tunic shirt and a fur coat with sandals and trousers instead of the skirt. "Shall we?" He opened his hand, asking for the money.

"Perhaps if I add a little more, you can find your way to Queen's Hill instead?" Gytha asked.

"Oh, no. Not even adamantine would make me take that risk. Come on." He wiggled his fingers.

Gytha dumped ten silvers in his hand from the money Selina had buried in her satchel when she'd thought the sorceress hadn't been looking.

"I will be here when you're ready to continue your mission," Beleron said to her.

"Thank you," Gytha said, nodding at him before she took the mover's hand.

"Hold tight," the dwarf said.

CHAPTER
THIRTY-TWO

T he throne room came to attention. Damiran, Fiona, and the two lieutenants of the King's Guard in attendance bowed as King Ranald marched in and sat at his throne, still wearing his cuirass. He was the only one with a sword at his side. His eyes were still glassy, with dark rings around them, hinting at a lack of proper rest.

"I think I have waited long enough. It's time," the king said.

Fiona glanced at the king's advisor, then back at the king. "Time for what, Your Majesty?" she asked.

"Time to show the Order what I am made of. It appears they don't think I'm serious."

"Your Majesty, considering what happened the last time they were here, I believe they understand just how serious you are."

"No. No, they do not. And besides, I don't need them to understand I'm serious. I'm not some child making noise to get attention from some menace. I am the bloody menace. This is my kingdom."

"It is, Your Majesty," Fiona said.

King Ranald looked at the lieutenants standing in his court. "You, Clemon," he pointed at the buffer one with the scar on his brow.

"Your Majesty." Clemon bowed.

"I am making you Commander of the King's Guards."

Clemon looked up sharply, glancing at the other lieutenant. Then he dropped to one knee. "Thank you, Your Majesty. I shall continue to serve, protect, and defend the kingdom with all my might. I swear to you," he said.

"Good, because now your job begins," the king said. The commander rose to his feet, and the man who had been his lieutenant only a moment before took a step backwards. "The Order of the Red Flame has enjoyed enough of my inaction. Prepare your men. The Den of the Flame will be invaded in two days unless the Order declares their complete surrender to me."

Clemon swallowed hard as he eyed the palatine and the king's advisor, who both looked shocked.

"Either the flame surrenders, or it dies," Ranald said.

* * *

Mary lifted her eyes from the doll in her hand as the figure appeared. Mary stared, not knowing where the woman had come from. The little girl got up from the chair. "Who are you?" she asked.

Gytha couldn't remember ever seeing a child with William. "I'm Gytha. Where is William?"

Almost immediately, the door opened, and a familiar, striking face appeared. Isabelle had surprise written on her face at the sight of the Grand Sorceress. She stepped towards Gytha. "Grand sorceress," she said. "It's good to see you."

Gytha could have guessed Isabelle's presence, but the child was still a mystery. "It's good to see you too, though I wish it were under better circumstances," she answered.

Isabelle frowned. "Is everything okay?"

"I need to get to Queen's Hill right away."

"William is —" Isabelle was cut short by the sound of a galloping horse as William rode onto the property. "There he is."

William brought the beast to a stop and dismounted, expression part smile and part worry at the sight of their guest. "Gytha?"

"William," she said.

"To what do we owe the visit? Is everything well?" he asked.

"Not quite, from what I've heard. I hope I'm wrong, though."

"What's the matter?"

"I need to get to Queen's Hill to see my son. His traveller companion visited me with news. He's been troubled. His magic may be consuming him."

William and Isabelle straightened at the same time, both understanding the severity of what that meant.

"You weren't with him? I thought you were going to remain for a while?"

"I had to leave. Business took me to Edenborough. My ship ran into some trouble. I was unconscious for five days. I'm still quite drained and cannot get there on my own, which is why I'm here. I need you to take me to Queen's Hill right away. Please," she said.

William nodded with a glance at Isabelle and Mary standing by the door. "Of course, certainly."

"I'm sorry, Gytha. I hope your son is alright," Isabelle said as William walked into the house.

"Thank you. I hope he is too."

"If there is anything you need me to do ..."

Gytha nodded. "I appreciate it, but I just need to go and see him for myself. I believe that's what he needs right now. But if you would let me borrow William for a little while, that would certainly help."

William returned with a coat. He stopped abruptly as Mary held him by a sleeve. "Mary?" he said, turning and kneeling in front of her.

Isabelle turned, her heart dropping as she moved towards them.

"Is he coming back?" Mary asked, the question directed at the stranger standing outside the house. She looked back to William. "Are you coming back?"

"Of course I will, Mary." William took the girl by the shoulders and stared into her eyes. "I'm coming back."

"He will be back," Isabelle echoed, knowing how much this hurt. Mary had only lost her father a week ago.

"You have to promise?" The teary-eyed child asked as she threw her arms around William.

William glanced up at Isabelle and then Gytha. "I promise, little one, I'll only be gone for a short while. I have to help a friend. I'll be back before you even notice I'm gone," he said.

As Gytha stared at them, she became even more eager to return to Queen's Hill to her son, whom she'd once again left without a goodbye. It didn't matter that Olinander was now over two decades old. He was still her child.

William stood, and Mary reluctantly relinquished her hold. He took Isabelle's hands, looking intently into her eyes before he turned to the Grand Sorceress.

* * *

"Your Majesty, I believe we must reconsider. It's one thing to talk about the war against the Red Flame, but preparing to invade the Den of the Order is something else entirely," Fiona said.

"Are you telling me you don't have the stomach for it, Fiona? Is my palatine quivering at the thought of bringing down the Order turned traitor to this crown?" the king asked.

"Your Highness, it would be a lie to say I'm not concerned about declaring war on the Order. We know what they're capable of, especially given their foothold in the kingdom. We don't know where they are lurking among the common people," Fiona answered.

"And either they all surrender, or we will weed them out. I don't understand why you question my decision, Fiona. Were you not here in this very room when they came for my head? Was it not you who brought the people who saved me?"

The palatine nodded. "Yes, Your Majesty, I was. That's not something I would forget easily. But you appointed me as your palatine, and it's my duty to advise you when I believe there's a need to reconsider a decision, such as now," Fiona said.

Damiran stepped forward. "Your Majesty, it's unlikely that giving the Order an ultimatum will make them surrender. Instead, it may force them to do something rash. You should reconsider. The kingdom cannot afford a war, not with everything else that has happened."

"Do not tell me what my kingdom can or cannot afford, cousin!" the king answered. "Who is the king? Who wears the crown?"

Damiran shook his head. "Of course, it is you, Your Majesty."

"Then remember that. Now, I have had enough of this! I have made my decision, and it is final. They're confident, thinking all I do is roar. I will show them what it means to snuff out not just a flame but the entire bloody fire. I won't hear any more arguments." King Ranald exhaled deeply, leaning his head back and placing his hands on the arms of the throne.

Damiran eyed the king's hand. He still wore the ring that had killed the past Lord Watcher with the kiss of death. He glanced at the palatine and shook his head before he bowed to the throne and exited the room. Fiona followed suit, and he turned to her once they were out the door.

"Remember, you agreed to the Indulgence, but you weren't there when it happened and what he did there . . . and now this is because the Indulgence riled him up. You wanted him to face it; now he has, and this is what has come of it. I hope you're prepared. If not, then I suggest you head back in there and try whatever you can to make him listen because if the king goes to war against the Order, then Queen's Hill will burn," he said.

Fiona stared at Damiran, taking a moment to think of what he'd said. Then she turned around and opened the door to the throne room.

King Ranald had already moved from the throne. He was now standing by window closest to the door, looking down with his back half-turned to the door so he wouldn't be blinded. He saw the palatine the moment she stepped in.

"Fiona."

"Your Majesty." She stood by the door, keeping her distance until the king waved her closer.

"You really don't think we need them gone?" he asked.

"Your Majesty, I think your desire for vengeance is justified. What they did is certainly unforgivable. Even my husband was a victim."

"So you understand." Ranald's flushed eyes widened.

The palatine shook her head slowly. "My lord —"

The king wiped his face with his hand and bit his lower lip. "How is your daughter?" he asked.

The question caught Fiona off guard. "She's well. Safe."

"You remember what it felt like when you didn't know what had happened to her, do you not? When you thought it might have been the Red Flame?"

"Yes, Your Majesty, I remember. But it wasn't the Red Flame."

"No, it was a man who took your daughter because of the Red Flame. You know, I believe you would have done whatever was necessary to that shepherd you suspected if you hadn't found your daughter. He would be dead, even if you kept it from me."

He knew, of course, he knew. "Your Majesty —"

322

"You don't owe me any explanation, Fiona. I trusted you would do whatever was needed to find your child. That same determination drives me. I feel it too – the same thing you felt when you didn't know if the menace called the Order had taken your child for no reason other than that they could. It's what drives me to want them dead," he said. "I think you should know. I've already begun to weed out those I believe don't have the interest of this kingdom at heart. Starting with Alderman Kon."

Fiona frowned. "My Lord, I don't believe I understand what you mean."

"I'm sure he was a watcher, working for the Red Flame. I could tell. It was in his eyes, how he looked at me, and how he questioned everything I said. He was in my court, feeding them information. He was one of them, Fiona."

"It was in his eyes?"

"Yes, it was. I could see it. I don't know how I'd missed the signs before, but I could see it once I paid enough attention. He had the same eyes as the others – the guards who tried to kill me, the Lord Watcher I killed. They all had the same look, and I could tell. It was right there. But see, I came back to my senses quickly enough, and, just like I with the Lord Watcher, I made sure to remain ahead of whatever the Order has planned. I had him dealt with."

"Alderman Kon is dead, Your Majesty."

"Yes, that's what he got for being part of the Order."

Fiona couldn't believe it. She felt her body stiffen. He peered at her with wide eyes. Kon's body had been found at dawn, and the news had spread. No one knew who was responsible. She'd thought it was the watchers beginning their revenge for the king's actions, but no. It had been the king. He'd had the alderman murdered on a hunch. The king had killed a man merely because he'd thought he'd seen it in his eyes that he'd been a watcher.

She'd hoped to make the king see reason. Help him believe the Red Flame was no longer after him. If there were no more attacks, then an understanding could be reached. But in less than two days, he had poisoned and beheaded one man and had another killed.

"Your daughter is safe, Fiona. If you wish for her to remain so, then you need to understand why the Red Flame must end and why it must end now," the king said to his speechless palatine.

* * *

Damiran's heart was beating, threatening to fall out of his chest as he rode hard and fast on his horse away from the palace. He had all but broken through the palace gates on his way out. Damiran continued to glance back as his horse galloped, hoping he wouldn't see men wearing the colours of the King's Guard following him.

He had dismissed the guards at the door right after Fiona had returned to the throne room. Once they'd left, he'd pressed himself to the door so he could listen to their conversation. Fortunately, they were close enough to the door. He'd been seething at how ineffective the palatine's argument was until the king revealed the truth that had almost made his knees collapse. Damiran had been with Kon merely hours before he'd been killed on their clandestine trip to the prince's castle. He'd been the one to convince Kon to make the journey. But the king had been convinced that Kon was plotting for the Red Flame. If the king got wind that Damiran had ridden with the alderman that night, he was dead.

The horse trotted to a stop, and Damiran dismounted as the servant opened the latch. He didn't wait to be led as he hurried into the castle.

Price Petr jerked his head towards the door. His mutt barked as Damiran barrelled into the living chamber. His hair was dishevelled, and his hands were practically trembling.

"Lord Damiran, what is this? Did I not make myself clear? Do I have to banish you from my castle or go to the king about your harassment?" the prince asked, setting his goblet on the stool next to his seat and then snapping his fingers at the dog to quiet.

"He's dead, did you know?"

"The alderman? I heard. Is that why you've barged into my castle? To bring me stale news?"

"Did you know the king had him killed?" Damiran asked.

Petr's face went blank as he stared at him. "Cousin, have you decided to descend into unfounded accusations so that you can get a reaction from me?"

"This is not a ploy to get you to come to the palace, Petr. This is not an accusation!" Damiran said. "I just heard it with my own ears. The king was telling Fiona what he had done. He killed Kon because he saw in his eyes that he was Red Flame. In his eyes, Prince Petr! That's all it took," Damiran said. "He didn't ask. He didn't confirm. He just had the man killed. A man who was returning from this castle with me. He took him to be a watcher because of his eyes."

Prince Petr stared at his cousin, concern in his own eyes.

"Do you still think your brother isn't going mad?"

CHAPTER
THIRTY-THREE

L evyna knocked on the door but got no response. She
knew he was inside; she could sense him. She stood at the
threshold and considered walking away, but the idea left her
head as quickly as it had come. Levyna knocked a little harder
than the last, but she still got no response.

"Olin?" she said. Silence answered.

Levyna sensed he was there but couldn't hear a reaction. She let out a deep sigh before she turned the knob of the door, even though she could just as well have used her spectre. The door was unlocked, and she opened it slowly till it was wide enough to slip through.

Levyna stepped into the room and finally realized why Olin hadn't responded. He was half-on the bed, with his right leg touching the ground, his left still on the bed. He wore his boots and belt as though sleep had been an accident he hadn't been expecting.

Levyna let out a soundless sigh at the sight. She'd been gravely concerned about his lack of sleep, and she had half a mind leave and let him rest, but then she looked at him again. She walked carefully until she stood beside him. His brown, curly hair spread around his face like a halo, and his expression was no longer stiff and angry like she'd last seen him.

Levyna wrapped her arm around herself as she watched him. Whatever had become of Olin, whatever he had been going through, she still knew he would walk himself through hell if she needed him, even if she told him not to. She rubbed slowly at her arm as she remembered what she'd said to him. It had been wrong and unfair.

She wanted to take his shoes off and lift his leg to the bed so he could sleep more comfortably. He had taken on the role of warrior and protector. She didn't even know if he was fully conscious of it. It was hard for her to imagine what it would be like if he lost himself. She knew it would even be harder if she played a role in why he couldn't get back to who he'd been before. Had it been her on the bed, she knew he would make certain that she was comfortable. He would throw a blanket over her. She'd caught him doing that more than once. And then he'd take a seat in the closest chair he could find and sketch away at scroll – of a picture of Yondi, a creature she didn't know, or a fiery bird.

But if she touched him, he might wake up from the first sleep he'd had in nearly three days. She couldn't risk it. Levyna stepped closer, gently reached across his body, and grabbed the blanket on the other side of the bed. Then she gently laid it across him, first over his legs and waist so that she could draw it over his chest, careful not to brush too hard against his skin. Levyna thought she had escaped touching him until she rested her hand over Olin's chest and her face pinched.

She couldn't sense him anymore. He wasn't there. She was looking at him, Olin, the same young man she knew, who she'd sensed from behind a closed door a moment ago, and it didn't feel like him anymore. Like someone else was on the bed, someone who looked familiar but wasn't Olin. Levyna didn't understand what was going on. The only way she could think this would be possible was if . . .

Levyna pulled the blanket away and placed her head on his chest where his heart would be. Her own heart drummed at the silence, and then she was yanked off him and held at arm's length. Levyna gasped as Olin's hands held her in place, leaning over his body. But it hadn't been the sudden jolt that had shocked her. It had been the utter blackness of his eyes.

The black was gone now, and she could sense him again. She didn't know why she was still holding her breath – if it had something to do with the suddenness of his movement or the way their eyes looked now. They locked gazes, and Olin's eyes were still flushed even as he looked back at her. Then he frowned, and she felt his grip ease from around her arms, and he let go.

"What are you doing here?" he asked her.

"Checking on you," she said.

"You shouldn't. You should be resting," Olin said, bringing his other leg down, so he was sitting on the bed.

"I am rested. Besides, how is it fair that you get to check on me and I can't do the same?" she asked.

"You shouldn't be here. You should go," Olin said, rising to his feet and walking towards the door.

"You don't mean that." Levyna frowned, shaking her head. "You do not."

"I do," Olin answered assuredly enough that it terrified her.

She gasped and grabbed his arm before he made another step towards the door. "I'm sorry for what I said, Olin. I truly am. It was wrong and unfair of me to say it. You are not a killer," she said.

He looked down at her hand and back up at her face. "It doesn't matter."

"But it does! It does . . ." She moved to stand in front of him. "I know what you are, and you can read my mind now. You know that I don't think that about you."

He glanced at her, then looked away as though he wasn't willing to let himself hear whatever she wouldn't say with her words. "You really should leave, Levyna," he said.

She reluctantly let go of his arm and stepped back, away and towards the door. She opened it, looked back at him, and then walked out.

Levyna, half-angry and half-tearful, left the guest quarters. She made it back to her chamber, anger brewing, partly at herself and partly at Olin. She didn't know where the rage was coming from. She was angry at the Red Flame for what it had done, what it had taken away from him, and what it was taking away from her. Levyna's breathing grew heavy, and she clenched her fist. The water in the washbowl in the corner stirred. She was angry at the Order for killing her father; she was angry at him for being gone; she was angry that someone else she cared about was hurting and couldn't help him. She stared at the bowl, and the water inside started to bubble.

"Levyna?"

She turned to find her mother standing behind her.

"Is everything alright?" Fiona asked, walking up to her.

Levyna wanted to lie but couldn't muster the strength to. "No."

"What is it?"

"It's Olin. He's upset, not himself, and I might have made it worse," Levyna answered.

Fiona had come looking for her daughter. She'd been worried before, but since the king's declaration and confession, she couldn't stop herself from seeking her out. "Whatever happened, I'm sure you will be fine."

Levyna frowned. "That doesn't sound like an attempt to help, Mother. I know you still distrust him, but Olin is my friend. I care about him, and I'm worried about him."

Fiona closed the distance between them and took her daughter's hands. "I'm sorry. I don't mean to dismiss your worries, and I might be critical of Olin for a good reason after what happened, but that doesn't mean I don't trust him or that I don't care what happens to him. It's very much the opposite. You care about him, so I do too. And he brought you back to me, so he has earned himself even more of my good grace."

"I worry about him. He looks beside himself. And then earlier, I said something, and he got upset."

"Do you want to tell me what you said?"

Levyna couldn't bring herself to say it. "I would rather not. I feel guilty enough."

Fiona nodded. "Fine. It's impossible to take back words, but you can try to let new words heal them. If he is upset, perhaps give him some time. Then you can apologize and let him know you understand your words were wrong."

"But I have told him several times. He doesn't hear me."

"Because his emotions are still raw. But given what you share, you have something not many . . . friends have. You can talk to each other without words, without having to open your mouths, and without having to be in the same room. It's an unfair advantage and one you must learn to use wisely and respectfully. Continue to remind him of how sorry you are and that you are there, and soon it will pass."

"You believe so?"

"Yes, I do." Fiona held her daughter's hands tight and then gripped her shoulders. As she looked into her daughter's eyes, she remembered King Ranald and the looming chaos. "What if we decided to take a break from all of this? Away from Queen's Hill?"

"What? Where would we go?"

"Anywhere. We could go to Edenborough, or Maedro, or somewhere far, somewhere without watchers and Orders and deaths and the threats of war."

"What threats of war?" Levyna asked, and Fiona's face pinched. She hadn't meant to let that slip.

Fiona sighed. She couldn't tell her daughter everything she'd heard from the king, but she could tell her some of it. "King Ranald is unwavering in his conflict with the Red Flame. He is preparing to invade the Order's Den. War is coming to Queen's Hill."

Levyna frowned. "How soon?"

"A matter of days."

"Oh."

"So you see, maybe we should go —"

"And abandon the kingdom? You are the palatine, Mother, the king's right hand. How can we ignore everything?"

"Yes, Levyna, I am the king's right hand, but first, before anything else, I am your mother. And the mere thought of something happening to you again, of losing you too . . . it's unbearable to me," Fiona said.

Levyna shook her head. "You won't lose me, Mother. Not anytime soon. But you can't expect me to hide. I can't leave everything behind, everyone. Before war comes, we will do whatever we can to stop the Red Flame. And if war does come, then we will pick up arms, and we will fight."

Fiona smiled as she stared at her daughter. There was no doubt where that courage came from. "It amazes me. The woman you're becoming."

"I know who I take after."

They were interrupted by a knock at the door. Fiona answered, and a maid stepped in.

"Lady Palatine," she curtseyed. "Forgive me, but there is someone in the palace asking for Miss Levyna."

"Who is it?" Levyna asked.

"I believe she said her name is Gytha," the maid said.

CHAPTER
THIRTY-FOUR

O lin was still seated on the bed, head bowed, as the door opened. He knew she was at the door; he could sense her, but he wasn't willing to listen to her thoughts. If he looked at her, he would snap at her again.

"Olinander."

That wasn't Levyna.

Olin jerked his head up. His mother. He was seeing his mother for the second time in over a fortnight. He wasn't willing to show his excitement, even as his heart fluttered at seeing her after her abrupt departure. He gawked at her. He wasn't even sure if she was real or if his mind was playing tricks on him. A few days ago, there'd been a time when he would have jumped at the chance to imagine something as real as this. He wouldn't have believed anything. He'd been so desperate. Now, he stared at her as she stood by the door. Levyna waited just behind her, furtively trying to hide her face.

"Olinander, it's me," Gytha said, guessing what was going on in his head. He looked both doubtful and confused.

"Mother," he said, getting to his feet. "Where have you been?"

"It has been quite the ordeal, but I've been in Edenborough," Gytha said as she stepped towards him, holding herself back from the urge to throw her arms around him.

"Edenborough?" he asked. "What's in Edenborough?" His expression and tone was a demand. He wasn't simply curious.

"Thorne," Gytha answered.

"The Lord Watcher?"

"He didn't die in Ravinshore, and he didn't return to Walera. He escaped to Edenborough, and I followed him on a ship. He realized I was there and managed to wreck the ship before he vanished. I couldn't abandon the passengers to sink with the ship, so I moved them all to land, to Edenborough. But there were consequences. I was unconscious for five days afterwards.

The day after I woke up, Levyna's spectre found me," Gytha said.

"And you didn't think to tell me where you were going? Let me know, so I wouldn't lose my mind and torture myself. You didn't think I deserved to be spared going through this again?" her son asked.

"I'm sorry, Olin. I was only supposed to be gone for a day, perhaps two, at the most. That's why I didn't think to tell you. And I didn't want you to worry about Thorne at all."

Olin shook his head slowly. "You could have said something. You could have left a message, a clue. Just anything so I would at least know where you had gone. You have no idea what I've gone through since you left."

"I erred, Olinander. It was selfish and thoughtless of me not to have considered telling you," Gytha said.

Olin walked towards the window and stared out for a moment before he spoke. "No one knew where you were. You left a child with Old Ron, and then you disappeared. I went searching but found nothing. No one knew anything. Not even Levyna could find you or your dreams."

"She couldn't, not when I was unconscious. I wasn't merely asleep – consciousness is linked with the essence of one's magic. What I did took every bit of strength my essence could muster, and I was left with almost nothing."

"So you almost died?"

"I . . . I did not die, Olin. I am here, alive. And I would have been here much sooner, but my magic still needed time to recover."

"What would have happened if you hadn't been able to get off the ship? If Thorne had done something?"

Gytha shook her head. "He couldn't. He couldn't do anything to me, which was why he attacked the ship and ran instead of facing me."

"You sound so sure of yourself!" he said, voice shaking.

"That's because I am. I made a mistake by not making sure he was completely dead last time, but that doesn't mean I have anything to fear from him, and he knows that. I was going to hunt him down, and I wasn't going to rest until I was sure he was dead until he'd paid for what he did to you, for what he did to Wylie," Gytha said. She saw the flicker in his gaze at the mention of his uncle's name. "But I should have told you so you'd know I didn't abandon you like before, but I needed to hunt that watcher down. And I still will. You were never far from my thoughts, Olinander."

* * *

"Perhaps it was only a matter of time before this happened," the Fourth Watcher said to the rest of the circle. They stood around the table with Gossie, the Lord Watcher, at the head, in the wake of the message from King Ranald declaring war and threatening an invasion of the Order's Den if the Red Flame did not surrender by dawn in two days. "The question now is: what will our response be?"

"We need to make a statement, to make the king realize he can't do what has never been done – give the Red Flame an ultimatum," the Sixth Watcher said.

"No, nothing like that will be done," the Lord Watcher said. "The Red Flame will not respond to the king or anyone else."

"My Lord, an entire garrison is preparing to attack the Den. Shall we do nothing?" Fourth asked.

Gossie, the oldest of the four watchers, kept his face steel behind his mask. "The Order has existed for six centuries, watcher. It's not some group of mercenaries flailing without course. Each one of you here has been a watcher for half the lifetime of the boys and so-called soldiers who wield swords in the king's name, wearing the king's colours for the garrison. Most of them were raised with the fear of the Red Flame in their minds. To stare at the walls of the Den is one thing. To step inside in battle against a Watcher of the Red Flame is another. Many of them would rather take their own lives when the time comes, and even more, will flee. And those that remain will be taken care of by ghosts in their midst. There is no way Ranald's call for war will be anything more than the flailing of a stupid child, and he doesn't even realize it.

"And, if the invasion happens for some reason, it will not end with the blood of the watchers and warriors. The king will learn the effectiveness of the Red Flame when the kingdom begins to bleed one village, one town, one shire at a time," Gossie said.

"The Order will turn on the people?" Sixth asked.

"It will do whatever is necessary to make the king understand he cannot win. When people begin to die, the kingdom will turn on the crown, and the Order will take control, just as intended," the Lord Watcher answered, his hands behind his back. The others stood courteously in his presence. "But of course, this will only happen if the current plan fails, which is unlikely."

"Perhaps then, Lord Watcher, we could consider the possibility of moving our plan forward before the king gets the bright idea of invading the den before the two days are over," Fifth asked. "It's clear his mind and reason have fled his body. He had his alderman killed. He's sent the rest of them hunting for watchers . . . there's no telling what he'll do next."

"The plan will happen when it's meant to – not long now. Not long at all. And if the king does change his mind, it won't change the plan. It will just mean we act in the middle of a war he shall not win. Now, are your men ready?" Gossie asked.

"Every watcher is poised, Lord Watcher," Fourth answered.

"And the ghosts?"

"They have received word across the kingdom," Fifth answered.

"And what of those mysterious hunters after the Red Flame?" Gossie asked.

"It turned out to be just one man, a potter from Sallen who went by the name Eusa."

Gossie frowned. "One man?"

"Yes, a shifter and a leihcon – a possessor," Fifth continued. "He managed to hunt a handful of watchers. He wanted to kill the Red Flame – something to do with his son and wife being killed by watchers years ago."

"Why?" the Lord Watcher asked.

"The child was a shifter."

Nothing more needed to be said. Gossie understood. The Red Flame had fought many like that – people who were looking to get revenge on the Order of the Red Flame for some slight against a loved one. Over six centuries, Red Flame was bound to gather a number of enemies, individuals and groups alike. But those enemies always met terrible fates, with consequences they could never escape. But for one man, this Eusa the porter had surely left his mark, having taken four ghost watchers.

"How did the man survive the first time?" the Lord Watcher asked.

"No one knows. He was left to burn in a fire that consumed everything, and he managed to make it out," Fifth said.

"Such a shame," Gossie said. "Had he been found sooner, he would have been a watcher to remember – a Red Flame fire couldn't kill."

"But he was a shifter, Lord Watcher?" Fourth asked.

"Yes, he was, and it would have made him even more perfect," Gossie answered. "So, who finally killed him?"

"The sciff from Ravinshore killed him," Fifth answered.

CHAPTER
THIRTY-FIVE

"**Y**ou still don't want to talk to me?" Levyna asked. Gytha had just left to see Posdel to find out if her reappearance had any effect on Olin's mood.

Olin glanced at her quiet but looked away as he returned to the bed. Levyna exhaled, disappointed, frustrated and then she remembered what her mother had said.

You'll forgive me, eventually, won't you? she asked silently. She kept her eyes fixed on him, standing silently, holding her arm and rubbing it gently. When she didn't get anything response apart from his cold glance, she turned and moved towards the door.

"Thank you for finding her," he said suddenly.

Levyna's heart galloped as she turned back to find him looking at her. His eyes were still flushed but no longer carried that coldness. "You never have to thank me, Olin. I only wish I had been able to do it sooner," she said.

He sighed. "You did it now. That's all that matters."

She nodded briskly, her stance cautious. She didn't know if they were back to normal yet. "It helped that she is what is, I suppose," she said. Gytha's power, and the fact that Levyna had connected with it before, made it easier. Olin fell silent, and it seemed like her grace had expired. "Can I apologize again?" she asked.

Olin shook his head. "That won't be necessary. You weren't completely wrong if I'm being honest."

"No. No, I was." She moved to sit next to him on the bed. "It's not true."

"I have killed people, haven't I?"

"Only because you had to. You've only taken lives to protect yourself or someone else, Olin."

Olin turned his palms up on his legs. "What about the ones who haven't died from my hands but from my actions?" he asked, looking at his hands.

Levyna knew who he meant. She looked at his hands and shook her head. "No. You mustn't do that to yourself, please. What happened doesn't make you evil, Olin. You must forgive yourself because you cannot control everything. I know because when you've had the chance, you've done everything you can to protect others, too, to protect me. So please, banish the thought and forget my horrible words."

He looked at her, meeting her eyes for a moment. "You're thinking of him, the shifter."

"Yes, I am. And not because I want to have another argument," Levyna answered. "It's because of the dream I've been seeing."

"The phoenix?"

"Yes."

"What about it?

"When I met him, it crossed my mind. It could be him."

"You think the shifter is the phoenix from your dreams?"

"I think so. I thought it was possible when he revealed his face and told me his story. It would make sense. The Red Flame burned him in a fire that burned everything but him, and he survived and came back different. If ever there was a way a human could be seen as a phoenix, it would take a rebirth like that."

"But something doesn't fit?"

"No. Since I've been free, I thought that was it, but then I dreamt of it again last night. I saw the phoenix just before. I even saw it again this morning, and I'm sure that if I closed my eyes now, it would come," she said.

"Then we continue as planned – go to Kelegro," Olin answered. Just then, someone knocked on the door. Gytha opened it and stepped in.

"Should I come back another time?" she asked.

"No, it's fine," Olin said. "We were just talking about going to Kelegro. Levyna has been having a dream. We don't know who it is pointing to."

"What are you seeing?" Gytha asked.

"A phoenix."

"Ah, the legendary bird."

"Yes, I've been seeing it form from its ashes for a while now. I've dreamt of nothing else since it started. It has never happened like this before. At first, I thought it meant the shifter who took me, but he's dead and yet I dreamed it last night. Before everything happened, we'd planned to go to Kelegro to find a seer who could tell us the meaning. And now we think we should. If I keep seeing it, it must be important, right?" Levyna said, looking from Gytha to her son and back.

"I suppose."

"And perhaps the sooner, the better," Olin said.

"Yes," Levyna said.

Gytha nodded. "I agree. Only I will be the one to go with Levyna to Kelegro."

"What? No, why?" Olin answered, anger returning to his voice.

"Because I have just talked to Posdel about what happened, and I'm doing everything I can to hide how worried I am, and the fact that you look like you haven't slept in days means I must insist that you stay behind and rest. Preferably try to get some sleep."

"But I don't need it. I feel fine."

"And your eyes betray your words," Gytha answered her son, and Levyna looked briskly from Olin to the sorceress.

Olin sighed. "How is this fair?"

"I don't care if it's fair, Olinander. I care that you are well. Kelegro might be part of Queen's Hill, but the journey can be very demanding."

"I can handle whatever it is."

"Yes, you can when you don't look like this," Gytha answered. "The second and less important reason you cannot come is that we will not be going by road. My friend William is still here and can only take two other people. If we leave now, we should be back in no time."

"I will have to inform my mother," Levyna said.

"I wouldn't have it any other way," Gytha answered.

Levyna looked from her to a sulking Olin. "We won't be long, I promise."

* * *

Ranald was confident in his course of action, and they had to let him. Gossie had to let him. The Lord Watcher had come close to ruining everything when the king had decapitated Eden in front of him, but he had remembered what was to come and held himself back. Whether or not the ruler of Queen's Hill had genuinely gone insane or was simply reacting out of fear – it didn't matter. He would soon learn that he'd never stood a chance of winning a war against the Order.

The Lord Watcher turned away from the window after the rest of the circle departed. The room was empty, and he exhaled, regarding the empty table for a moment before he stepped forward. Gossie walked to the east wall and stood in front of an empty torch holder. He raised his hand to tilt the frame to the left. As he did, the wall creaked in front of him, and Gossie stepped forward and pulled at the wall, turning it like it was a door. Behind the wall was a passage lit by a single touch on the wall. The Lord Watcher entered, pulling the wall closed behind him.

If only Ronald knew that one shouldn't boast of a basket full of eggs before the chickens were visited by the wolf.

The passage continued for a while before Gossie descended the last few steps and came to a large room. The torches here weren't lit, but daylight filtered in from the opening on the roof, looking out over the side of the mountain. The cave had become part of the building of the Watcher's Den. Gossie stepped forward towards the cliff until his feet were inches from the edge. One wrong move would mean certain death, without magic at least. But neither the thrill of the heights nor the view of the mountainside had brought him here. Gossie turned away and left in the opposite direction of the path he'd come down.

There was another passage. Another torch marked the beginning. The Lord Watcher plucked the torch to light his path, and he journeyed through the dead walls.

King Ranald was doing everything he could to keep the Red Flame at bay. He thought they couldn't reach him. He thought he could destroy the Order from inside the walls of his throne room. His brush with death had given him insight like none other – though it may have taken his mind in the process. The king was sure he knew just what the Order would do, thought they would attack just as they had before. He thought he could find the truth of it in the eyes like he'd seen in Eden's eyes when he'd made him kiss death. King Ranald, the omniscient.

Gossie came to the end of the passage to a door made of silver and Akearian steel. He reached into his pocket and brought out a key, sliding it into the keyhole and turning it. The door clicked, and he pushed it open, walking in. There were no windows or doors, no holes or cracks to let light into the room. Without the torch in his hand, it would have felt like standing in a void.

Gossie moved the torch to the left and saw nothing. He turned it to the right, grip tightening at the sight of layers of shed skin lining the floor. He took a step towards the slough and kneeled to look closer. The Lord Watcher pulled a knife from his belt, and just as he reached to touch the skin, the flame in his hand died.

"Exonus!" he said as he stepped back. Immediately the torch relit, and this time the Lord Watcher held it in place at the realization of what was in front of him. Without the light, it might be mistaken for a human if it was just a shadow. But the flame revealed its true form. Some of it.

It had no eyes and no nose, and its mouth was twice the size of any human. But what should be its face was hardly the source of the gripping fear. Its arms stretched to its knees, and its legs were thin beneath its form. Its skin glistened in the light of the flame, and the membrane that covered its flesh was such that the demon's insides could be seen.

"How much longer?" Gossie asked.

The demon tilted its head to the right and then the left as it gently circled him, like a predator searching, watching for the right moment to strike its prey. Gossie moved the torch as swiftly as he could to match the demon's speed till it finally stopped.

"How much longer?" he asked again.

"Patience . . . Lord Watcher. Not long now . . . the son of the flame will rise soon," the demon said.

CHAPTER
THIRTY-SIX

K elegro smelled like mushrooms and wet earth. William stood to the right of the two women as they appeared. Levyna turned, looking around. It looked quite different from what she knew of Queen's Hill. Kelegro was still part of the kingdom of the hills, but it lay on the furthest edge of the rest of Queen's Hill society.

"It looks . . ." She didn't know what word to use.

"Don't try to wrestle for the perfect word to describe it. Trust me when I say that many have tried and have fallen short," Gytha said.

"Or simply fallen," William added.

"True," Gytha said.

"What does that mean?" Levyna asked, wondering if it had anything to do with stepping wrongly. She followed them to the edge of the structures.

"It means when you're here, you have to try not to pay attention to the things around you. Only focus on why you are here or where you are headed," Gytha answered.

Levyna frowned at the statement. Then they passed a man walking on air – his feet weren't touching the ground. She looked at Gytha.

"Kelegro is a village made up of a special kind of people, some of whose magic is in tune with a plane of reality different from this realm."

"Is that why it's called the ghost village?" Levyna asked.

"Yes. Not because the people are made of ghosts."

From the trees to the hills, to the fields and even the clouds in the sky – it was as though everything in the village was alive, was moving. Levyna realized how true that was when she looked at a very tall tree, and it turned in her direction. It wasn't so much terrifying as it was odd. Still, she looked away at once. As they passed, figures glanced at them from every direction, and every time she forgot what she was supposed to be focusing on. As soon as she remembered, she would see something that threatened to make her stop in her tracks. Levyna eventually stopped looking around until they reached a house that looked like the roots of a giant tree.

Gytha knocked, and a short pale man opened the door. Though he was pale, unlike Eusa and Moreen, he didn't look like death was at his door. He regarded the Grand Sorceress, the sorcerer, and the traveller before ushering them in. If Gytha hadn't explained beforehand, she would have thought she was in a dream. The inside of the house was three times as large as it looked from the outside.

The pale man led them into a room, where a grey-haired woman sat on the wooden floor. She was holding an oro in her hand and stroking it gently. As they entered, the old woman grunted and tilted her head. Her eyes were pale, just like Moreen's had been, but Levyna guessed that she wasn't just a walking body that had been possessed.

"Sorcerers and another." The old woman stopped petting the oro and raised her hand towards Levyna. From the way she moved, Levyna inferred the woman was blind. "I don't need eyes to see you. Take my hand. Let me know who this is."

Levyna looked to Gytha, who nodded. Leaning down, Levyna took the blind woman's hand.

"Oh . . ." the old woman said. "I didn't think I would ever get to meet your kind in my lifetime. A dreamer and – and a traveller," she said. The pale man gasped, and when Levyna turned, she saw his gaze was fixed on them. A smile hinting at excitement flashed across the old woman's face, revealing two crooked front teeth. "To what do I owe the pleasure of your visit?" she asked.

"The dreamer has a dream. She doesn't know the meaning of it or who it belongs to," Gytha said. "She hopes that you can see it and tell her why it troubles her."

"Is that true, child? This troubles you?" the old woman asked Levyna.

"Yes, it does. I haven't had any other dreams besides this one for days now. I can't close my eyes without seeing it," Levyna said.

"And why does a dreamer wish to see who the death belongs to? Shall you not merely let it pass and move on?"

"I want to. I need to. I would move on if I could, but I cannot, please."

The old woman sighed again. "And what is the dream?"

"It's of a phoenix," Levyna answered.

The old woman's thin brows creased on her forehead. "The mark of rebirth," she said. "Very well, if you wish me to help, you must prepare yourself. This will not be pleasant."

Levyna swallowed hard and held her breath. She looked back at Gytha and William, both of whom nodded at her. Whatever it was, she wanted to find out. She needed to find out. "I'm ready," she said.

The pale man appeared, seemingly out of nowhere, and gestured to Gytha and William. When they looked at him, he pointed them towards a bench against the wall, signing with his hands the need for them to remain in their seats no matter what happened.

"If you don't think you can stand it, you should wait in the street," he signed, and neither of the sorcerers moved. The pale man then moved toward Levyna and positioned her lying face-up in front of the old woman. Then, he took the oro from the woman's hands and placed it in a jar.

Levyna didn't protest as the slimy and smelly hands that had held the slug hovered over her head and held her left hand.

"You hold your breath and don't let go of my hand."

Levyna didn't get a chance to respond before the seer placed her hand on her forehead. Then Levyna felt her body being sucked into the ground as the tree branches and roots wrapped, folded, and twisted around her.

William glanced at Gytha as they watched Levyna begin to convulse.

Gytha's remembered the man's warning to stay seated, though her first instinct was to reach for the girl. She was trembling as bad as the King of Ravinshore had when she'd healed him of the Egro, and it was hard to watch. Looking at Levyna, Gytha saw Olin in her mind and the look on his face and his hesitation to part with Levyna. She saw Fiona and the look in the eyes of a mother who was seemingly helpless to how strong her child was, merely a day after she had returned from captivity. Gytha saw her vulnerability. She held her breath as Levyna writhed, gasped aloud, and then fell quiet under the seer's hands.

A voice called Levyna's name, and it felt like a thousand mallets slapping against the inside of the skull. She slowly opened her eyes. The daylight was torture. Slowly, the pale man helped her sit up. Gytha rose, and William followed.

"What happened? What did you see?" Levyna asked.

Levyna had told the details of the dream when the seer had taken her. Now she wanted to know the meaning. That was why they had come all this way.

"The phoenix is real. Not the animal, but a person. Someone consumed by that which he is, who returns from the ashes of his self."

Levyna frowned. "I don't understand."

"He faces a death he cannot escape. A death that will consume him and everything else. Your phoenix faces death," the seer said.

Levyna got on her feet and glanced at Gytha and William. They looked worried. "You speak in riddles, seer. Tell me in true words."

"You aren't blind, dreamer. Your phoenix is right next to you. It doesn't leave. It's why you have been so troubled. It's as though he is standing with you now."

He does not leave.

Levyna's eyes widened as he looked from the seer to the face of the mother of the phoenix she had been dreaming of. Gytha gasped.

***

No one understood the mystery of death. Fiona certainly didn't.

Fredric had died a fortnight ago. The night he'd died, she'd seen him moments before everything had changed. A change ushered in by death. It wasn't how he'd died – it was what his death had brought her. Fiona stood at the door of the washroom where her husband had died, staring at the bathing bowl where he'd drowned, and she wondered what course life would have taken if that hadn't happened.

If Fredric had listened to their daughter, if Fiona had made him listen, then perhaps he would have been more cautious. He would have had a guard at the door and a servant inside with him. He would have finished his bath, dressed for the night, and slept in bed. Guards at the door and more at the windows, and Fredric would have lived the night, knowing death was lurking nearby. But for how long? Fiona had never been able to answer that question. She grieved the love of her life, yet his death plunged her and their daughter into chaos and danger.

Fiona was no longer just a lady, wife to the palatine. She was now the woman who held the power of Queen's Hill's throne in the king's absence. That would never have happened if her husband still lived. And Levyna, their daughter, had taken the grief of her father's death and used it as a mantle to climb out of her silence, out of her lonesomeness. She has used it to challenge everything around her, which led her to a companion she now all but breathed. One who had imprinted on her as though they had grown up knowing each other. Levyna had morphed into her father's fearlessness too. Levyna was prepared to fight the Order of the Red Flame should it come to war.

But there was no version of reality where that type of bravery didn't terrify a mother. The Red Flame would not rob her of her child. She didn't care what fate had in store.

Palatine Fiona of Queen's Hill turned sharply at the sound of hurried footsteps approaching.

* * *

Yondi had come to the mage as a seventeen-year-old candle burning at both ends. Yondi's magic had been looking to die inside of him before he'd become Posdel's apprentice. Yondi's flame hadn't known where to burn when he'd been sent out of his family home. He had been shy, afraid, and wasting away before Posdel had tossed him into the world and forced the boy out of his shell.

Despite all the ways in which Posdel had fallen short of being the perfect master, Yondi had learned on his feet, never complained, and never stopped being annoying.

Would Posdel choose the same fate a second time?

To have his unstoppable apprentice find a stray sciff by the bank of Black River, bring him home and never return? Would Posdel choose to have Olin, an impossible boy from Ravinshore, take the place of his apprentice? Even if it meant always remaining on guard whenever the sciff went out, only to bring back trouble at his heels?

Posdel couldn't deny that he'd almost forgotten this part of him existed – the man he'd been over the last fortnight. Posdel has fought watchers and saved the life of a king. He has spent many days sober because of that boy under his roof. If he had a chance, would he change fate, trade what had to happen for this chance to feel alive again?

He surely wouldn't. Posdel wouldn't allow fate to take away his annoying apprentice. If he could change it, he would have paid more attention and wouldn't have assumed Yondi would find his way on his own. He would have been sober that day when Yondi had needed him and would have fended off fate.

But that didn't mean he would reject the chance to be where he was now, old but not precarious, and healing from his injury gained by following that impossible skiff. Because from the first moment he'd met Olin that day at his house, he hadn't been able to shake the feeling that this boy would break everything down with his bare hands, anything and everything that got in the way of doing what he believed was right even if the broken shards hurt him or those around him.

Now that fate had taken the choice out of his hands, Posdel wondered if fate was going to make him watch this candle raze itself to the ground before the flame could even catch.

Posdel stood in Olin's chamber, staring at an empty bed. Beside it, a jug had tipped over, spilling water across the table and floor. There was no sign of Olin, and Posdel jerked his head around at the sound of heavy steps.

CHAPTER
THIRTY-SEVEN

Olin's eyes seemed to open by themselves the moment he closed them. The blurriness at the corners of his vision pulsed with the same rhythm of his heartbeat. He felt sweaty, even though it was supposed to be cold. He raised his hand to his forehead to find it matted with sweat as he'd been underwater. Olin turned on the bed and turned the other way a moment later. He felt parched like it had been days since he'd had something to drink. He managed to push himself up, his bare feet hitting the ground. It felt like broken shells beneath his feet as he walked to the table, pouring himself a cup of water with a trembling hand.

He downed the water and then tried to place the cup on the table but dropped it when his hand missed and found the edge. He moved back to the bed and sat for a moment before laying down again, hoping for whatever it was to pass. But Olin's eyes snapped open the moment he closed them, and this time the blurriness at the edges had only worsened. He shook his head, trying to shake whatever it was off. He was already thirsty again.

Olin got back up, despite the room spinning around him. He shook his head again. His steps were heavier as he moved towards the table.

Killer.

Olin heard it. In his head. His face contorted into a frown. He closed his eyes as hard as he could, and when they snapped open again, all he could see was blurriness. He reached for the water to quench his thirst, but his hand knocked over the jug instead. He heard the water spill to the floor. Olin tried again to blink the blurriness away, but all he saw was pulses of images of the room around him. As he turned to return to the bed, the first step felt alien, like it was someone else's leg. And when he tried to take the second step, his leg collapsed, and he crashed to the floor like a felled log.

* * *

It didn't matter if Petr was convinced – the news had taken him by surprise. He hadn't remotely considered the idea that his brother could have killed Kon. Even though he knew what

Ranald had done to the Lord Watcher, he wanted to believe that whatever Ranald had done, it had been his right as the king. Eden had represented something he detested, something that irked him – the Order of the Red Flame that had tried to kill him, and his action was vengeance, a justice only the king could give. But the alderman's death was something else entirely. It was as if this single act had put everything else Damiran had been begging him to see right inside his head, and now he couldn't ignore them and claim indifference.

Petr told his cousin to relay exactly what the king had said, after which Petr made him swear it was the truth. Damiran had sworn on his life that the king had described his elimination of Kon. Afterwards, Damiran relayed the king's most recent orders and his plan to invade the Den of the Flame in two dawns with a new commander for the garrison. The danger was real now, and Petr realized his abstinence was worth nothing.

And so, he fetched his horse and, with the king's advisor by his side in the convoy, they headed to the palace so he could see for himself what had become of his brother, the king. The gates opened at the sight of the flag his convoy bore – the prince and the royal family crest.

Damiran, for his part, was getting what he had hoped for all along. He would have to let the queen know of his success, but a part of him couldn't have cared less how Queen Katina felt. He rode through the palace gatehouse, swallowing hard and holding his breath. Deep down inside, there was a tremble he couldn't control – fear at the chance the king knew he had been in the company of Alderman Kon that evening before he'd died. The king wouldn't listen to reason, not the man who had poisoned the one who had kissed his ring and then beheaded him with an axe. Damiran was terrified.

* * *

From the moment they stepped out of the house in the tree, Levyna thought the seer had to be wrong. The old blind mage had to have seen something else, or he had to be mistaken. That was the only explanation she could accept. It was the only one that would make sense to her.

In the midst of the seer's riddled words, the only thing she understood was that the one who would not leave her side would find death. He would because he was the phoenix. It wasn't the man who had abducted her, who had risen from the ruins and the fire meant to consume him. It was Olin, her companion who had an affinity with flames, who burnt his enemies to ash. The seer had seen Olin, but Levyna wouldn't believe it.

Gytha's heart had been in her mouth from that same moment. She hadn't ever considered that her son – her son whose father had turned to ash when he'd died at her hands – would be the phoenix Levyna had dreamed of. She couldn't begin to comprehend what they had just been told. She could comprehend that she had chosen to chase after a man that had hurt her son while leaving her son, the most important thing to her, alone again.

The seer hadn't known what would happen or when. But that didn't matter. Saying her son would find death was horrifying enough. The Grand Sorceress was prepared to give her own life to stop that from happening if it came to it.

William could see that determination in her eyes as he held the woman and departed the ghost village.

* * *

History was going to remember him as the man who ended the Order of the Red Flame and made certain that their evil met its doom during his reign. There was no denying it. He was sure.

King Ranald thought of how it had all come to this; how he'd shown the Red Flame couldn't touch him once he'd discovered their treachery. Killing Eden had been only the beginning. No one realized that. If the Order didn't surrender to his ultimatum, he would ensure the war ended them all. And if they were foolish enough to surrender, he'd have all of their heads, even then. Whatever happened, the history of Red Flame would come to an end with their greatest error – crossing King Ranald.

It would be a glorious day when he quenched the flames of the Order for good and liberated his people, his kingdom, and his crown.

King Ranald, forever in his cuirass and gauntlet with a sword at his belt, looked out from his palace on the hill as the clouds gathered for an approaching sunset. From where he stood, with his back to the throne as he peered out the window, he caught sight of the figure arriving through the door of the throne room. Ranald's hand reflexively reached for his sword, and then, recognizing the figure, he lowered his guard, smiled widely, and beckoned.

* * *

Levyna was first through the door. Gytha, William, Fiona and Posdel flooded in after her, closely followed by Damiran and the king's brother, Prince Petr. They all reached the throne in time to witness it.

Levyna's hands trembled, and her legs nearly gave way as she saw the scene before her.

Olinander had horror in his eyes as he looked from the floor up to the audience, up to her face. He brought his gaze back down to the king's body, laying grotesquely on the floor as blood pooled around him from his slit throat. And the sciff lifted his hand to the bloody dagger.

T he end was on his heels. There was nowhere else to go. Olin's thoughts were jagged, breath laboured, heart racing. There was no home to return to. No comfort for evil. He had been promised one here, but what would it be? The sword or the blanket?

He looked behind to the distant hills of the kingdom of Queen's Hill, then turned ahead to the view of Black Castle gates. Panting, he took a step but felt a sharp pain in his chest. Olinander lifted his hand to his chest and felt his heart stop. He fell to his knees, then face-down on the earth.

Thank you to all those who helped throughout the writing and editing process. Without you, this book wouldn't be here today.

Thank you to the beta readers who helped refine the story and pick up on some plot holes that I missed; oops.

The editors that I had The pleasure of working with helped me trim up and refine the story to what it is today. Thank you so much.

Originally from Alice Springs, Australia, A.M. Dyer currently resides in Broken Hill with his spouse and biggest fan, Buddy the Kelpie cross. Dyer works in the Broken Hill mines as an Electrician and volunteers with St. John Ambulance to provide medical aid at events. Though Dyer is passionate about helping others, he always felt the urge to pursue the creative outlet of writing as well. With the drive to craft his stories pushing him and the knowledge that there was never a perfect time, Dyer saw no reason to procrastinate on his dream. He set to work. The culmination of his efforts, a debut Young Adult fantasy novel, released in May 2022.

Lord of the Three, Book 3 in The Ash and Stone series will be in stores soon.